The Picket 'Napping

By

Bridget Schabron

Albany County
Public Library
Laramie, Wyoming

Cover design and all illustrations in the book were made by Bridget Schabron.

This is a fiction novel. Any similarity to names of real-life persons is entirely coincidental and unintentional.

Copyright © 2008 by Bridget Schabron

All rights reserved, including the right to reproduce this book or any portions of it in any form at all. For permissions or more information, email the author at <bridgetschabron@yahoo.com>.

Published in 2009 by Mountain Country Publishers.

Mountain Country Publishers is a trademark company of Bridget Schabron. Logo and publishing company copyright 2009, all rights reserved.

Library of Congress Cataloging-in-Publication Data
The Picket 'Napping/Bridget Schabron—1st ed.

ISBN 1441491791

EAN-13 is 9781441491794.

1.   Fiction   2.   Christian   3.   Romance
1.   Title

Printed in the United States of America

Marlene Henders always dreamed of adventure, but she never dreamed of being kidnapped...

"Git outta here!" Sam shouted, slamming the door.

As he closed the door, he heard the sound of shattering glass. A young man hopped through the window and dodged Gruff's fist. McGee picked up his gun. The front door swung back open and the suited man stepped in, holding a pistol. "Put the gun down, McGee," Detective Arsward ordered. McGee acted as if he would, then raised it back up and fired as Arsward fired. Frank always carried a pistol with him. He never knew when he might need it in his line of work.

Frank fell to the floor. Another man dove in through the window and tackled Gruff, who was fighting the other young man. When Curt took over on the fight with Gruff, Arthur raced to the two girls tied to the chair on the floor. Before he could reach them, however, Sam Henders barreled into him. Arthur let out a gasp. Marlene watched, excited, as the cowboy she had seen from the truck rose up to punch Sam.

And so begins the adventure of a lifetime for Marlene Rose Picket and Arthur Pressed in *The Picket 'Napping.*

Chapter One

Marlene Rose Picket was a quiet girl. She never had many friends growing up. Instead, her best friend was a book. She loved to sit down and snuggle in a blanket in the big rocking chair at her parents' house and read an exciting novel. She would picture herself as a fair western girl in a Zane Grey book, or a detective in a mystery. Her favorite book to read was *Majesty's Rancho*. Many a time Marlene wished she had grown up in the 1920's or earlier, in time to be involved in the thrilling west.

Instead of being a cowgirl on a ranch back in those tumultuous days, Marlene was a college girl in a small Wyoming town. She was never faced with big troubles or dangers, and, with the way things were, it was likely she never would be. Sighing at the thought, she stood up from her chair. It was summer break, and she was going to Cheyenne with her mother to shop.

As Mrs. Picket pulled out of the driveway with her daughter, she did not notice a strange grey truck in the rear view mirror. Marlene Rose was deep into her book by the time they reached the highway, otherwise she might have observed the vehicle on their tail. "How's the book, Marlene?" her mother asked.

Marlene's mind was on the adventure. She was a beautiful rancher's daughter, riding after a handsome cowboy. "Marlene." Marlene glanced up from the pages.

"It's good, Mom."

"You have got to be the only twenty year old girl I know who reads westerns that thoroughly."

"Aw, Mom, please don't lecture me agin. I reckon I can't take it." Marlene grinned at her mother as she spoke.

Mrs. Picket looked riled. "Now see here, Marlene, you're even talking like your books now. If you would just take a break once in a while and hang out with some friends, then I'd leave you alone."

"I don't have any close friends."

"Yes you do. What about Sandy?"

"She's off in Montana for college. She's trying to catch up on her classes. And so is Judy Frankridge."

"So? There's plenty of other kids around."

"I'm not a kid, Mom." Marlene gave her mother an aggravated stare.

"You still are to me. Won't you please try to find some people to do stuff with this summer? Last summer you were bored."

"I was working, Mom. I didn't have time to hang out with anyone."

"Yes you did. And you were bored."

"Can I please read, Mom?" Marlene pleaded, growing tired of the conversation that seemed to repeat itself every time she was alone with her mother.

"Alright!" her mother snapped.

The rest of the drive was quiet. Marlene knew she should just agree with her mother so she would stop sitting sulkily, but she was too stubborn.

Though she was a quite intelligent and sharp girl, who valued her family, she was always off dreaming about some adventure. That annoyed her parents. Her parents would rather her be sensible, and go to movies and basketball games with friends and plan for her future.

In Cheyenne Mrs. Picket took the exit which led them to Central. It was not long before they arrived at the mall parking lot. "Come on, Marlene," she called to her daughter as she stepped out. Marlene placed a bookmark in the middle of her book and set it down. She slid down onto the pavement. Neither she nor her mother noticed a truck parking across from them.

Fifty-one year old Gruff Henders pulled down the parking brake and nudged his sleeping son. "Wake up, Sam," he grunted. Samuel Henders sat up, rubbing his eyes. Sometimes Gruff could not believe his son was a law student. The Henders did not believe in laws, not since they began rustling cattle back in the late eighteen hundreds.

The two stepped out of the truck and watched as two women strutted towards the mall entrance. "When do we nab her, Pa?" Samuel asked. He always obeyed his father, no matter what. Never did the young man even blink at breaking the law, despite his future as a lawyer. Whenever he wanted something, he usually got it.

Marlene and her mother walked into the clothes store entrance at the front of the mall. Marlene almost tripped on a little boy who was running wildly about the store, dodging his mother who carried a shirt for him in her arms. "Timmy, get back here!" she cried, racing after him. Marlene chuckled and smiled at her mom. It was plain to see Mrs. Picket was also amused.

"Now, let's look around for something nice to add to your wardrobe," Mrs. Picket told her daughter.

Stepping away the entrance, Marlene started looking at a rack of dress pants. "Don't you already have several pair?" her mother asked. Marlene nodded. "How about finding a nice dress? Who knows if you'll get asked to a dance one of these days."

Marlene was studying a dress on one of the racks when she saw someone running out of the corner of her eye. When she turned a man knocked her over and picked her up. As Marlene screamed the young, bulky man carried her out of the store. Her mother watched, horrified and frozen. Her legs turned to stone, though she wanted to run after her daughter and stop the man.

"Don't try to follow!" threatened an older man. His menacing eyes danced and he scratched his grey beard as he shouted before following the kidnapper out. Everyone in the store watched but obeyed, confused. Finally Mrs. Picket broke down and dropped to her knees, sobbing. The mall officer ran to her, sensing she could help him.

"That man, who was he?" the officer questioned her.

"I don't know!" cried Mrs. Picket, shaking her head. "But he just kidnapped my daughter!"

Chapter Two

Arthur Pressed was just loading a bale of hay in his truck late into the afternoon when he saw a truck slow down to halt at the stop sign. Normally he would not have taken much notice. But when he saw a girl wearing a mess of tangled hair inside, pounding furiously at her side window to get his attention, he sensed something was wrong. Before he could run over to the truck it was gone, leaving a trail of flying dust and gravel behind it.

Scratching his chin, Arthur pondered over what he had just seen. He did not feel like chasing after the truck, considering he did not know the circumstances, or what was really going on. After a few moments, he dismissed the event from his mind and continued to load bales into his truck. Curt Hawk would be waiting with his baled hay five miles down the road and would be impatient and furious if Arthur took too long.

Arthur was a regular cowboy. He wore chaps and boots with spurs to work, and loved to ride his horse, Belle. Though twenty-two, he had never been to college, and did not plan to go. Ranching was his life. He loved the mountain country he called home. He would always love it, and try to stay here, though trouble was facing his ranch lately. The bank was threatening to foreclose his horse and cattle ranch soon if he did not pay more on his mortgage. Arthur did not like banks; they always seemed to be threatening him. If he had not been such a meek character, he would have long ago told the banker, Mr. Stevens, what he thought of him. As it was, Arthur was a calm, shy fellow, most of the time. He never bragged much and did not take kindly to liars. Never a great studier of the English language, his talk was full of accent and slang. Therefore, when trouble came to Arthur in the past, he usually shied away. The exception to that was when he was on his horse, on the range with the cattle. Only then did he feel confident and unafraid.

Arthur closed the back of the bed with a thump and hopped into the front seat of his old, dented truck. Blue paint was peeling off the outside, and rust claimed to take to the curbs over his wheels off, but he did not mind so long as the engine still ran smoothly. Arthur was a pretty content fellow, over all, though lately a longing came over him for something new.

"'Bout time ya got here," Curt called as Arthur pressed on the brakes. Hawk walked around to the back as Arthur stepped out. Between the two of them, they got the rectangular bales loaded in a few minutes.

"Alright, let's git back ta the ranch," Arthur ordered, sitting behind the wheel.

"Ahh, Boss! Can't we just hop inta town real quick?"

"Why? So you can spend that paycheck I gave ya this mornin'?"

"I gotta put it in the bank, Arthur."

"Alrighty. We'll stop over in Meeteetse fer a few. But I ain't loanin' ya anythin' if ya spend it all," Arthur told his friend, grinning at him. Curt scowled.

Curt Hawk had worked for Arthur for two years. Though he was a year older than his boss, Curt was respectful. His short brown wavy hair blew around as he stuck his head out the window. He was a lean man, tan from hard work outside. Curt could be both bold and stupid at times. Hawk was a bit of a mystery to Arthur, since Arthur never pressed for details when he hired him. Arthur just needed an honest, hard-working cow puncher to help him out. Though he was behind on the mortgage, he still managed to pay Curt for his work.

At the age of seventeen, Curt Hawk ran away from home. Mistakes and hard times had made it easy for some men to frame Curt for a bank robbery. Since then Mr. Hawk had traveled from town to town, eventually making his way to Wyoming. He had used fake names such as Troy Liken, Ralf Sanders, and Jake Pullsor, to keep any authorities from catching him. A fugitive from justice, which had so wrongly convicted him at court, Curt just wanted to stop somewhere and feel honest again. He had escaped the courtroom those five years ago, and never stopped running until he met Arthur Pressed. Arthur was a trusting man, and did not ask him many questions.

Curt told Arthur his real name, figuring he had come far enough west and been out of the papers long enough to not be questioned. The little, old fashioned bank in Meeteetse did not make background checks on its customers. They only required identification of some sort. This made it easy for Curt to save up his money.

When the men had set Curt up, he was furious. They made threats on his life to speak about it, and made such a convincing case against him, that Curt had no way to fight it. He never could stand bullies. He was disappointed to find out Cindy, a girl back home in Massachusetts, who he trusted and thought he loved, had betrayed him. She was in on the frame-up, along with Luke Watkins, her no-good brother, and his pal Charlie. It was then Hawk admitted he just had no luck with girls.

In town Curt ran into the bank to drop off his check. Arthur waited patiently in the truck. He had no interest in facing Mr. Stevens in there. He turned up the volume on the radio and propped his feet up on the dashboard. His wrist thumped against the door with the rhythm of the country music. Someone tapped at his window, causing him to jump.

Arthur turned off the radio and rolled down his window. A man with graying black hair, wearing a pressed black suit, bent to peer in at him. "Sir, I noticed you just got into town," the man commented.

"Yep, I reckon that's so. Anything wrong, Sir?" Arthur replied, casually.

The man nodded. "There's been a kidnapping down at the capitol, and I was told to look out for anyone in a truck. Apparently two men kidnapped a girl and headed north," he explained.

"Well, I'm not your man. I'm just in town 'cause my friend had to cash a check, and, as you can plainly see, there's no girl around."

"We'll see about that. Step out sir," the man ordered.

"On what authority? I don't see no badge!"

The man slipped out his wallet to show his detective license. "Detective Frank Arsward."

When Curt walked out of the bank, he stopped in puzzlement. A man was searching Arthur's car while Arthur stood against it, hands up. At first Curt worried the man was looking for him, but then he saw that Arthur was motioning for him. He had to trust him.

"Who are you?" Curt queried as the man got back out, apparently done with his search.

Frank looked him up and down. "Detective Frank Arsward. You two don't even meet the description."

"Can we go, now?" Arthur asked, annoyed.

"Sure, you're clean. Sorry about that, but I just didn't know."

"It's okay." A thought struck Arthur. "Say, what did the girl look like?"

Frank was walking away when Arthur spoke. He stopped and spun around on his heels. "She had brown hair. About medium height. Twenty years old."

Arthur nodded, smiling. "I think I saw her. But I didn't see the men in the car. She was on the passenger side."

Detective Arsward nearly jumped. "Where at?"

"At an intersection of the road to Meeteetse and the road to Pitchfork Ranch. He turned right, away from Pitchfork."

"Are there any places they might stay at?" Frank asked, observing that the sun was setting.

"Yeah, a few. My ranch is near the road, so I know it pretty well," Arthur told him.

"Could you show me?"

Arthur gulped. "Well, ah, maybe Curt could. I don't think I could—" he trailed off. He really did not want to run into danger. It seemed as stupid to him as running into a burning barn.

"Let's all go. If we catch 'em, Detective, you'll want us to help," Hawk offered.

"Sounds good. Can we go in your truck? I don't think my little Plymouth can take much more of these rough country roads."

As they drove down the road, Hawk talked with Arsward. "So, Mr. Arsward, I hear you're pretty famous in mid-Wyomin'," he mentioned.

"I suppose so. But this is my last case. I'm planning on retiring. My wife wants me to enjoy the grandkids while they're little. I couldn't agree with her more."

"Family man, eh?" Curt replied, smiling. "Say, I have a question."

"Yeah?"

"If I end up helping you save this girl and jail them crooks, would you do me a favor?"

"Depends. Can you tell me what it is?"

"I don't know," Curt answered, hesitantly. Arthur eyed him a moment.

"Does this have something to do with your deep, dark past, Curt?" Arthur questioned.

Frank's eyes grew wider. He studied Curt Hawk carefully. "What's your last name, Curt?" he asked.

Curt groaned. He should have kept his mouth shut. This man would jail him for sure. Arthur stopped the car and stared at Curt, along with Frank. He knew he had to answer. "Hawk."

The detective frowned. Everyone was silent. "Well, well, well. I'm in the midst of at least one fugitive. Curt Hawk. The famous seventeen year old bank robber," he laughed suddenly.

"What?!" exclaimed Arthur. He looked bewildered. Tipping his cowboy hat back he kept his gaze on Curt, as if watching a criminal.

"Please don't throw me in jail," Curt begged, sounding more like a boy than a grown man. "I didn't do it. I was set up, I swear!"

Frank eyed the younger man. He was always keen on his job, so keen, in fact, that he tended to study cases states away. Curt's had been one of them. Frank was no fool, but a most observant, studious investigator who did not miss much. He had found many details about Curt's case interesting, especially the ones that did not catch the Massachusetts' investigators eyes. He knew Curt was innocent, and was outraged when the boy was convicted. But he could do nothing.

"I'm not going to throw you in jail, Curt. I've studied your case. I know you're innocent. The whole trial was rigged and the witnesses were bribed," Frank told the nervous young man.

Curt let out a long sigh of relief. "Then you won't give me away?" he asked.

"What's the favor you want, Curt? Is it to have your name cleared, so you don't have to go on hiding from the law?" the detective queried.

Curt nodded. "Yeah, I reckon thet's just what I was hopin'."

"Tell ya what. You help me, both of you, in whatever way I need you to, and I'll clear your name Curt. Do you need an incentive, Arthur?"

Arthur wiggled in his seat. "Can't I just stay out of it?"

"Sure," Frank replied.

Arthur sat silent a moment, hesitating. He did not dream it could be so easy. The girl's face floated before his eyes. Never before had he thought of facing danger, but thinking of that girl changed his mind. "Never mind," Arthur mumbled. He turned the key. As the engine roared he added, "I'll come along." He had no idea what he was getting into, and he was not sure he wanted to know. Arthur only knew he wanted to save the poor girl.

Chapter Three

Marlene struggled against the force of the big man's grip. She screamed and kicked as he held her arms tight against her chest and carried her out to the parking lot, to a dark truck. A grey haired, balding man joined them and opened the door to the truck. The younger man tossed her in. He pulled out a roll of duct tape and wrapped it around her ankles, so she could not run away. "Git in front with me, Sam," the older man ordered.

Marlene sat solemnly in back as the truck rolled down the highway. She wrinkled her nose as a pungent odor from the two men wafted back to her. It was a smell of sweat, mixed with the smell of calf and cow, and of oats and feed. She could guess from the smells that these men spent many a day on a ranch. Tears rolled down her cheeks as she wondered what would happen to her.

Several hours of silence passed as they sped down the paved road. "So, do we ransom her, Pa?" Sam asked.

"Yep," Sam's father replied.

"Who are you?" Marlene asked, bemused and uncertain.

Samuel glanced back at her and laughed at her teary face. "Yer shore a wimpy girl," he told her. "I'm Samuel Henders, and this here's my pa, Gruff Henders."

Marlene turned pale at hearing the names. She had heard of some robberies and other crimes in the past linked with those names. The courts were never able to prove their guilt, however, and they always got off free. She recognized Sam's face now. "Do I know you?" she asked Sam.

Sam grinned, still staring at her with hungry eyes. "We met, once, on campus."

Marlene recalled seeing the young man walking behind her and a friend one day. He seemed friendly enough, so she briefly spoke with him. She barely remembered joking to her friend about being from a rich family. Marlene was not from a rich family, but her friend always insisted that she must be, having such manners as she did. Sam Henders must have taken her literally.

As Sam turned back around to face the front window, he mentioned, "We'll git a lot a money off a ya." He and his pa laughed at this.

It was late in the day when they stopped at a stop sign. Marlene's eyes were growing heavy, but she felt she must stay awake. She had to be ready to run away. She feared what the men might do to her when they found out her family was not rich. The look Samuel had given her was not comforting. His sneaky disposition and snake-like eyes made her nervous. He might try anything to make the kidnapping worthwhile.

Marlene glanced out the window. She saw a tall, slim, muscular cowboy throwing a bale of hay into the back of a pickup. Now was her chance for escape. She tried to open the door, but the men had put the child-safety lock on. Pounding at the window, Marlene hoped to get the man's attention. He stood erect and turned around to see her. She watched the puzzled look on his face turn into a blur as Gruff drove her away.

They finally stopped at a ranch, and Sam Henders yanked Marlene out of the cab and tossed her onto the ground. She cried out as her arm struck a boulder. "Ah, shet up," Gruff yelled. Sam dragged her to an old, broken down ranch house. Marlene guessed that this must be their ranch. She lay on the floor as the two men walked out and back in with back packs and saddles. Gruff opened his backpack and spilled the contents on the table.

"We got at least a couple hundred bucks from thet register at the gas station, Son," he called to his son as he walked in.

"Great, Pa. Now, we have a stamp ta put on the ransom letter, right?"

"Yeah," Gruff growled, "but ya gotta write it first. How many times have I told ya, one thang at a time?"

"Right, Pa." Sam slammed the front door shut. "I'm gonna bolt it, Pa."

"Good, Son. Now yer thinkin' right."

Gruff closed the musty old curtains on the three windows in the house that was more like a cabin. The red glow of the sunset shone through the chinks between the bleached logs. Marlene felt a draft coming from above. It was no wonder. The patched roof over her head had many a hole that still needed to be fixed. Two of the walls were slanted and looked as if they would fall over at any moment.

Marlene sighed, feeling her throbbing arm to see if it was broken. The arm was okay, though bloody. As the girl lay on the floor, she wondered over her situation. It was as if she had been picked up from the twenty first century and tossed down into the early twentieth century. The house looked to be at least a hundred years old. She suspected the ranch had been operating here for at least as long. If Marlene ever made it out of here, she sure would have a story to tell.

The last light of the sun drifted away, and the cabin turned dark. Gruff lit a small oil lamp for Sam to write by. He then proceeded to grab a blanket from a pile and tossed it towards Marlene. Sam walked over to Marlene and dragged her further from the door. He threw the blanket over her. "Go to sleep," he ordered reaching down towards her. Marlene tried to resist as he felt her face, brushing away the hair. She could tell how tempted he was to do more.

"Son, write thet letter," Gruff shouted.

Sam walked away, but not before he gave Marlene a sly smile. Marlene grimaced. Sam sickened her. She closed her eyes, in the pretense of sleeping, and waited. Maybe she could stay awake until they had fallen asleep. Then she could escape and.... Marlene had been more tired than she thought. She quickly fell asleep. The image of the young man on the side of the road glowed in her mind. She dreamed about him, imagining him saving her from this ghastly situation.

Chapter Four

Nancy Favors heard the truck driving towards the Henders' ranch that evening. She looked out her window and watched as Gruff and Samuel stepped out. Nancy wanted to run out to meet Sam, but she did not. Quickly she closed her curtains, lest Gruff see her looking. Gruff had forbid his son to see Nancy, since she was African-American. Gruff's family had lived in the south for a hundred years before his great-great-grandfather moved west, to Wyoming. Though Gruff had never been to his family's old farm in South Carolina, he proudly called himself a southerner. Though his father was a racist man, Sam did not share the same ideals. Every night, after dark, he would sneak out of the house to meet Nancy, since she moved near him that summer. She had a job at the library in Meeteetse, yet wanted to have a home away from any towns. When she met Sam, she thought she was in love. She let him kiss her some nights, when he whispered of marriage.

Nancy was an openly honest girl, rather brutal in her words and opinions at times. That is why Sam liked her. She fought him sometimes, and he liked that in a girl. Nancy listened to every word Sam said, though she did not always trust him. If she had known he was a criminal, she would not have ever spoken with him. Nancy appreciated Sam at first just for his friendship. She had had only one friend before, back in high school. Marlene Rose Picket, a quiet, studious girl, was the first to greet Nancy when she met her her sophomore year. The two talked about books at lunch time and studied together in study hall.

When Nancy graduated from high school, she forgot about Marlene. Marlene had gone off to college. Nancy could not afford college when she graduated at seventeen, and so she moved to the old ranch house up north. She was eighteen years old now, and, by the end of the summer, would have enough money for her first year of college in Sheridan. Nancy loved to cook, and she planned to work in a bakery or restaurant with high pay some day. For now, working at the library and reading books to pass the time sufficed.

It was late in the night when Nancy ran out on bare feet to their usual meeting place. There she waited, by the rushing water of the river, beneath the cover of the tall willow. Near her, a homemade bridge consisting of several longs laid from one bank to the other made passage across possible.

Time seemed to pass slowly as she waited for Sam. A cool wind blew, and a hooting owl in the tree caused Nancy to gaze upward. Between the leaf-covered branches the stars sparkled in the dark blue sky. An illuminated cloud concealed the moon. Nancy glanced back down at her feet. She sat down, not worrying about her slacks getting dirty. The ground was cold and a bit soggy from a recent rain. Crickets chirped at random intervals all around. Suddenly Nancy heard a frightening scream.

As fast as she could, Nancy took off running toward the scream. There was one more scream, muffled at the end, and then a voice Nancy recognized shouted, "Quiet!" That was Samuel's voice. Nancy's heart beat wildly as she pumped her arms and bounded on her feet. Maybe Sam was in danger.

Marlene woke up a couple hours after she had fallen asleep. At first she thought she was at home, until she felt the cold, hard, wood plank floor beneath her. In the dark, she scanned around with her eyes. She remembered her situation now. Her ears were alert. No one stirred. Deep breathing came from near her, before the door she suspected. Loud snoring arose from the left of the room. It was husky and deep and rumbling. That was the noise that had woken her up.

Quickly, Marlene stood up and let her eyes continue to adjust to the darkness. A little light streamed through the cracks between the door and its frame. Marlene walked softly and carefully on her toes. She watched ahead of her and slowly stepped over Samuel Henders' sleeping form. She reached for the door handle and took one more step. The floor creaked beneath her weight and she turned the handle.

Suddenly Sam shot up from the darkness and grabbed her by the arm. Marlene screamed in shock and fright. Sam took her in his arms as she tried to run out the door. She screamed once more before he covered her mouth with his broad hand. Her next attempt was muffled. Marlene fainted and Sam set her on the floor.

Gruff woke up and stared through the darkness at the figure he took to be his son. "What the—" Gruff began.

"Don't worry, Pa. I got it taken care of," Sam told him.

As Gruff lay his head back down, the door swung open. "Stop!" Sam yelled sleepily, thinking it was Marlene escaping. But Marlene lay on the floor, unconscious.

The person who opened the door tripped over Marlene and fell into Sam's open arms with a little cry. Sam recognized Nancy immediately. He held Nancy in his arms and spoke softly. "Nancy, what are you doing here?"

Nancy whispered back, "I heard a scream. Are you in trouble?"

"No," Sam told her. He studied her eyes, trying to see what she knew in them. It was possible she had seen Marlene earlier.

The room grew lighter. Sam turned his head with a bewildered look on his face. His father blew out the match he had used to light the lantern. "On the contrary, little Nancy, he is," Gruff spoke angrily. Then he laughed a sly laugh. "Guess you're stayin' the night too. Can't have you talking."

"But Pa—"

"I'll have words with you later, Son. Huggin' and datin' a black girl."

"That's enough, Pa!"

"Shet up, Son. She'll be part of the ransom," Gruff growled.

"Mr. Henders, your son intends to marry me," Nancy told Gruff, hoping to get away safely. She was afraid, but she hoped Gruff would not harm her if he thought she was Sam's fiancée.

"That true, Son?" Gruff looked intently at Sam.

Sam could feel his father's eyes, burning into him. He could not bear to face him. Turning his back to everyone and letting go of Nancy he replied, "No Pa, it's a lie." His face was red.

Nancy grabbed Sam's shoulders and swung him around. She slapped him soundly across the cheek. Gruff reached her in several strides and knocked her off her feet with one big, trunk of an arm. Nancy let out a gasp as she fell to the floor.

On the ground Nancy noticed Marlene. "Marlene!" she cried. Marlene stirred and weakly opened her eyes to peer back at Nancy. "Oh, Marlene, what are you doing here?"

Marlene could not believe it. Her old friend was staring at her. Where had she come from so suddenly? "I've been kidnapped," Marlene whispered, as if it was a secret.

"Oh no!" Nancy gasped.

"You're both our captives, now," Gruff said with a laugh.

"And don't try any more a yer escapes," Sam added, grinning at his father.

Nancy and Marlene exchanged glances. "I thought Sam was a nice boy," Nancy whispered.

"I did too, when I first met him. Now we both know the truth."

"Quiet!" Sam yelled.

The road was bumpy and jolted Curt against Frank. Curt sat in the middle, to be squished between the other two men. "How far do you think we'll have to go to find them?" Frank asked.

"Don't ask me. You're the detective. You must have some inkling as to where they were headed.

"He didn't, Arthur, remember? He—ow! He needed our help to even get goin' in the right direc—ow! Direction."

There were some deep dips before the road smoothed down a bit more. Heavy rains had washed out gullies in random lengths of the road. Curt's side was already beginning to ach from Arthur's constant elbowing.

"We'll find them, somehow. You just help me look," Frank told them.

"Say, do we even know what these fellows look like?" Arthur asked.

"One is an older fella, and the other is a young guy, like around your age," Frank replied.

"Oh, that helps a lot. We just need to find a father and son in a truck and hope there's a girl with them," Curt retorted, sarcastically.

"The young guy, who nabbed the girl, had on a grey college sweatshirt, according to her mom. That's all the info I got," Frank returned, ignoring the sarcasm. "Say, can you speed it up a bit, Arthur? We'll never catch 'em at this speed."

"Please, no faster," Curt Hawk begged.

"Hey, do you want me to clear your name or not?" the detective snapped. He glared at Curt.

"Well sure, but I don't want to have to be tortured to do it. I'm getting all sore from being jolted around in here."

"I thought you two were cowboys," Frank replied, now grinning at Curt who turned red in the face.

"We shore are. Come on, Curt, it's no worse than a day in the saddle," Arthur told his friend, gently nudging him before a dip caused him to lean forward and his shoulder to hit Curt's neck.

"Alright," Curt groaned, throwing up his hands.

A couple hours down the road Arthur's truck broke down. As sunset was nearing, Arthur, Frank, and Curt decided to camp off the side of the road. In the morning they would decide what to do. Arthur had a box of granola bars and a bag of old beef jerky under the seat of his one cab truck. He and Curt eagerly devoured the jerky and some of the granola bars as their ration for the night, but Frank politely declined. He found a lollipop his youngest daughter had stuck in his left pant pocket and ate that.

Meanwhile, the sheriff in Cheyenne was sending out dispatches to his men. Immediately after the kidnapping, Sheriff Ralf Kieler radioed his men to keep a lookout, and he alerted other stations around the state as well. No one had reported anything, yet. Now that it was dark, the sheriff told his men and advised those around Wyoming to wait until morning to continue their search. The few news stations around the state broadcast the story several times before switching to their planned topics.

Pam Picket and her husband, George, Marlene's parents, waited anxiously near the telephone all day once the police dropped Pam off at home. As the hours passed Pam grew more discouraged. "What if we never see her again?" Pam sobbed. She had held up strong after she left the mall, but now she broke down.

"Don't worry, honey. The cops know what they're doing. Marlene will be fine," George comforted her. He was just as worried, however.

Marlene was the youngest of five. Her parents did not tell her siblings yet of the kidnapping, as they did not want to worry them. The phone rang. At the same time a car drove up and parked in front of the house. As George picked up the phone, someone knocked at the door.

Pam answered the door to see her youngest son standing on the front welcome mat. "Mom, why didn't you tell me Marlene's been kidnapped?" he cried, stepping forward to hug his tear-faced mother.

"Oh, Ryan," Pam bawled. She lay limply in her son's strong arms.

George heard a familiar voice on the phone. "Dad, it's me, Nate. I just heard on the news that Marlene's been kidnapped. Is there any news as to where she's at?"

"No, Son. We just have to wait," George replied, trying to hide his fear in his deep voice.

Nate could hear the trembling in his father's voice. "Dad—Dad she's okay, right?"

"Sure, Son, sure. We just don't know if she's alright," George replied. He could no longer think straight.

"I'm heading home," Nate told him.

"No, Son," George refused. "You'll just miss school." Nate was a senior at Washington State University. He was taking a few summer classes to catch up, since he changed degrees after his freshman year.

"Come on, Dad. I've gotta. We need to stick together."

"No, Son. You can't do anything for her now, anyway. Just stay where you're at. We'll call you the moment we hear anything," George returned.

"Okay, Dad. But I'll be waitin' by this phone, so you call me, okay?" Nate relented.

"Okay."

When Nate hung up he slumped into the only chair in his one room apartment. He let out a long sigh. "I wish I hadn't picked on Marlene so much," he mumbled. Nate was a year older than Ryan. Ryan and Nate had always been close, playing football together and telling each other about the girls they were dating. But Marlene was left out. Back in elementary school, the three of them stuck together, but once the two boys hit junior high they took to picking on her. She got them back by teasing them about their girlfriends, and sometimes sabotaging their dates. By high school Marlene was sick of Nate's teasing, but he kept on with it until he left for college. After that they had not had much time to talk.

Ryan was a junior at the same college as Marlene, but he lived at his own apartment, full time. He was just driving home from a movie with a few of his friends when the announcement about Marlene's kidnapping rang over the air. Ryan turned his car around and headed down the highway, straight for his parent's house.

Ryan sat down at the table with his mother and father. Pam told him the details of the kidnapping, and what little the police had gathered. No one knew where the kidnappers had gone. They had simply vanished.

Pam asked Ryan not to call the two oldest, Sue and Albert, until the morning. Ryan spent the night at his parents' house. Pam tried to sleep, but her thoughts kept her restless. She kept replaying the day's event in her head. Again and again she wished she had run to stop the men, rather than freeze and fall. She also regretted arguing with Marlene that morning. How many times had she nagged Marlene about not getting out more, instead of enjoying the time she had with her daughter? Sadly she realized that today might be the last time she would see her daughter. Maybe she should not have insisted on her daughter studying so hard and seeing friends. After all, Marlene loved to read and write. She may have been quiet, but Pam knew she was smart. She picked up on different writing strategies from her books. Marlene studied hard during the school year, so why should she not get a break from it all? Pam decided that when she got her daughter back, things would be different between them. She wanted to believe her daughter would return, no matter how much doubt crept in.

George had always insisted that Marlene plan for the future. His younger brother had dropped out of school and now worked at a grocery store with low pay. He did not want his own daughter turning out like that, just because she was always dreaming. George believed his daughter still had a lot to learn. He sometimes thought she had not learned much from school, and then Marlene would make some clever comment or observation that changed his mind. Now he wished he had let Marlene know how much he loved her and how his insisting on her making goals was for her own good. One thing he was glad about, though, was that he had bought her a few of those books she cherished so, despite his fear that she would dream her way through life.

Sue and Albert had both been sensible. Sue was now a teacher in New Mexico, and owned her own house. Albert lived in Ontario and worked for the Canadian government. He had majored in political science and gotten his masters in business. His income was more than enough to support his wife and four kids. He was the oldest of the family, and, when he was home, was always giving Marlene advice about her stories. Both George and Pam could see how much Marlene looked up to Albert. Sue tried to persuade Marlene to become a teacher like her, but Marlene was not sure what she wanted to do.

Marlene's parents were so upset over losing her that they exaggerated any wrongs done to her. They had always been kind and generous to her, supplying her with writing supplies and giving her more Zane Grey books for her birthday. Marlene never had a doubt her parents loved her. Though Pam often insisted her daughter go to games with friends, she just as often asked Marlene to tell her about the books she was reading and drove to the mountains with her to walk. George read some of Marlene's books after her, as he loved westerns too. And though Marlene's siblings had all picked on her at one time or another, they had all bonded with her and each other through growing up together. Ryan and Nate always included Marlene in playing video games and board games with their friends. Albert and Sue loved to help Marlene with her homework, when she needed it, before they moved away. Despite all the good things they had done with Marlene, fear of losing her played a funny trick on the minds of the Picket family.

Chapter Five

The next morning Arthur found himself filled with energy. Curt, eager to clear his name, suggested they walk on down the dirt road, looking for the truck. It was still early yet, the sky still grey with dawn. Surely, Curt reasoned, the kidnappers spent the night somewhere nearby and would still be there. Arthur's mind lingered on the beautiful girl. All he had was a glance of her fine, soft face, but it was enough.

Pam was still awake, full of guilt, regrets and fear, when she heard the paperboy ride up on his squeaky-wheeled bike and throw the paper at the front door with a thump. She crept out of the room, not wanting to disturb George, who was snoring heavily, and she wearily stepped down the stairs to the door. The door creaked as Pam opened it, and she picked up the paper.

As she walked back up the stairs, Pam rolled off the rubber band around the paper and straightened out the bulk to read the front page. Her dropping eyelids raised and her hand flew to her chin. The front line read:

Girl kidnapped. Police ponder on motive behind Picket 'Napping.

Pam sat down in the rocking chair in the corner of the living room. She scanned the next lines with her eyes.

> Yesterday college-student Marlene Picket was kidnapped. She was taken from the Cheyenne mall. Police are unsure of the motive. Governor Franklin promises that Wyoming's police force will track down kidnappers. A search is underway for the victim, if she is still alive, or for her body. Suspects are....

Tears streamed from Pam's eyes, blurring her vision. The thick newspaper slid from her lap to the floor. She could not stand the thought that the kidnappers could also be murderers. "You alright, Hon?" George's voice wafted over to her as she fainted in the chair.

When Marlene awoke, she found she was tied to a chair. Nancy, who was tied right next to her, was staring at her. "Why did they kidnap you?" she asked Marlene.

"They want me for ransom," Marlene explained.

"But your parents don't have that much money," Nancy whispered. "Shhh! Don't let them know that," Marlene whispered back, nodding her head towards Sam and Gruff, who were sitting at their bare wooden table, talking.

"You sure that Mike fellow will get the letter to them, without spillin' the beans?" Gruff asked his son.

"Of course, Pa. Mike's smart. You remember that last job he helped us carry out."

"Oh, yeah. I fergot about that. He did a good job sneakin' them cows outta that corral. And he arranged it nicely with thet stationmaster," Gruff recalled, scratching his scruffy beard.

"Ya see? Of course we kin trust him. He told me he'd be by this mornin'," Sam returned. "But Pa, what'll we do about Nancy?" His tawny, clean face showed anticipation.

"They seemed to know each other."

"Who?"

"Marlene and Nancy. We'll add a few thousand bucks to Marlene's ransom for Nancy. Her parents will pay it all," Gruff explained. He brushed his straggling hair back from his face.

"I'm nervous, Pa. What if somethin' goes wrong? What if this doesn't pan out?"

"Sam, no one follared us and no one knows where we are, 'cept Mike. Stop worrin'" Gruff reasoned.

Arthur led the way along a cow trail that ran parallel to the road. They had started out walking on the side of the road, but when a car honked and almost hit Frank, it was decided they would stay off the road. After a few miles they reached a large ranch. Curt stayed out by the road, keeping his eyes open in case the suspects would come down it, while Frank and Arthur took the path made by a heavily laden horse trailer driving along the same route over and over. It led them to the ranch house, where a family Arthur knew well lived.

The house looked like something off a Wyoming postcard. A red barn lay a hundred yards to the left of it, picturesque with its clean, white borders painted on it and tall, wide doors. The ranch house had neat, white walls and blue trim. The brown roof was obviously very new, and a stone path greeted them a few feet from the front door. Arthur knocked.

A short chubby woman hopped down the stairs and peered at Arthur and the detective a moment before she opened the door. "Arthur Pressed! Well, I'll be! We haven't seen you since the Christmas party," the woman greeted. Her cheeks were rosy and she wore a smile on her fat lips.

"Howdy, Mrs. Jertenson. It's good to see you too," Arthur greeted. "Oh, and this is my friend, Frank Arsward," he added, seeing the woman's curiosity at seeing Frank.

Mrs. Jertenson extended her hand to shake Frank's. "Nice to meet you, Mr. Arsward. You're mighty dressed up for the country. May I ask what you do?"

"I'm a detective," Frank replied, courteously. It was obvious that he wanted to get moving on.

"Oh?" Mrs. Jertenson glanced over at Arthur.

"Mrs. Jertenson, we're lookin' for some men that drove down this road. They kidnapped a young woman earlier yesterday. Have you seen anything?" Arthur asked. Frank eyed the woman intently. She shook off his gaze.

"No, Arthur. I wish I could help you. That's just awful. Is she a friend of yours?" Her voice shook with concern. Having children of her own, she shuddered at the thought of someone kidnapping one of them.

"No, Ma'am. Just saw her in the truck about fifty or more miles back, and Frank, here, wanted my help."

"Where's your truck, Arthur?" Mrs. Jertenson asked, looking behind them.

"Let's go, Arthur. We're wastin' time," Frank interfered.

"My truck broke down, Mrs. Jertenson. We've been walkin' since mornin'," Arthur replied.

"Wall, that isn't pleasant. You'll never catch them 'nappers at this rate," Mrs. Jertenson told him. "Walter's out with the car, right now, otherwise I'd lend it to ya." She was silent a moment and Arthur turned around, murmuring his goodbyes. Then an idea struck her. "Say, you could borrow our harses."

Arthur spun on his heel to face her. "Really?"

"Sure."

"Where are they?"

"In the barn. You can take the two fastest, Barney and Tony."

"We got another fellow with us too. You remember Curt Hawk."

"Shore. Take the little mare, June, also. She's almost as fast as the boys."

"Much obliged, Ma'am," Frank thanked her, imitating her kind of talk. He tipped his hat as he spoke.

Curt was pleased to see Frank and Arthur with three horses behind them. "Now yer talkin'!" he shouted. Arthur instructed Frank on how to mount up, while Curt hopped into the saddle of the little mare, swinging his leg over. "Ye-Haw!" he exclaimed with glee.

Early in the afternoon, as Pam was resting in the rocking chair, a car drove up to their house. She stood up, and George, who had taken the day off to wait for information, ran down the stairs. The doorbell rang as he reached the front door. He swung it open, but there was no one there. On the step lay an envelope, with simply one word on it: Picket. George picked it up and tore it open. Upon reading the letter inside, he raced up to his wife.

"Look at this, Pam!" he cried, tossing the letter to her. Pam held the paper in shaky hands. The letter read:

Dear Mr. and Mrs. Picket,

This is to inform you that your daughter, Marlene, is safe and being held for ransom. She is in an undisclosed location. We want fifty thousand dollars for Marlene, and four thousand more for Nancy Favors. Leave money in post office box 307 in Sheridan, Wyoming, on July third, at three-thirty in the afternoon. Do not bring police into this. If you try to track us down, you'll never see your daughter and her friend again.

Sincerely,

S. and G.

"Oh my God!" Pam exclaimed. "Where are we going to get the money, George?"

George gazed steadily at his wife. Her eyes were dark with shadows beneath. His face was drawn and serious. They had two days to pay the men, including this day. "I don't know, Pam. I guess I could get a loan from the bank."

"What bank would lend us that much? We're still paying off the mortgage on this house. And somehow they got her friend, Nancy, too. What will they do to them if we don't pay?"

George shuddered. "I don't even want to guess. Come on, let's go to the bank and ask them." Ryan heard his parents talking and came out of his room.

"We should call the police!" Ryan suggested.

"No, we can't. They said in the letter not to," George rumbled sternly.

"Then what will we do?" Ryan asked. He looked agitated and angry.

Chapter Six

Frank bounced up and down on the saddle of his horse, while Arthur and Curt seemed to be enjoying the ride. "I hope we don't have to go much farther," he complained.

They had not seen any houses for the past ten miles, and it was long past noon. "Arthur, we should a had lunch at that last ranch we stopped at," Curt added.

"We can't afford to stop. We need to catch them. Besides, I didn't even know the people at that place. I couldn't ask them for food."

"Those criminals probably are long gone by now," Curt replied.

"I'm not so sure about that. Look!" Arthur called. Curt rode up to get beside him, and Frank joined them.

"Who lives there?" Frank asked, gazing at the old cabin next to a collapsing barn. The curtains were drawn and smoke was slowly rising from the chimney.

"I don't know, but there's a grey truck outside. I think it's worth a shot," Arthur commented.

He led the way as they left the trail they were making parallel to the road. "Bang!" Arthur jumped off his horse after a bullet whizzed by his ear.

"You were saying?" Curt replied, smart-aleckly.

"Get down!" Arthur shouted, ducking behind his horse. Curt hopped down and reached Frank to pull him down. The old detective looked stunned and confused.

"Git off our property, ya tresssss-passers!" a scruffy voice called from inside the cabin.

"I think we better go," Arthur whispered.

"No way. This must be them," Frank argued.

"Come on, let's go," Curt snapped, waving his arm.

They walked to the side of the horses, using the animals as cover as they walked forward, turning away from the house. Apparently the shooter thought they were leaving, because he did not yell any more threats. "We don't have guns. How're we gonna git to them?" Curt asked, once they had moved a couple hundred yards east of the cabin.

"I've got an idea," Arthur replied. "Here's what we do."

Gruff had heard the pounding of hooves as he sat at the table. When he peered out between the curtains, he was astonished to see three riders, approaching his house. He nudged Mike McGee, known to the Henders, and others who had dealt with him, as One-Eyed McGee.

McGee had first learned how to shoot when he was drafted for the Vietnam War. He lost his right eye in a battle in swampy land in northern Vietnam, and amazed his peers as he aimed with his left eye squinted to take out the man who had done the job. The man was an army sergeant, also from the United States. He had accidently hit McGee. Mike missed hitting the sergeant then, but he kept on practicing his aim until the day when they met again. Then Mike would have his revenge. Mike was just eighteen years old then. The wound he received on that day would haunt him the rest of his life. The army discharged Private McGee honorably, ignoring the fact that he had tried to shoot a fellow soldier.

After the war, McGee hired himself out as a business associate, using his gun skills and clever thinking to earn him money. Not since he started his jobs had he worked an honest one. The Henders had first met him five years ago and had quickly earned his friendship. Just a year ago they hired him to help with a job. He visited often, using their cabin as a hideout between jobs. Gruff treated Mike like he was a son, despite the fact that McGee was just ten years younger and that his hair was starting to grey.

"McGee, there's some men out there. Would ya scare 'em?" Gruff asked.

McGee did not answer. Instead, he hurriedly grabbed his gun and aimed, resting his rifle on the windowsill. The shot did indeed scare the riders. When McGee yelled out to them they quickly changed direction. Pleased, McGee set his gun down and let the curtain fall back to its place.

Marlene was startled when the strange man shot from the window. She would have screamed, except Sam had covered her mouth with duct tape. Her face fell when Gruff commented that the riders were leaving. The men outside might have helped her escape, but it was too late now. She exchanged glances with Nancy, who had had the same hope.

Mike McGee stared at Marlene. When Marlene looked up to see him, her eyes grew wide, and she looked terrified. He was not that tall a man, but the way he walked around you would think he was a giant. A scar ran down from his closed right eye to his cheek. His cheeks were sunken and you could see the bones beneath them jutting out. The crooked nose and yellow-stained teeth did not help his impression on her. His chin was freshly shaven, however, and his hair cut short, unlike Gruff Henders. One-Eyed McGee had a tantalizing look in his eye that frightened both Marlene and Nancy. But it did not bother Mike. He did not need to make any more friends. In his business, he had more enemies than friends. The Henders were some of the few people he trusted. It had been that way ever since his own brother tried to turn him in for stealing, fifteen years ago. Now his brother was a forty-three-year-old broker on Wall Street in New York.

The hours passed slowly for Marlene, and she did not know the time until the sun once again dipped back down and left its purple glow to shine through the curtains. The room grew dim, and Gruff lit his lantern. "So, what date did ya set, Gruff?" Mike called.

"The third, Mike."

"What'm I gittin'?"

"Five thou, fer now, unless we need yer help some more," Gruff told him. He took a sip of coffee from his mug.

"Ten thou, or I walk out now and—"

"Alright, ten thou." Gruff glared at Mike, who stared coldly back. Mike took a bite of his stale ham sandwich, made with canned ham. He smiled with a full mouth, feeling victorious. Gruff picked up his poker hand to organize it.

Marlene gazed at the men silently as they sat around the table, playing cards. Sam noticed her and left the table. He squatted down to stare at her. "You're pretty," he commented, smiling friendlily.

Marlene was not in a friendly mood. She scowled with her face, since she could not talk. Sam bent over her. "I wish I coulda dated ya before this," he whispered. Marlene wrinkled her nose. Sam's breath smelled awful, like stinking fish. He reached for her and laid his hands on her shoulders, drinking in her beauty. If Marlene's hands were not tied to the chair, she would have slapped him. Nancy watched Sam, feeling a tinge of jealously, though she hated him now. She realized he never meant to marry her.

Sam ripped off the duct tape and kissed Marlene. She bit him on the lip. "Ow!" he shouted, standing up.

"Don't you dare kiss me, you scum!" Marlene yelled.

Sam kicked her with a booted foot. His foot hit her under her chin and she cried out. "Don't hurt her too bad, Sam!" Gruff called from the table.

"Just lettin' her know who's boss!" Sam replied, turning away from Marlene.

"You won't get any money!" Nancy exclaimed, infuriated. Sam had not put tape over her mouth. Sam swerved back to gaze down at her.

"What do ya mean?" Sam asked.

"Quiet!" Marlene shouted.

"Marlene's not rich, you idiot!" Nancy answered. "Now, let us go!"

"Oh, no, we won't be doin' that," Gruff growled from the table. "We'll git our money."

Sam glanced at Marlene. He had a feeling Nancy was telling the truth. His father did not believe her. Marlene tried to look innocent, but it was clear Nancy's words had struck her dumb.

A knock sounded on the door before Sam could think anymore. He answered it to see a suited man before him. "Yes?" Sam said nervously.

"I'm sorry to bother you, but I'm trying to find Meeteetse. You see, I got lost at the last turn I think, and it's getting dark and—"

"Git outta here!" Sam shouted, slamming the door.

As he closed the door, he heard the sound of shattering glass. A young man hopped through the window and dodged Gruff's fist. McGee picked up his gun. The front door swung back open and the suited man stepped in, holding a pistol. "Put the gun down, McGee," Detective Arsward ordered. McGee acted as if he would, then raised it back up and fired as Arsward fired. Frank always carried a pistol with him. He never knew when he might need it in his line of work.

Frank fell to the floor. Another man dove in through the window and tackled Gruff, who was fighting the other young man. When Curt took over on the fight with Gruff, Arthur raced to the two girls tied to the chair on the floor. Before he could reach them, however, Sam Henders barreled into him. Arthur let out a gasp. Marlene watched, excited, as the cowboy she had seen from the truck rose up to punch Sam.

Curt knocked Gruff to the floor. Gruff jumped back up and grabbed a chair. He broke it over Curt, knocking Curt to the ground, unconscious. Frank, though conscious, was doubled on the floor, holding his stomach. The blood kept flowing from the wound in his abdomen, despite his efforts to stop it with his hand. Arthur hit Sam on the chin with a left hook.

Marlene cried out, "Watch out!" as Gruff came up behind him with a chair leg. She wished she could help the cowboy.

Gruff hit Arthur on the side of the head as he turned to face him. Arthur started to fall when he grabbed the edge of the table. He rose back up and swung at Gruff's stomach. He made contact with a loud smack, and Gruff doubled over. Arthur ducked just in time as Sam swung at him. The two kept swinging and dodging and hitting until Gruff stopped them. "Put yer hands up, stranger!" Gruff ordered.

Arthur did as the man said, seeing that he held McGee's rifle. The cowboy watched out of the corner of his eye as Frank slid his gun along the floor. Arthur fell to the floor on purpose as Gruff fired. Grabbing the gun, Arthur stood back up. Sam knocked the pistol out of his hand. A thousand thoughts ran through Arthur's mind as he faced Gruff's gun barrel. Never before had Arthur found himself in such a situation. Two days ago he would have given up now, and hoped things would turn out all right. But he had changed, now, and he was ready to face the danger.

Marlene rubbed her ropes up and down and back and forth against the squared leg of the chair. Her wrists were growing raw from the effort, but she did not care. There was trouble in the cowboy's eyes, and she feared he would act drastically. The corner slowly cut through the ropes as Arthur stood frozen, staring intently at his newfound enemy.

"Sit down," Gruff told Arthur. McGee stared, amusement showing on his face. Instead of obeying, Arthur jumped towards Gruff. Gruff was surprised and caught off guard. Arthur managed to knock the gun from his hands and knocked his forehead against Gruff's. The older man grew dizzy quickly and fell down. McGee ran at Arthur, but Arthur was ready. He reached down and grabbed the rifle. Swinging the gun, he smacked McGee across the neck with the barrel. Mike fell to the ground, groaning and gasping for air.

As Arthur turned to face Sam, a gun went off. Marlene screamed and Arthur cried out hoarsely as he fell to the floor. Smoke wisped from the front of the pistol in Sam's hand. He looked shocked and almost dropped the gun at his action. Sam glanced at Marlene. She looked horrified. Arthur lay on the floor, gripping his chest.

Before Sam could swivel back around, Arthur grabbed Sam's leg and yanked hard. Unexpectedly Sam fell to the floor. The cowboy reached for Sam's gun and Sam knocked it away. It slid to their right. Both men reached for it.

The ropes snapped. Marlene reached for her ankles and quickly untied the ropes binding them together. Sam and Arthur were struggling for the gun when Marlene picked up the rifle and hit Sam's back with the body of the gun. He groaned and rolled over. Marlene rotated the gun around and aimed the barrel at Sam. "Stay down there, Sam!" she scowled.

Arthur rolled over to look up at the girl. She bent down to grab the pistol, and then asked him, "Are you okay?"

"Yep," Arthur moaned. He held a hand over his chest, just below his shoulder.

Marlene stuck the small gun in her pocket. She offered Arthur her hand, which he took. When he stood up she said, "Will you help me tie them up or something?"

Arthur nodded. They worked together to tie the three criminals up. Curt woke up and helped them get Frank onto a horse. Nancy followed Curt around, doing whatever he asked. He told her to sit on the horse with Frank, and hold him on. They would need to get Frank to a hospital soon. All the while Arthur was growing weaker and weaker. Once Frank was on the horse, Arthur's legs buckled.

Marlene let out a cry as the cowboy fell. She dropped down to help him up. Holding him against her, she stood back up. She could feel the wetness of the blood from his chest soak into her shirt. Curt helped her get Arthur onto a horse.

"Say, Miss, I think you should ride with him and hold him on," Curt suggested.

"Okay," Marlene agreed. "But I've never ridden a horse before."

Curt laughed as he helped her hop on behind Arthur, who stared at her, dazed. "Jest hold onto them reigns with one hand and my pal with the other."

Marlene held on tight, worried that she would fall off. Arthur leaned against her. "I feel like I'm going to bounce right off," Marlene complained to him.

He just laughed. "Thet's how ya always feel, until ya git used ta ridin' with the horse," he told her. His voice was deep and calm. Marlene loved how he spoke.

Marlene smiled. "What's your name?" she asked the cowboy.

"Arthur Pressed," he told her, closing his eyes. The scenery ahead did not interest him. "What's yours?"

"Marlene Rose Picket," Marlene told him.

Her voice sounded like honey to him. It was a western name, yet she had never ridden a horse. "Where are ya from?" Arthur asked. Dizziness swept over him.

"Wyomin'" Marlene replied. "How about you?"

Arthur did not answer. He was unconscious. The pain and dizziness had been too much for him. Marlene held him tightly against her. He smelled like cows and hay, but this time those smells did not bother her. She felt like the character in one of the westerns she had read. Never had she imagined, even when she was kidnapped, that she would be saved by a cowboy from any situation.

Chapter Seven

Pam, George, and Ryan were trying to take their minds off of the kidnapping by playing monopoly when the phone rang. They all raced for it and Ryan won. He picked up the phone and said, "Hello?"

"Is this the Picket residence?" a strange voice on the other end replied.

Thinking it was one of the kidnappers, Ryan answered, "Yes, and we'll get the money."

"What? What money?" the voice returned. "This is Sheriff Ralf Kieler."

"Oh. Sorry."

"I'm guessing the Henders must have asked for ransom money?"

"Well, er, yes. But we are supposed to keep the police out of it."

"You mean you were. I called to tell you we have word that your daughter is in good hands and that the three kidnappers have been apprehended. Several hours ago a Sheridan squad car was called to a ranch, where the men had been tied up."

"Holy cow! Mom, Dad, Marlene's okay! The police saved her!" Ryan shouted to his parents as he still held the phone.

"Not exactly us, Mr. Picket. But the point is your sister is fine. She's at the Sheridan hospital."

"Is she hurt?" Ryan questioned, feeling panicky.

"I don't think so. But the doctors wanted to check. We didn't get full details, but you can drive up to Sheridan to see her. They'll tell you what room she's in at the front desk in the hospital. Good bye."

When Ryan hung up the phone, he turned towards his parents. Pam had fainted into her chair and George was jumping up and down like a kid. Ryan glanced at the clock on the wall. It was ten o' clock in the morning. He and his father woke up Pam and the three of them jumped into the van.

They were quiet at first, as George started driving, but once they hit the highway it was as if a spell had been broken. "I'm so glad she's okay," Pam said, excitedly.

"It's funny. I thought that was the kidnappers calling. I guess the men must have been the Henders that the sheriff mentioned," Ryan added.

"I've heard of the Henders. The courts all around Wyoming have been trying to pin that father and son team for long about ten years now. I wonder why they kidnapped Marlene," George replied.

"Who knows? But at least Marlene's safe," Pam mentioned. "And I'm guessing Nancy's fine, too."

It was hard to avoid rabbit holes in the dark, so after Curt's horse almost pitched, he advised they ride on the road. Marlene was growing sleepy, but she kept holding on tight to Arthur. Nancy glanced at Marlene and smiled. She remembered back in high school when Marlene would tell her how she wished she had grown up in the eighteen hundreds. Nancy was always happy being in the twenty-first century—though she did wish her family had more money. She bent her head down to stare at Frank. His eyes were closed and his breathing was a rasping sound.

Curt gazed at Nancy for a moment. She was a pretty girl, from what he had seen of her in the cabin. Maybe life had finally turned around for him today. He hoped Frank would be alright, considering he wanted to see him get back to his wife and family. Plus he secretly hoped Frank would keep his promise and clear Curt's name. Then Curt could truly move on with his life.

Only one car came down the road the whole time they were riding. It cut through the darkness with its headlights about a mile before it reached them, driving towards them. Curt urged everyone off the road and then waved his arms, hoping the car would stop. The driver, however, did not seem to care. He only sped up as he grew closer, and his car shot dirt and rocks at Curt.

They rode slowly, so as not to worsen Frank and Arthur's wounds. Rain started pouring soon after they saw the car, and it kept on falling during the whole ride. Early in the morning they reached the Jertenson's house. Jenny Jertenson woke up her husband, Walter, as soon as she heard the hooves pounding the earth. These were the only people down this road that Curt knew. He knocked on the door and Walter immediately answered.

"Wall, hello Curt. Did ya catch the 'nappers?" Walter asked in a long, easy drawl.

Curt nodded as he said, "Yes, Sir, we did. But we got two wounded badly. My friend Arthur got hit near the shoulder and the detective with us got hit in the chest." He tipped his hat to Jenny, who stood behind Walter. Rain dripped off the hat and splashed his boot.

"I'll get my bag. Bring them in," Mr. Jertenson told him. Mr. Jertenson was a big animal vet, though he sometimes paid visits to neighbors when they were ailing. He was just two years short of becoming a doctor, in residency, when he switched to veterinary work.

Curt carried Frank inside, while Nancy and Marlene worked together to bring Arthur in. Arthur woke up on a couch in the Jertenson's living room. Walter was bent over Frank on the floor. "Walter? How did I git here?" Arthur asked.

Jenny walked into the room with hot cloths that she handed to Walter. "So, you're awake Arthur. Glad to see that."

"You rode with me on a horse here," a new voice called, answering his query.

Arthur turned his head and looked down to see Marlene kneeling by the couch. He marveled at her pink, young face, bordered by her wet dark hair that ran down to her shoulders. Splotches of mud decked her face, and there were dark circles under her hazel eyes.

"Marlene, could you tear off Arthur's shirt and start washing his wound?" Walter called. Marlene's small nose wrinkled. She reached up and grabbed both sides of Arthur's shirt.

Arthur put his hands on Marlene's to stop her. Her hands were cold. She was dripping water onto him, and he realized he was soaked, too. A red blotch stained her blue shirt up on her chest. "This is my favorite shirt," Arthur pleaded as Marlene paused.

Marlene smiled at Arthur, understanding. "I'm sorry, Arthur, but you're going to have to bear it. I could sew it up for you later, if you want."

She gently pushed his hands away and tore the shirt. The buttons flew everywhere. Arthur sighed, staring down at the remnants of his light brown cotton shirt.

Shivering, Marlene took one of the hot cloths from Jenny and laid them over Arthur's chest. He groaned in pain. "Sorry," she mumbled. She carefully rubbed the cloth over the hole made by the bullet as Arthur ground his teeth. "Have you ever been shot before?" Marlene asked, curiously.

Arthur shook his head. Jenny noticed how badly Marlene was shaking. "Marlene, why don't ya go git a blanket and sit by the fire. I'll have Curt and Nancy help," Jenny offered.

Marlene stared into Arthur's eyes. They were pleading that she stay. "No. I'll fix Arthur up first." Arthur's eyes opened wider. He was astonished that she actually would stay to finish the job.

"Marlene," Dr. Jertenson called.

"Yes?"

"I've got a lotta work ta do on Frank here. Can you try to get the bullet out of Arthur?"

"Shouldn't we just take them to the hospital?" Curt asked. He was sitting next to Nancy by the fire. The two were huddled together in a blanket.

"Nearest good hospital is a couple hours away, and Frank needs attention—ugh, there we go—now," the doctor replied. "I got the bullet out."

Frank's breathing was still a little raspy, and the doctor worked urgently. He called his wife to help him. She had often helped him in jobs before, like setting an animal's leg. "Curt, Nancy, could you get more of those cloths out of the boiling water?" Jenny asked.

Curt stood up and helped Nancy up. As they walked to the kitchen, Nancy asked, "Where are ya from, Curt?"

"Massachusetts. How 'bout you?" Curt asked.

"Well, I was born in Saratoga, Wyoming, but then we moved to South Dakota. Eventually we went to Indianapolis. But the living was too expensive there, so we followed my dad's job to a suburb of Chicago. We came back to Wyoming when I was in high school."

"Wow. You've been around a bit."

"I've never been as far east as Massachusetts, though. How'd you end up here?" Nancy queried.

"We better get these cloths over to the Jertenson's. They're beginning to burn my hands," Curt complained, changing the subject.

When they were heading back to the kitchen the second time, this time to grab some soap, Curt continued the conversation. "So, are you going to college?" he asked Nancy.

"No, not yet. I've been working at a library for a year, saving up."

"I thought you said you were eighteen."

"I am. I graduated at seventeen. I skipped eighth grade. It was kinda weird being in a class with older kids at first, but then I wasn't at that school long anyhow."

"Oh. Smart kid, eh? Well, I wish I had skipped a grade. Then I'd have a high school degree."

"Dropped out?"

"Sorta."

"You should go back. Or at least get your G.E.D. Anyway, what made you leave Massachusetts in the first place?"

"I ran away from home. Long story. But to sum it up, some supposed pals of mine set me up. They threatened me to not tell who really robbed the bank."

Nancy put her hand to her mouth, forgetting she had a bar of soap in it. After spitting into the sink, she said, "So you've been running away, ever since?"

"Yep. But Frank here promised to help me prove my innocence."

"I'm glad. You're a nice guy." Nancy put her arm in Curt's. He turned her towards him and kissed her, on impulse.

"What was that for?"

"I don't know. For believing in me, I guess. It's been a long time since I've had a girl believe in me."

After delivering the soap and pulling out the ointments and bandages from a bag for the doctor, Nancy and Curt returned to the fire. Marlene tried to listen in as she held a pair of tweezers in her hand, but she could not hear their words over the roar of the fire. She looked down at Arthur, who was watching her carefully. "This is going to hurt," she warned him.

Marlene slowly lowered the large pair of tweezers and reached them into the hole in Arthur's chest. She felt around with them until she gripped two sides of the bullet. Quickly she yanked the bullet out. Arthur cried out and grabbed her arms. "Good God!" he gasped. Marlene lowered him back down and set the tweezers and bullet on the cloth-covered table. She took a second glance at the bullet. Funny, it was somewhat round, like a musket ball, yet still had the shape of a shell. Mike McGee had a pretty old fashioned gun.

Arthur was dazed. He kept his eyes on Marlene, even when she turned from him to get another hot cloth. She laid it on his chest and wiped the blood from it. Then she reached for a squeeze bottle and squirted ointment over the wound. Marlene had no idea what she was doing, and she was still shivering, yet she tried to act confident. She may even had had a fever, yet that did not stop her. Arthur was impressed by how she ignored her own problem to help him.

Once the wound was dressed, Marlene wrapped a long cloth tape around Arthur's chest. He put his arms around her and held onto her for support as she wound the cloth behind his back. Then he lay back down on the couch and smiled at her. Marlene smiled back. She started to stand up when he stopped her with a hand on her forearm.

"Will you stay and talk a little?" he asked. Marlene nodded. Arthur scoot his legs to the back of the couch to make room. "You can sit down." She sat down on the couch, beside him.

"Thanks for saving my life," he told her. Marlene looked surprised.

"You saved my life," she replied.

"Well, I don't know about thet."

"You did. I've never met such a brave cowboy."

Arthur blushed. "I've never done anything like this before."

"You never had to save a girl in distress before?" Marlene joked.

"Nope. Yer the first one. Say, what's yer whole name again, Marlene?"

"Marlene Rose Picket."

"You sure are pretty, Miss Picket."

Now it was Marlene's turn to blush. "You needn't call me 'Miss Picket.' Just keep calling me Marlene."

"Okay. Say, you ever been on a ranch before?"

"No, not until now. Though I loved reading about it in wes—oh but you wouldn't be interested."

"Sure I am. You read westerns?"

"Yeah. I always dreamed of being a cowgirl on a ranch."

"After this is all over, you could come visit me, if you want. I've got a small ranch near Meeteetse."

"Really? Oh that'd be wonderful!" Marlene shouted, forgetting there were other people in the room. She threw her arms around Arthur's neck and hugged him.

"Ow!"

"Oh, sorry."

"It's okay."

Marlene and Arthur talked until Arthur fell asleep. Then Jenny showed Marlene to the bathroom and offered her a dress to change into. All Jenny's other clothes were dirty. Jenny was going to do the wash the next day.

Chapter Eight

When Arthur awoke, he was in a small, clean hospital room. It was somewhat dark, and his vision was a little fuzzy at first, so he blinked. Looking around, he observed a small nightstand beside him, a chair in the corner, and a girl sleeping in the chair. Rays of light were pouring in from a window behind him, giving the only light in the room. A white sheet covered him, and a pillow lay behind his head. He looked under the sheet to see that he was dressed in a hospital gown. He could hear voices murmuring in the hallway.

The girl awoke and looked across the room at him. It was Marlene. She stood up and walked over to stand by his bedside. "I'm glad you're awake, Arthur," she told him. Arthur did not reply. He only stared. This clean and beautiful girl was more radiant than the one he had rescued not long ago. Her face was shiny, the dark circles under her eyes were less apparent, and her hair looked soft and brown. Even more amazing was that instead of the soaked blue shirt and dark blue jeans, she had on a pale pink dress. She looked just like a settler in the west.

"Arthur? Are you alright?" she asked him, concerned that he had not moved, or even spoken.

"You're—you're beautiful," he told her.

Marlene blushed. It was just one compliment after another from this cowboy, as if he was making up for all the years she had longed for a compliment from a nice guy. "We're in Sheridan now," she replied, trying to shift his attention from her.

"Ah. That explains the hospital gown."

She giggled. "Arthur, you sure are funny."

"Not you. You look like someone from one of your westerns."

Marlene nodded. "Too bad you're not still in your cowboy garb, or we'd make a fine couple," she laughed. She covered her mouth after her last words.

Arthur turned serious. "Say, that gives me an idea. Can I take you out ta dinner sometime?"

"Sure." Marlene stared at him, surprised. She liked his drawl.

The door handle turned and a doctor walked into the room. "Miss, your boyfriend will be just fine, but I need you to leave now. Visiting hours are over," he told her. He was a handsome, tall man, wearing a white jacket and black pants. A smile from him revealed a set of white, straight teeth. Marlene smiled back. Arthur sighed. He never did have any luck.

"You don't understand, Sir. I—he—" Marlene began.

"I don't need to hear any explanations. You've got to leave. You can wait in the waiting room if you want. I've got to do a checkup on him."

Marlene left the room without any argument. The doctor checked Arthur's pulse, and he changed the IV that was hooked up to him. Then Arthur was left alone in the room. He listened to the ticking of the clock on the table beside him, and the dripping of the IV on his other side. Arthur thought about Marlene. She would probably fall for that doctor. That would be his luck.

She was a different kind of girl than any he had ever met before. When they had talked earlier, she had told him all about her family. She lovingly talked of her two closest brothers, who always teased her. Laughing, she had told him about a date she had ruined for one of them, Ryan, by coming into the restaurant and sitting at his table. She was good friends with the girl he was dating at the time and talked with her the whole time while Ryan sat sullenly. Arthur had asked her why she did it, and she told him that Ryan had threatened a boy she liked, just that morning. "You stay away from my little sister, or I'll knock your face in," Ryan had told the guy.

Arthur liked Marlene's feisty, yet kind spirit. She listened quietly when he told her about his younger brother, who was in college in Montana. He and his brother had fought a lot over girls in high school. Jim, his brother, usually won. He was the handsome basketball star of the family, and all the girls fell for him. Arthur was simply the quiet, shy guy, who played tic-tac-toe with a friend in study hall while Jim told wild stories to his friends.

Jim, Arthur, and Arthur's twin sister, Jill, drove from their parent's ranch into town every weekday, in Arthur's truck. At home in the winter, Arthur would gladly get up early in the morning to break the ice in the water troughs, before warming up the car. Jill was always the last one to get up, and sometimes Jim would complain that he was late to class because of her. Arthur sometimes teased her about it, too, but usually he would pick on Jim to take the pressure off Jill.

Jill Pressed got married right out of high school to Arthur's best friend, Robert, and she now lived in Butte, Montana. Jim visited her more often than he would visit Arthur, but Arthur did not mind. After saving up from working various jobs in high school, Arthur bought a ranch two months after graduation. His parents were disappointed that he did not want to go to college, but they did not bother him about it.

Marlene was in the waiting room when her parents and Ryan walked in. "Marlene!" Pam rejoiced, and she ran to hug her daughter. Her father was close behind, followed by Ryan.

"Glad to see you safe, Sis," Ryan told his sister.

"Are you sure, Ryan? I might sabotage more of your dates," Marlene replied grinning.

Ryan snickered. "That'd be pretty hard, considering I'm engaged now."

Marlene sat down, wide-eyed. "What? When'd that happen?"

"Guess he was so afraid he might lose you that he started to take life seriously. He called up his girlfriend last night and proposed," George explained, slapping Ryan on the back.

"So, how'd you get free of the kidnappers, Sis? The sheriff said the police weren't involved."

"Two cowboys and a detective saved me. One of the cowboys and the detective got shot fighting my captors," Marlene detailed.

"Really? How are they?"

"They're okay. We rode to a vet's ranch, and he worked on the detective, Mr. Arsward, while I had to get the bullet out of Arthur."

"Who's Arthur?" Ryan queried.

"The cowboy," Marlene replied with a dreamy look on her face.

Chapter Nine

"So, now that you're cleared, are staying here?" Arthur asked Curt as they walked down the steps of the courthouse.

"Well, for a short while, to visit. But I was hoping I still had a job in Wyoming," Curt replied, glancing at Arthur.

"Curt, wait up!" a voice called behind them. They stopped. Curt glanced back as Nancy raced down the steps to him.

"Oh, hi Nancy. I didn't see you in the room."

"I told you I'd be there."

Arthur watched as Curt offered Nancy his arm and she took it. "Sure, you still have a job, Curt. Thank goodness the Pickets gave me a reward, or those bankers would have gotten me for sure."

"You're forgetting some of that reward money invested is mine," Curt replied.

"So, I guess we both have a share in it, like partners. Which reminds me, are you still working at the library, Nancy?"

"Yep, until the wedding."

"You know, Curt, you two won't have much privacy if you stay at my house," Arthur told him.

"Oh, don't worry. I'm gonna start my own ranch, once we git some profits. Then that ranch will be all yours again."

"Sounds good to me. Although it'll be awfully lonely, not having Nancy visiting anymore."

"Listen to this guy. First he complains that having Nancy over all the time is eating him out of house and home, and now he wants us to stick around."

"You two are good friends of mine, Curt."

Curt laughed. "I know, Arthur, and don't worry. We'll visit. And we'll even have you over. Say, you should git yerself a girl, so you won't be always callin' us up."

Arthur looked down as he hit the last step. "I tried."

"Whatever happened to her, Arthur?"

"I don't know. It was a year ago. Marlene probably doesn't even remember my name," Arthur spoke softly. He and Marlene had gone on one date a week after he got out of the hospital. The next time he called her, her father told him she was studying, but that he would have her call him. That was in the fall. She never called him. Arthur did not try to call again. He just figured she did not want to see him again. After all, he did not quite fit into her lifestyle. Arthur never went to college, nor did he care too. He was used to hard work of pitching hay, riding horses, and throwing ropes. She was used to punching numbers into a calculator, solving math problems, and writing papers. His hands were callused and dry from hard work, his face set serious from facing problems on the range, while she was calm and humorous, her hands soft and warm from rubbing on cream before she left for school to study. You did not get blisters and calluses from the hard work of testing and using your mind, and writing with a pencil.

"Well, see ya later, Arthur," Curt called as he and Nancy headed down the street. Arthur snapped out of his remembrance to wave goodbye. He jumped into his car and it rumbled out of town, towards the airport. Heavy clouds hung overhead. It would be a rainy afternoon here.

They had just finished a trial during which Frank Arsward proved Curt's innocence. Arthur was heading back to Wyoming now, from Massachusetts. Curt and Nancy were taking a plane too, after they spent a few days visiting his folks. His parents were shocked and pleased to hear his voice when he called that morning. They never did believe that Curt was guilty. Arthur was glad the detective had kept his word.

Marlene was in her room, studying, when the phone rang. She answered it. "Is this Marlene?" a voice on the other end asked.

"Yes," she replied.

"This is Brad Tooth. I was the doctor you met in Sheridan, remember?"

"Yes, I remember."

"I'm in your town, and I was wondering if you'd like to go out for dinner tonight, say in two hours?"

"Sure, I'd love to," Marlene replied. She tried to hide her disappointment. Secretly she had hoped it would be Arthur Pressed. When her father gave her the message from Arthur a year ago, she was eager to call him back. Unfortunately, however, she had lost his phone number. She waited, day after day, for him to call again, but he never did. Marlene had no idea where he lived, but she thought about driving to Meeteetse to ask the townspeople about him. When she finally got the courage to go, her dad refused to let her borrow the van or grey Oldsmobile to go. After all, she had school to go to the next day, and, even if she went on the weekend, where would she stay? Marlene had forgotten to get Nancy's phone number or address, so she had no answer to that question.

Sighing, Marlene sat on her bed, thinking. She wondered why she kept on hoping Arthur would call her back. Did he really mean something to her? Maybe it was just the way they met that kept the image of him in the back of her mind. That soft spoken cowboy, who seemed awkward and afraid when he first jumped into the room, quickly turned to action when he saw her. It was as if seeing her for the second time made him brave enough to fight. But she had another opinion as to why. Marlene had been feeling quite lonely and scared when Nancy entered the picture. After that, somehow, Marlene remembered God. When she and Nancy were being tied to the chair, she was silently praying for someone to save them. Maybe, thought Marlene, I should pray about Arthur.

She prayed for a moment, and then turned back to her studies. Though it was summer, she was still taking classes from the University of Wyoming. She wanted to get ahead in her studying, so that she could take one less class in the fall when her friends returned. Plus, she had a few friends in the class she was taking now. It was odd how calculus could actually be fun with a few people you knew taking it too.

Since that memorable summer event where she ended up in northern Wyoming, Marlene had become more outgoing. She made several friends and made it a point to call them at least once a week and get together. Memories of funny movies, watching wet swim meets, cheering loudly for basketball players shooting the hoops until she was nearly hoarse and deaf, playing big group games, and eating out floated through her mind as she punched in numbers into her calculator and wrote down results. Finally Marlene had found herself, she felt. She still read westerns, of course, but that did not take so much of her time now. Marlene had discovered that to truly enjoy her life and to really live it, she had to throw herself into it, not hide away behind some cardboard cover. All it took was a couple of rough men to tear her out of her own world and show her what it was like to be trapped in a different one. Marlene decided not to let herself get trapped in any one 'world.' If she wanted to do some good for people, she had to make sure she was available to do it.

Marlene still remembered how awesome she felt, not to mention tired, when Arthur, Curt, and Frank rode in to save her and her friend. She loved to relive that time, in her mind, over and over. It was the one time she felt she was in a real, old-fashioned western land. A tear escaped from her glimmering eyes to splash upon the paper. Marlene tried to brush it off the paper, and it smeared the pencil lead. She wished the adventure could have gone on and had more than just simply 'a happy ending.' Every western she read had some part in it where the cowboy kissed the girl and at least hinted of marriage. But how could she think of that? After all, she had barely met Arthur. She had no way of knowing if he was the right one. It was good she was going out on a date with a nice guy. Then she could stop worrying about the cowboy.

The plane was delayed an hour, so Arthur moseyed around the airport, trying to think of something to do to pass the time. It was late afternoon, and the shadows were growing longer. Arthur switched his gaze back and forth, noticing departure areas and fast food restaurants. Maybe he would get a bite to eat. After all, he still had not eaten lunch. But for some reason Arthur did not feel hungry. Ahead he spotted an elderly man who was trying to lift his bags quick enough to get to the boarding area leading to a departing plane. Arthur raced to the man, as if it were some emergency in his life.

"Here, let me help you," Arthur said to the old man, reaching for his luggage.

The older man looked up, and Arthur saw that he had the white collar under his black suit. "Why thank you, young man," the priest replied, letting go of his heavy bags. He had a frail, wiry frame and short white hair that made Arthur wonder why he continued to serve. By that age many Americans had long been retired.

Arthur followed the priest, who seemed to trust him, though they had only just met. As Arthur plopped down the bags by the counter, near the departure ramp, the old man turned to him. "Thank you, uh, I don't think I caught your name," the priest told Arthur, smiling kindly.

Arthur tipped his worn, bleached Stetson. "My name's Arthur Pressed. And yours?"

"Father Matthew. Might I ask where you're from, son?" the priest replied, not in a hurry to get in the lengthening line to get on board.

"Wyoming."

"Oh, so are you on this flight, too?" Matthew asked.

"No, why?"

"This flight goes to Denver."

"Oh. I was going on a different plane to Denver, but my flight's been delayed," Arthur explained.

"Say, that's funny. This flight was delayed, too. Why don't you see if they'll board you here," Father Matthew suggested, with a twinkle in his eye.

"I don't know if they have any more—"

"Say Miss," Matthew called to the busy flight attendant who was checking people in.

She turned to him and smiled. She had been watching as the young cowboy had patiently carried the old priest's bag for him to the loading area. "Yes, Father?"

"Can you get this young man on my flight?"

The flight attendant turned a pair of lovely blue eyes to Arthur. Arthur smiled politely at her and watched as she blushed. Her eyes peered down at the flight schedule a moment before returning to Arthur. "Can we get going?" grumbled an impatient man gripping the hand of his eight year old son. His wife behind him shushed him.

"It looks like we have just one more seat, sir. May I see your old ticket?"

Arthur handed her the dog-eared ticket and she exchanged it for a new, flat ticket. She handed it to Arthur, who held her hand just a moment longer than she anticipated. Once again she blushed. "Where are you from, Mr. Pressed?" she whispered.

"Wyoming."

Then Arthur picked up the priest's bag and his own, small bag and followed Matthew onto the plane. They headed toward the back of the plane, where the same mother Arthur had seen earlier was anxiously trying to quiet her two year old daughter in her arms and the impatient father was disciplining the rebelling boy who was threatening to stick his chewed gum on the back of the seat ahead of him.

As Matthew sat down, Arthur hefted his bag into the slot above him. He was just about to continue on to his seat, when he noticed the number on the chair next to Matthew. "Hey! Number twenty-three! I'm right next to you, Father Matthew."

"Well, what do you know about that!" the priest exclaimed, surprised.

Back in the loading area, a man jumped to the end of the line. He took the last bite of his egg sandwich before handing the flight attendant his ticket. "Why this is for the other Denver flight," she told him, starting to hand it back.

"I know, Miss, Miss Fult," the man spoke with a full mouth, reading her name tag, "But I gotta get to the meeting on time in Denver, and the other flight's delayed. Can you get me in on this one?"

Miss Fult shook her head, glancing down at his warped, grease-stained ticket to read the man's name. She looked back up. "I'm sorry Mr. Debutrain, but we're full. You're just going to have to—"

"Listen!" the man interrupted. "I've got to get this flight! I need that contract, or I may lose my job!"

"I'm sorry, I can't help you," she replied, looking rather upset.

The irritated Mr. Debutrain stamped his foot and scowled at her. "Don't you know how important the stocks are these days? My stocks alone are worth more than your measly job!"

Tears started to flow from Jane Fult's eyes. "I'm sorry sir, but I have to go."

"Darn it lady!" The man looked infuriated. He pulled his arm back and looked as if he would swing at her when Arthur walked out from the narrow passageway. Mr. Debutrain peered at the cowboy as he walked between him and the flight attendant.

"Excuse me, sir," Arthur intervened, facing the man, "I couldn't help but hear your shouting from the plane. He noticed the broker's frozen position. "Were you going to hit her, over a stupid ticket? Well, if that's the problem," Arthur told him, pulling his ticket from his pocket.

A security officer walked over. "Is there a problem?"

"Yes," Jane told him. "This man is very upset. I've tried to tell him we have no more room on the flight. He was going to hit me I think."

"Let's go buddy. We'll get you on your flight," the officer ordered, grabbing Debutrain's arm and, with a quick motion, turning him away.

Jane batted her eyes at Arthur as she whispered, "Thank you."

Arthur simply tipped his hat and walked back onto the plane. When he sat down, Jane eyed him gratefully for a moment, before helping a child riding alone buckle his seatbelt. "I think you made her day," Matthew said, nudging Arthur in the ribs.

Why did Arthur think of Marlene as he stared at this girl, who looked quite different in her pressed blue and red uniform, dark blue cap, and shining blue eyes? "I don't know about that. Say, what do you mean?" Arthur turned to stare at the priest.

"We could all hear the man shouting at the nice lady, and I saw you walk out there, instead of sitting down. I'm quite sure it was your voice I heard, telling him off."

"I was just going to give him my ticket, so he'd leave her alone."

"That was nice of you. Confidentially though, I'm glad you didn't. I find your company much nicer."

"Thank you. Hey, where are you from?"

"Wyoming. I was just visiting my sister and her family in the east," Father Matthew described. "Her kids are ten and twelve. A smart little boy and a clever little girl, who is already almost a teenager. I can hardly believe she's been married fourteen years."

"Wow. Younger or older sister?"

"Younger. After I saw her take her vows, I flew to Missouri to take my own."

"So, you're a Catholic priest? You can never tell for sure these days, considering other religions dress similar."

"Yep. I've been the priest in Gillette for some years now."

"Oh. I haven't been to church for a long time," Arthur confessed.

"Really? Would you join me at St. Mary's tomorrow for mass, if you're around Cheyenne?"

"Well, I can't promise that, Father. I'm heading to my ranch near Meeteetse."

"Say, that's where those kidnappers were caught a year ago, wasn't it?"

"Yep."

"I was praying that the girl would come home safe. Some cowboys and a detective saved her, didn't they?"

"Yep." Arthur turned his head away. He stared at the floor of the isle as Marlene's face drifted from a lost cavern of his memory. Her tender eyes, the soft cheeks, her soft hair falling to her shoulders, and the dress she wore that day making her look so much younger, yet emphasizing her figure somehow. The priest was quiet, but Arthur could feel him watching him.

"Have you seen her since?" Matthew asked out of the clear blue.

The question pierced Arthur's recollection, and he nearly jumped out of his seat. As he gazed at that wrinkled, laughing face, Arthur wondered if the man could read minds. "How did you know?" His lips were dry as he spoke.

"After you mentioned that town, I remembered why I recognized your name. A young fellar was in the Rawlins prison and asked for me when I came visiting. He had a lot on his mind, and he just needed to talk. He told me about the kidnapping, which I had briefly heard about on the news. Then he mentioned how Marlene would be better off with the cowboy. When I asked him who, he mentioned your name. His name was—"

"Sam Henders?"

"Yeah, that's it."

"That's odd. He didn't seem to like me when we first met. Of course, that might be because we were fighting each other at the time." Arthur paused. "Well, I only saw Marlene twice after the adventure, once in court and once on a date."

"Yet you still looked like you think of her."

"Sometimes. When I git lonely I guess. But I'm not her style."

"How do you know?"

"She's a pencil pusher and I'm a cattle pusher. My mom was raised on a ranch when she met my dad. He majored in agriculture. I don't know what major she is, only that she isn't interested in me. Never called me back when I called her," Arthur described. The priest encouraged Arthur to continue, and Arthur found himself pouring out his life story to the kind old man.

When the plane landed and Arthur was walking out to his truck, he noticed the priest following him, dragging his bag behind him. Arthur stopped to help him. The priest was panting from the effort. "Where's your car, Father?"

"Down there," Matthew pointed. It was the opposite direction Arthur was planning to go, but he decided to help the priest out a little more.

Once Arthur had loaded Matthew's bag into the trunk of his red Subaru, Matthew turned to him. They shook hands. "I'll see you at St. Mary's," Matthew told him. Before Arthur could reply, Matthew sped like a young man to the front of his car and hopped in. He drove off waving to

Arthur. Arthur waved back and sighed. Maybe he should go to mass. But it did not have to be St. Mary's.

The sky to the west was bright red, and the thin clouds seemed to soak in the color. The Rockies jutted up from the earth, looming in the distance. They cut a jagged pattern into the sky. Arthur stood and just watched the sunset, thoughtfully. A plane roared close overhead, but Arthur did not seem to hear it. He blocked out all the sounds, turning what Matthew had last said over and over in his mind. The red started to fade, and purple began to take its place. Before long all the wonderful colors were gone and the blue sky was darkening in tone.

Chapter Ten

Marlene was curling her hair when someone knocked at her door. "Who is it?" she called.

"It's Nate," a voice called back.

"Oh!" Marlene dropped the iron and ran to the door to answer it. "What are you doing here?"

Nate had been coming to visit Marlene and their parents more often now, and he loved to surprise Marlene unexpectedly. Marlene always asked him the same question, before he asked her to go to a movie or something. "I just visited Mom and Dad, and I thought I'd drop by and see how things are going."

"You usually have a plan, Nate," Marlene insisted.

Nate threw his arms in the air. "Why do I try to be clever? Okay, I was wondering if you wanted to go up to St. Mary's in Cheyenne."

"What? I just went to mass last night. Besides, why would I want to drive all the way to Cheyenne to—"

"Because, that priest who married Sue and Charles is visiting. He called me on my cell," Nate interrupted.

"In that case, I'll come," Marlene replied. "What time is it?"

"Nine. The mass is at ten-thirty."

"Okay. Just let me finish curling my hair real quick and change to nicer clothes. It'll only take about five minutes."

Marlene was true to her word. Less than ten minutes late she was following her brother outside to his blazer. He clicked a button on his key chain to unlock the door and she hopped in. In less than an hour they arrived in Cheyenne. They hit a detour on the way to St. Mary's, however, that delayed them.

Marlene's sister Sue met a nice young man who was teaching fourth grade at the school she was at just two years ago. She did not tell her family about the teacher, Charles, until they got engaged. A month ago Sue and Charles traveled up to Wyoming to get married. A visiting priest, Father Matthew, married them at St. Mary's. He and Nate had a long talk after the reception that caused Nate to change his major once more. Nate was in electrical engineering to make plenty of money for the family he hoped to have in the future, but he changed to become a history teacher. Matthew had told him about his love for history, and how he involved his own history major into his sermons. Nate remembered how much he had enjoyed learning about the history of Rome in high school, and decided he wanted to pass on his own enthusiasm for history. Since then Nate and Matthew had talked a few times over the phone, the older man giving Nathan advice and encouraging him.

The choir was already signing, and the church was crowded when Marlene and Nate entered. They quietly walked up the pews, looking for some small space where they could squeeze in. A man with a cowboy hat resting on his lap had his face turned to the stained glass windows on the other end of the room. Marlene gazed at the windows as well. The mid-morning light was pouring colors through, onto the polished tile floor. Images of saints, including some apostles, glowed before Marlene's eyes. It was the most beautiful sight she had ever seen. She was still staring at one of the windows when Nate tugged on her sleeve. "Move in here, Sis," he whispered.

Marlene suddenly realized that the choir had stopped singing and that the priest had made his way to the front. She sat down on the bench and scooted down to make room for her brother. Turning, she saw that they were sitting next to the cowboy. As Father Matthew started speaking, the cowboy turned his head. Marlene could not help but gape. She cried out, "Arthur!" Matthew continued, ignoring the interruption.

When Arthur looked, he was astonished to see that the tall, slender girl who sat next to him was Marlene. She seemed more her age now, and more happy. "Marlene?" he whispered.

Marlene's eyes danced. Arthur grinned at her before glancing up ahead. Did he just see the priest wink at him? Suddenly Arthur was glad he had ended up at St. Mary's. He had not planned to, even when Matthew said it a second time.

Arthur had been driving along calmly the evening before, when he saw the lights of Cheyenne ahead. He was going to continue on up north when his check engine light came on. Sighing, he started to turn towards a gas station exit. A hummer swerved in before him and he rear-ended it. The other car was fine, but Arthur's truck had shrunk about two feet in length. He sat for a moment, watching the front end smoking, before the hummer driver knocked on his window.

"Are you okay, mister?" the man asked. Funny, Arthur would have been ticked if someone had rear-ended his car. Arthur nodded. "I sure hope you have insurance. You dented the back bumper," the man added. Now the cowboy groaned.

A tow-truck took Arthur's compressed truck to a cheap repair shop, and then took him to the nearest hotel. It would be at least a week before his vehicle would be repaired. "That's what I git fer trying to skip church," Arthur mumbled to himself as he walked into a hotel room. The air smelled like Lysol, and the carpet was thin and worn. A small, square TV sat on an antique-looking table. Arthur slumped down on the bed, and cringed at the sound of creaking springs. This just was not his night.

He managed to sleep anyhow, despite the squeaking, bumpy bed and the buzzing and brightness of a florescent light that just happened to be on outside his window. The room was cold half the night, but the heating system turned on around four in the morning, and the temperature was just right when Arthur woke up.

"Hi, Marlene," Arthur whispered, amazed that she still remembered him.

"I, I tried to call you, but I lost your phone number," Marlene whispered back.

Arthur gazed at her, noting her pressed red shirt with Capri-style sleeves and her stiff brown pants ending with her white and orange running shoes. Marlene stared back at him, surveying his brown leather vest over a white shirt with blue stripes down it. His hair was slicked back with gel.

On his lap sat a fading Stetson that made his average blue jeans look nice. She returned her eyes to his face. He smiled at her. How she loved his smile. His fine chin tightened. His face seemed to be chiseled out of marble until he smiled, and then the glowing of life melted away that persona to reveal a kind, lovable cowboy. Marlene's smile back made Arthur's heart race. He was sure she could hear the loud pounding of his heart over the singing of the church members.

Nate stared at the two for a moment, and then looked back ahead. It was mysterious. The guy Marlene had told him about last night when she called was a doctor, not a cowboy. The two seemed to know each other well, yet seemed to mystify one another and fill them with questions. A reader stepped forward and read from the Corinthians. Then the people burst into song again. Now it was time for the Gospel. Matthew took his gaze off the young couple near the middle pew of the church and stood up, beckoning everyone to do the same. Arthur and Marlene joined them, and Matthew chuckled as he glanced once more at the two to see Arthur grasp Marlene's hand.

As mass ended Arthur walked outside with Marlene, once again holding her hand. Nate confronted the two. "Who are you?" he asked.

Arthur put on his hat with his free hand and tipped it down. "Arthur Pressed. And who might you be?" Suddenly he feared the other man may be Marlene's boyfriend.

Marlene saw the look on Arthur's face. "Oh, this is my brother, Nate," she hurriedly introduced.

"Are you that cowboy who saved my sister?"

"Yep, I reckon so."

"I thought I recognized the name. I want to shake your hand." After they shook hands, Nate added, "So, are you sweet on my sister?"

"Nate!" Both men glanced at Marlene to see she was blushing rather badly.

Arthur grinned as he turned his gaze back to Nate. "Why, yes, yes I am."

Marlene let go of Arthur's hand to turn face him. "Why didn't you call me?" she questioned, her face returning to peach and a new light in her eyes.

"I figured you didn't want to see me again. 'Sides, I lost yer number."

"I lost yours, too. Otherwise I would've called you."

"You told me that already. Say, did you want to go walkin' downtown?"

Marlene turned to her brother. "When do you have to get home, Nate?"

Nate shrugged. "I'm staying over at Mom and Dad's, tonight, so it doesn't matter."

"Would you and Marlene like to go out to lunch?" Arthur offered.

Nate grinned. This guy was smooth, and he did not seem to mind an extra wheel. "Sure."

"Oh, and can I get a ride there? My truck's gettin' fixed," Arthur added.

"What happened?" Marlene questioned. She looked concerned.

"Just had a little accident."

"Are you okay?"

"Sure. I'm fine, Marlene," Arthur reassured her.

The three had a fine time at the pizza place Nate picked out. Marlene laughed at Arthur as he tried to pick up his first slice and carry it to his mouth. Cheese dripped over his chin as he bit down. He clumsily held the piece, trying to imitate Nate who seemed so skilled at the art. "Haven't you ever eaten pizza before, Arthur?" Marlene asked.

Arthur shook his head, since his mouth was too full for him to answer. Once he had swallowed he replied, "All we ever had were roasts and steaks and burgers with pasta or rice or potatoes on the side. And all I eat at my ranch is ham, beans, and tomatoes, with the occasional roast on the side. I have to admit, it does get kind of old after awhile. It was sure nice those nights when Nancy came over to cook. She made spaghetti."

Marlene raised her eyebrows. Was Arthur hinting that he was dating Nancy? "Is Nancy still around that area?" she asked.

"Shore. After all, she's dating my pal, Curt. Though right now they're in Massachusetts." Marlene let out a sigh of relief.

"Why don't you buy something else to cook?" Nate suggested.

"I can't cook anything else."

"You mean you don't know how to cook?" Marlene laughed.

"Yep. Only know a few recipes, an' thet's it."

"I ought to teach you sometime," Marlene replied, looking very serious. Arthur grabbed her hand and replied, "I'll have to take you up on that."

The rest of the meal Nate was silent. He listened as Marlene related to Arthur what had happened in her life since they last saw each other. Arthur then proceeded to tell Marlene about his life on the ranch, and then about Curt and Nate. Time seemed to pass by too fast. Before they knew it, they were done with the pizza and were leaving. Arthur asked them to go to a movie as well, and Nate dropped the two off at a mall theater, while he drove over to visit a friend.

Arthur had never been shushed so much in his life as when he was in the theater with Marlene. They kept on talking, verging on their dreams, when someone begged them to stop again. Watching the movie, which was a comedy, Arthur started to comment on certain parts and laugh. Marlene laughed too, and joined in on the commentary.

Before Arthur knew it, Marlene was saying goodbye as she walked towards her brother's car. Arthur hesitated, then ran towards her. "Marlene, the offer still stands. If you ever want to visit…" Marlene listened carefully as he told her his address. Marlene then told him hers.

At the end of the week, Arthur's truck was ready. He drove up to Laramie, where Marlene was at, to visit her on his way home. Marlene was glad to see him, and they spent the afternoon talking as they sipped vanilla milkshakes in the prairie-like Laprele Park. It was a warm Saturday afternoon in July. Upon finishing their milkshakes, they took a walk around the park. Marlene glanced down at Spring Creek and laughed and pointed for Arthur to look. He looked to see two small ducks swimming side by side in the water, dipping their heads at intervals and disappearing completely under the water before reemerging. A throaty laugh escaped him, too.

Arthur found a Frisbee by a tree, and he threw it to Marlene. She struggled to catch it, and held it against her chest. "Throw it back," Arthur called from about fifty feet away.

Marlene gripped the Frisbee in one hand, staring down at it as if it were some complicated contraption. She looked back up and stared at Arthur, waving to her in the distance. "I don't know how," she called back. Grinning and throwing his arms up in the air, Arthur jogged over to her.

"You hold it like this in your hand and flick your wrist as you let go."

"Like this?" Marlene attempted a throw, swinging her whole arm. The Frisbee twisted in the air and landed five feet away.

Arthur grabbed it and handed it back to her. He stood behind her and held her hand on the Frisbee. "Don't use your whole arm. Just your wrist. Like this." He helped her flick it into the air and the Frisbee glided three times further than the first attempt. Marlene looked up at him. She wondered if he would kiss her. Instead Arthur turned her to hug her, telling her, "Good job."

After a few more tries, Marlene got the hang of it. They tossed the Frisbee back and forth until it started getting dark. "Oh, I forgot you were heading home today. It's already dark," Marlene told Arthur as they walked to his truck.

"It's okay," he replied, winking at her, "it was worth it."

Chapter Eleven

Marlene sped up on the highway as she exited the entrance ramp. On impulse she had decided to drive to Arthur's ranch. Her summer classes were over, so she did not have to worry about missing school. She had enough money with her to pay for gas and a few days stay at a hotel.

Arthur had called a few times since that day they spent at the park, and they had long talks, though to Marlene they seemed too short. Marlene's mind drifted back to the day at the hospital, when her parents first saw her again after the kidnapping.

Once Marlene had plied the bullet out of Arthur and Frank was in stable enough condition to be moved, Walter Jertenson drove Marlene, Arthur, and Frank to the hospital. Since Curt and Nancy were not hurt, they stayed behind. Marlene wanted to go to watch over Arthur, and to contact her parents. There was no phone at the Jertenson ranch.

Marlene had wanted to stay and visit Arthur as he recovered in the hospital, but her parents insisted she come home. After arguing for a while with her parents, Marlene dropped by Arthur's room one last time. Her parents wanted her home. That was that. She said goodbye to Arthur and he weakly asked her for her address. Apparently he wanted to write to her. She gave him her apartment address. Two weeks later Arthur showed up at her door to ask her on a date.

Willingly, Marlene had gone to a fast food restaurant with Arthur, and then to a movie. He let her pick the movie. She had enjoyed that date, and never wanted it to end, but it had. As she lingered on the step outside her apartment, Arthur asked for her phone number.

"Why didn't you ask for that before?" she asked, curiously.

"I didn't have a phone before. There aren't any phone lines near my ranch. But I just got a cell phone," Arthur replied.

Marlene smirked, sensing the reason Arthur had gotten the phone was because of her. She let him follow her into her apartment, where she found a scrap of paper to write down her number on. Pressing the paper into Arthur's hand, she asked, "Can I have your number, too?"

"Sure," Arthur responded, nodding. She handed him another scrap of paper on which he scribbled.

Then they stood there, staring at each other in an awkward silence. Arthur looked as if he wanted to kiss her, but Marlene was suddenly afraid. She stuck out her hand and he shook it, saying goodbye.

Marlene's parents were shocked and not very pleased when she called them on that Saturday after the last day of class to tell them she was driving up to Meeteetse. Before college, they had never allowed her to drive on the highway on her own. Once she started going to the university, they allowed enough highway driving for her to get to Cheyenne.

Ever since the kidnapping, her parents had been especially cautious. Marlene liked that they spent more time with her, and nagged her less about her reading habits and dreamy disposition, but she felt uncomfortable when they called her every day to check up on her. That action lasted the rest of the year.

Considering she was now twenty one, Marlene's parents felt they could not control her actions any longer. They told her on her birthday that she was all on her own. They never expected her to suddenly drive far away as a test of her independence. Marlene could hear the shock in her mother's voice as she answered and told her to drive carefully.

The highway seemed to wind its way slowly forward, like a snake. She approached a truck ahead that blocked her view. Marlene grew nervous as she put on her turn signal to pass the semi ahead of her. She did not like two lane highways. Swerving onto the other lane, she saw a car coming down the hill ahead, towards her. She had about half a mile between them. "God, help me pass this truck," she whispered anxiously.

Thankfully, the semi driver saw her in his mirror and slowed to let her pass. Marlene passed the truck and moved back into the right lane just a hundred meters before the car in the left sped by. "Thank you, God," Marlene whispered.

As a high school kid, Marlene stopped praying very often to God. She asked Him for things the few times she did, but then figured her life was up to her. She had her own dreams, and she did not want God ruining them. When she went to church, Marlene usually did not feel like praying, so she pretended to for her parents' sake.

Once college began, Marlene prayed more often and more earnestly. She was not sure what she wanted to major in, nor where she wanted to live after college. A rebellious spirit inside of her made her want to move to the east, to some populated city like New York. Then one day, Marlene found herself returning to reading books, as she had when she was in high school. It started when her father gave her a Zane Grey western, and she read the whole, three-hundred page book that night of her nineteenth birthday. From then she took to dreaming about the west, loving her homeland, and hoping she could one day meet a handsome cowboy who would ride with her to his ranch.

She started to trust God more and more, and asked Him to guide her, though she still had her own selfish dreams that did not include helping people. After the kidnapping, Marlene started to reevaluate her life. She made herself get out into the world more, and resisted the temptation to return back behind the cover of a book. She started to ask God to lead her so that she might truly help people. Whether that meant saving lives, making someone's life better, or something else she did not know.

Marlene now prayed day and night, even asking God to help her with little things she was frustrated about. It seemed only natural, then, that after passing the semi, Marlene would thank God and ask Him to watch over her as she headed up north.

Arthur was riding out on the range when he saw the dust of a car coming down the road. He could not tell what kind of car, as the afternoon sun glinted off the polished metal and glared into his eyes. He rode towards the fence near the road, about a mile down from the car. Waiting from his position by the fence, Arthur shielded his eyes from the burning light. It was not unusual that a car come down the road at this time. The drivers were probably just his neighbors, coming back from town.

As the car grew closer, the sun shone on it less, and Arthur could see that it was not his neighbors' Chevy blazer. Instead it was a small, grey Oldsmobile. He did not know anyone around these parts who owned an Oldsmobile. For some reason, though, he seemed to recognize that car. Strange, the car just turned down the road leading to his ranch. Maybe the driver needed directions.

After a long, dusty trip, Marlene saw the ranch she guessed to be Arthur's. When she slowed to stop and read the sign above a small road jutting out from the main one, she had to raise her hand up to her forehead to block the sun. Sure enough, the sign said, "Pressed Ranch," with an address below it. She spun the wheel and started down the road. This road was worse than the one she had just left, though she found that hard to believe. Her hands gripped the steering wheel as the tires tried to turn their own way and the car bounced up and down with every rain-washed gully.

Marlene flipped the cover in front of her to hide the sun and turned her head to the side, annoyed that the glare was making her eyes water. She looked in time to see a cowboy riding from the fence down towards the ranch. She wondered if that would be Arthur's friend, Curt. After glancing back at the gravel coated road, Marlene gazed once more at the cowboy, before he rode down a hill ahead, out of sight.

He watched as the car came down the road.

A few minutes later, Marlene parked her car. She almost fell upon stepping out, as she ran into the very cowboy she had seen on the range. Marlene's jaw dropped as she realized she was face to face with Arthur. Her lips were inches from his. Would he try to kiss her?

Instead of kissing Marlene as he felt tempted to, Arthur let out a whoop and took her in his arms. Marlene was amazed at his strong grasp that nearly took the breath out of her. She hoped, at this close proximity, that her deodorant had managed to hold up. After all, it had been a long ride, and the windows seemed to magnify the heat from the sun. It was a good thing she had added a little perfume, too.

Arthur held Marlene tightly in his arms for a moment, as if he would never let her go. As he rested his chin on her shoulder, he breathed in. A smell as sweet as honey wafted up to him. How it contrasted with the smell of horses, cows, sweat, and manure. It had seemed too long since he had smelled something that did not make his nose wrinkle. The strong perfume of flowers made his eyes water. He stepped back and took in the sight of Marlene.

Ever since that day at the park back in July he had kept that image in his mind, the one of Marlene laughing after she first tried to throw the Frisbee. He wondered every night how long it would be until he saw her again, if he saw her again. They had not discussed their relationship, yet. This seemed sure proof that Marlene felt as Arthur did about the two of them.

"Well, cowboy, I hope you don't mind me visiting," Marlene told him, warmth rising from her voice.

"No, I reckon it's a real pleasure. A real pleasure," Arthur replied, in his easy drawl.

"I reckon yer the cowboy I saw racin' me to this house?" Marlene asked, imitating his drawl.

"Yep. Say, why don't you come in?" Arthur returned. He led her to the house and opened the door.

Marlene's face crinkled as the smell of the house hit her. The small dose of man's sweat from toil coming off of Arthur had not bothered her, but the smell that came from the house was quite stronger. As the sun sparkled in through the windows in the opposite wall, it glinted off dust and dirt stirred from Marlene's feet brushing the floor. She glanced down to see rough, worn planks of wood under her feet, instead of the warm, fuzzy carpeting she was accustomed to.

From her world of comfort and ease, Marlene had stepped into Arthur's world of toil and bareness. A clock ticked steadily from somewhere in the room. Marlene scanned the bare room. Rough-hewn log walls sheltered her, a single painting decorating the left wall, two windows on the wall before her, their panes barely visible beneath the coat of dust and grime. A rocking chair sat near the lone painting, its style obviously antique.

Arthur nervously followed her glance. He had not swept and cleaned his place for a while. Noticing Marlene's eyes setting upon the chair, he told her, "That was my grandmother's chair. When I built this place, my parents gave it to me." As her eyes took in the table with two chairs near it, set in the middle of the room, he added, "And my parents gave me the table and chairs, too. That's the only furniture they had when they first got married."

Marlene turned to face him. "Do your parents live around here?" she asked, meeting his gaze.

"No. They live over in Montana. They used to live near Douglas, but when both my sister and brother headed to Montana, they wanted to be near most of the family."

"Oh," Marlene was quiet for a minute as she surveyed the rest of the room. A grey stone fireplace sat on the right wall, with a chimney leading up from it, marked by more large stones. Upon the mantel of the fireplace sat a small clock.

"I made that in woodshop," Arthur commented on the wooden piece with a small, round glass plate covering the ticking contraption.

After seeing a deer skin lying on the floor before the hearth, Marlene turned once again to face Arthur. She had a million questions she wanted to ask him. Starting with the easiest one, she asked, "Is your brother still in college?"

"Nope. Now he's a doctor in Butte. He loves his job, and is seriously dating a girl now."

"That's great! How about you? How have you been?"

"Fine, fine. Thanks to your parents I've gotten back on my feet again. I even got the mortgage I had on this place paid off. And Curt and Nancy are getting married in a couple weeks."

"Wonderful! You didn't tell me they were engaged," Marlene cried happily.

Arthur grinned as he returned, "Guess I was just so interested in gettin' ta know you thet I fergot to mention it."

"Well! You're not the shy cowboy I met a year ago," Marlene laughed, her face turning rosy as she blushed.

"How long are you staying, Marlene?" Arthur queried suddenly. He looked serious. Indeed he was. He wondered if Marlene was just passing through, or here to visit him.

"A couple of days. I'm going to find a room in Meeteetse tonight."

Arthur's face lit up into a familiar smile. "That's great. Who are you here to visit?"

Marlene reached out to poke Arthur in the ribs. "You, silly. And I want to see your ranch, if that's okay."

"Sure. This afternoon Curt's comin' over and we've got to ride over to talk to a neighbor about hay. But right now I'm free."

"Can I ride one of your horses?" Marlene found herself asking boldly.

Arthur nodded. "Sure, but not in those nice clothes. Did you bring anything old to wear?"

Marlene shook her head, her eyes turning downcast as a redness lit up her cheeks in her embarrassment. "No, I didn't," she replied meekly. She wore an ironed red shirt and brown dress pants. Marlene had wanted to impress Arthur. She never thought of bring clothes for ranch life.

"Wait right here." Arthur walked down a narrow hallway to the left. He entered his room as she stood by the doorway. A pile of dirty laundry stunk up the room, but he turned to his dresser. He found one pair of old, worn jeans and a blue and white striped button-up shirt in the top drawer. On top of the dresser was a pair of leather gloves. He decided to add them to his armload of clothing. She would need them more than him today.

"Here, you can change in the bathroom into these. Don't worry, they're clean," Arthur told her.

Marlene let out a gust of air. "What?" Arthur asked.

"I'm glad to hear you have a bathroom and not an outhouse. I was beginning to wonder."

"Yeah. And I've got electricity in the place, too. Just don't use it much in the daytime." Arthur pointed up at the ceiling. Marlene looked up to see a light fixture hanging down.

When Marlene walked out into the living room, minutes later, Arthur had to stifle a laugh. The tight-fit jeans looked baggy on her, and she was holding them up around her waist. "Maybe I should just stick with my dress-pants."

"Don't worry, I have a belt," Arthur snickered. Marlene eyed him suspiciously as he returned to his room. He seemed to be enjoying this.

Arthur returned and handed her the belt. "Here. This should do the trick." Once Marlene put the belt on, the pants hung to her hips. Arthur looked from her sneaker covered feet to her face. The shirt fit her quite nicely, showing her form better than the red one. Her eyes were glistening with excitement, and her mouth was drawn in a smile.

Marlene stared at Arthur as he seemed to be taking her in. It was funny how this once shy cowboy could look so intently at her, yet when other girls passed him back in her hometown, he hardly seemed to notice them. She liked his calm, strong personality, and the feeling she got from being around him that he would jump out to save her if she were ever in danger again. She felt safe around him. Unlike the doctor, who was boring and disgusting with his talk about surgeries he had performed the whole time she was trying to eat, Arthur cared about her and talked about things she wanted to hear. Plus, unlike a lot of the guys she had known before, he was not intent upon himself, acting cocky around others, and bragging to her. Instead, Arthur was humble and honest. He was who he was, whether or not she liked it. At times he did try to impress her, but that was by compliments and fine manners, which he did not seem wholly accustomed to giving and showing.

Arthur helped Marlene up onto his most trustworthy horse. As his hands left her waist once she was up on the saddle, Marlene reached out. Arthur stared up at this city girl, who looked beautiful even in his old clothes. Marlene squeezed his hand before she let go, feeling a shiver run up her spin as he slowly dropped his hand to rest at his side. It was not normal for her to reach for a guy's hand.

Quickly and smoothly Arthur swung himself onto his stallion, Gerome. The horse whinnied. Marlene's mare whinnied back and she grabbed the reigns just as she decided to take off. "Arthur!" Marlene cried. Belle galloped swiftly onto the meadow, with Marlene barely holding on.

Arthur chased after them, shouting, "Pull the reigns tight and yell 'whoa!'" Marlene tried to take his advice as the mare tore though sagebrush. The bushes scratched at the jeans as the wind whistled through Marlene's ears. She thought she heard Arthur shout more advice, but she could not hear him. Bouncing up and down in the saddle, Marlene held on to the reigns, though they did not seem to be holding her against the horse. Instead she was painfully jolted up and down, the horse's back slamming against her rear each time she landed. Belle was revolting against the tightened reigns. Marlene pulled tighter, just making Belle angrier. The bit was tight and rubbing in the mare's mouth, as the ropes rubbed against Marlene's tender hands. Arthur was approaching, full speed.

Suddenly Belle bucked, pitching Marlene into the air. Marlene could feel a scream escaping her as she watched the swiftly approaching ground with wild eyes. She momentarily heard Arthur riding up before the world spun away from her sight.

Arthur quickly hopped off his horse and ran the two steps over to Marlene. She lay unconscious on the ground. He reached a long arm back to his saddle and grabbed his canteen from the pack behind it. "Marlene, Marlene?" he called to her.

He began to panic. "Please, God, let Marlene be alright," he prayed under his breath as he watched her. Noticing her chest rise and fall in a steady breathing motion, he knelt down by her and tilted her head onto his lap. He unscrewed the cap of his grandfather's metal canteen from World War two and poured the cool water onto Marlene's forehead. The water ran in a stream down to Marlene's open mouth, and she choked and sputtered as it ran down her throat.

Marlene's eyes fluttered open. As the world stopped spinning, Marlene focused her sight on Arthur. "Arthur," she whispered. The back of her head throbbed and a headache pounded in her head as she stared into the handsome cowboy's eyes.

Arthur stared back, concerned. "Can you move?" he asked her. Marlene struggled to get up on her elbows. She cried out and fell back down against him. Feeling her right arm, Marlene found the bristly ends of cactus in it.

Arthur laughed easily when he saw her face. "You must've fallen on a cactus."

Marlene glared up at him. She scrambled to a sitting position, then turned about to face him. Before she snapped the words coming to her mind, she noticed that Arthur was wearing his light brown cotton shirt. Just as she promised, Marlene had sewed it back up and given it to Arthur at the courthouse where they had to testify against the Henders and McGee.

"Sorry, Marlene. I shouldn't have laughed. Are you all right?" Arthur asked, his face now serious again.

"You're wearing the shirt."

He glanced down and pulled at the cloth, as if just realizing he had a shirt on. "Why so I am. The last time I was wearing this, you tore it off of me." He paused and reached for her arm. She scooted closer as he pulled on her elbow. "I should git ya back to the house. I've got a pair a tweezers there to take these out. Does anything feel broken?"

Marlene shook her head. As she stood up, she started to feel dizzy again. Arthur caught her as her legs buckled under her. "Do your legs feel okay?" he questioned.

"Yeah. Just tell the world to stand still. It keeps spinning around me." Arthur chuckled as Marlene smiled at him. He helped her onto his stallion, and hopped up in front of her.

"I'll get Belle later. Let's just ride back on my horse."

Despite the stinging in Marlene's arm, she did not want the ride to end. "Can we ride a little more before heading back?" she asked, rubbing her bruised shin.

"Sure, if you really want to," Arthur answered without looking back. "You should probably hold on."

Marlene wrapped her arms around his waist. She leaned against his back. The back of his shirt was soaked with sweat, and it felt hot and sticky, but she did not care. She felt comfortable as she hugged on tight. Arthur whipped the reigns, yelling, "Ya!" The horse jolted from standing to an immediate gallop. The wind blew through Marlene's hair. She glanced down at ground that rushed by.

The ride was wonderful. Arthur liked the feeling of Marlene holding onto him, pressing against his back. He could smell her perfume as she tilted her head down, resting her chin on his shoulder. His spin tingled as her breath blew into his ear. It was hard to keep his mind focused on the view ahead. Temptation ran through him to stop the horse, turn around, and hold Marlene in his arms while he rapidly kissed her. His imagination soared at the thought, but then he told himself to stay steady, and remain a gentleman. Long ago his parents had warned him of the temptations he would face when dating, and the Christian way to act about them.

Marlene closed her eyes as they turned and the sun came face to face with them. The horse still bumped her up and down, but not as much now that she had Arthur to hold onto. The cowboy seemed to sit and ride so smoothly, as if he and the horse rode as one. Before she knew it Arthur was turning around. As they grew closer to the ranch house, riding swiftly, he slowed the horse, and it trotted leisurely towards the barn.

They entered the barn, ducking their heads, and stopped before Gerome's stall. Marlene blinked as she opened her eyes. She slid her arms off Arthur so he could hop down. He landed on the ground with a soft thump. He reached up and held her under her arms as she jumped off. Once again they were in a close proximity. Arthur decided this time he would kiss her.

As Arthur leaned close to Marlene, she suddenly grew frightened. She was not sure she wanted him to kiss her. Before his lips could touch hers, she took a step back. Arthur stared at her. His face grew flushed as he straightened back up. It was an awkward moment. They were both silent for a time.

"Well, I think I better head over to the hotel before it gets dark," Marlene mentioned, shattering the glass-like silence.

"What about those cactus thorns? I could get them out before you leave," Arthur offered, not wanting her to go just yet.

Marlene nodded, agreeing. She followed Arthur to the house, where he found tweezers in his bathroom. Sitting down on a chair at the table, she plopped her stinging arm on the table. Dabs of blood revealed where the almost clear needles poked into her tender skin. Arthur peered down and pulled them out quickly, one at a time. He pretended not to notice Marlene gritting her teeth as she held her arm steady and extended. Then he noticed how raw Marlene's hand was. He grabbed some band aids from the bathroom and taped them onto the blistered flesh that was covered with scabs.

"I guess those gloves didn't help much," he told her as he put the last band aid on.

"What gloves?" Marlene asked. Arthur realized then that he had left the gloves in his bedroom.

"The ones I forgot to give you," Arthur replied with a laugh. Marlene gave him a curious look before he asked, "Say, are you comin' by tomorrow?"

"Yes, unless I decide to head out. I hadn't really planned things out before I got here," Marlene replied.

"Not usual for you?"

"No. I usually don't go do things of this degree without taking a long time to plan them out. Of course, all the times I've planned trips out I've never managed to take them."

Arthur wanted to ask Marlene what places she had wanted to go to, but before he could reply, there was a knock at the door. Marlene stood up. "I guess I'd better go."

Arthur opened the door to see Curt, decked in his worn work clothes. "Hey there, Arthur. You look surprised ta see me!" he commented, staring at Arthur's surprised face.

Marlene walked up behind Arthur to peer over his shoulder at Curt. When Curt saw her, it was his turn to be surprised. "Well, now, who's this purdy lady?" he asked.

Glancing over his shoulder at Marlene, Arthur stepped to the side of the doorway. "Curt it's me, Marlene!" Marlene cried, with a smile.

Curt's eyes widened and a mischievous smile came upon his lips. He gave Arthur a sideways glance before returning his eyes to Marlene. "Say, that couldn't be true! Arthur told me there was no chance in a million you'd come ta see him! He was sure ya couldn't stand the hard work of bein' on a ranch!"

Marlene turned to Arthur with a glare. He seemed to shrink from her intense stare. "Really Arthur?" she spoke icily. Curt stepped back, realizing that he had made an error.

"I'll meet ya outside, Arthur, ifen yer still plannin' on gettin' hay today," Curt mumbled as he clumsily turned and stepped off the porch.

Marlene's eyes were still on Arthur. Arthur shrugged at her. "It's true. I didn't think ya'd ever come up here. It's tough. But you sure came, anyway, an' I'm glad."

His words were sincere, and they struck Marlene in such a way as to make her quiver. She was mad at this cowboy, who apparently did not think she had the strength to ride on a ranch, and yet his honesty refreshed her. She had expected him to deny any such words, and half wanted him to. Yet, yet she had also wanted to know what he thought of her. A wall of silence stood between them. A transformation seemed to come over Arthur as she continued to glare at him. From a frightened look he took on a guilty look, yet he stood tall and stared back boldly now, no longer shrinking back.

"I'm sorry if I insulted ya, Marlene," Arthur spoke calmly, his steely blue eyes piercing her, as if looking into her.

Marlene took a step toward him. Arthur dodged around her and stepped outside. "Might want to change back to yer city clothes 'fore ya go into town," he called, without looking back at her. "Hope ta see ya tomorrow."

After changing back into her pressed shirt and stiff pants, Marlene drove to Meeteese where she reserved a room. It was late afternoon by then, so she walked about the streets of the small town, greeting the town's friendly inhabitants. When dark fell she ate supper at a small restaurant, then retired to the comfort of her small room.

The lonely darkness surrounded Marlene as she stared up at the ceiling from the squeaky bed. A thousand thoughts reeled through her head. She tried to piece them together. Her sore, tired body made it difficult for her to stay awake.

Why was it she did not let Arthur kiss her? Since the last time she had seen him, she had longed for him to kiss her, and to tell her he loved her. She had found herself falling for this young cowboy, despite the fact that she had not gone on many dates with him. If she did not come to let him know how she felt about him, why did she come? And why had he not expected her to ever try ranch life?

This thought made her mouth taste bitter. Arthur did not think her good enough to ride the range. Just a weak city girl, he probably thought of her. The insult of Curt's remark, and the fact that Arthur did not deny it, made Marlene want to drive back early tomorrow morning. It was stupid and futile for her to come anyway. To even hope a courtship could arise out of a few dates and to think so positively about it as to come so far to see him again was foolish. Maybe Arthur did not even care for her. But if so, why did he try to kiss her? Could he just be attracted to her because she was a girl? If he just wanted to kiss her and hug her, and did not have any love for her, she did not want to stick around. Yet he had had other chances to kiss her, and he held back. Marlene thought to herself that she could go home tomorrow, and leave the nice image of Arthur in her mind, and she could go on with her life, remembering the nice cowboy.

She tried to close her eyes at this idea and rest. But her eyes fluttered open, and she drew her breath in deep. She would always wonder what might have happened between them if she did not find out now. She would never know how the cowboy felt about her, and what might have happened if she retreated. It would be smart to go back to his ranch, just once more. Then she could forget this feeling of longing she had felt ever since she met him, and go back home content. And there was one other reason for her to return. She had to prove to Arthur that this tenderfoot could ride like a true cowgirl, and take anything thrown at her. It was a rebellious spirit in her, the same spirit that had caused her to drive all this way. Still, she did not trust herself. She might get out of hand and do something courageously stupid, just to impress Arthur.

The thoughts continued and Marlene waged battle with herself. Upon finally deciding she would stay one more day, Marlene gave in to her exhaustion and fell into a deep slumber. She dreamed she was riding a horse, riding as if she had her whole life. And in the background, sitting upon a cross buck fence, with long legs dangling down toward the ground, was Arthur Pressed.

Chapter Twelve

Arthur was astounded the next day when he stepped out to see Marlene standing before him, wearing blue jeans and a yellow t-shirt. "You ready to take me riding?" she asked him, a smiled painted on her lips.

He looked down to see a new pair of boots on her feet, and his gaze shifted up, taking in the sight of her. "Haven't you had enough?" he asked, his face serious.

"I'll let you know when I have," Marlene replied curtly. "So? What are ya doin' today?"

"Curt an' I had planned ta round up an' count the cows. He's gonna bring his ta his ranch perdy soon, now thet the roof is up."

"Can I help?"

"It's not work fer tenderfeet." Marlene's soft hazel eyes took on a sharper, intense look.

She frowned at Arthur, who crossed his arms and stared stolidly back. "I don't care. I'm comin'."

Arthur shook his head. "No way I'm lettin' ya ride with Curt and me. You have no idea—"

"I'm not giving up, Arthur. You don't think I can handle it. Well, I've got to warn you—I'm stubborn. I even wore riding clothes today."

"That ya did. Ya sure are stubborn," Arthur relented, dropping his arms to his side. "But you'll want ta tie thet hair up."

"Do you have a rubber band?"

"Why?"

"I don't have a hair-tie."

Arthur scrummaged around until he found a rubber band in a kitchen drawer. Marlene studied the kitchen after tying her hair back. She had not seen it earlier. A small stove, two sided sink, and cabinets ran the border of the small room. Just her and Arthur in the room together felt crowded. The counters were clean, and, in fact, the whole house now smelled of soap. Marlene waited in the living room as Arthur grabbed his riding gloves. She stared down at the floor. The dirt clods and dust that had been there yesterday were missing.

Arthur glanced out of his bedroom window at the laundry line. His whole wardrobe was hung up, other than the clothes he wore now. Embarrassed that Marlene had come on the day he did his laundry, he determined to keep her from that side of the house. That would be an easy task, considering the barn was on the opposite side.

When he walked out from the hallway, Marlene greeted him by the door. "Did you clean up around here?" she asked.

He nodded shyly and handed her the gloves. "You have a nice house, Arthur."

Curt showed up a half hour later, and they saddled up. Despite the soreness of Marlene's palms, she gripped the reigns and spoke confidently. Arthur took a moment to show Marlene how to use a rope, though he was sure the lesson would not be enough for her to actually use a rope on this day. The three rode out to the range with the hot sun glaring down at them. Marlene held the reigns tight as she tried to keep up with Curt and Arthur.

Curt was almost as smooth on a horse as Arthur, his body rising and falling naturally with the horse. But it was clear Arthur had had years of riding experience. While Marlene's sore rear end and quad muscles repeatedly bumped the saddle and bounced back up again, Arthur mostly kept contact with the saddle and raised himself up with each stride of the stallion.

The cattle moved along slowly and lazily as Arthur and Curt rode behind them, steering them towards the corral down in the valley. Marlene mainly just followed Arthur around, until he started barking orders, telling her to get behind that left group of cattle, or to round up that lone calf lingering behind. Then she rose into action, and whipped her reigns to speed her horse towards the cows. By now she was growing used to the rhythm of the saddle, and good at ignoring the pain in her muscles from the day before. Her hands clenched the leather straps, and her keen eyesight led her to the calf a mile back. She ignored the growing blisters from the rubbing of her feet against the new, stiff material of the boots she had bought in Meeteetse.

Midway through the day Marlene's stomach was growling, and she felt starved. Curt teased her when she asked about lunch, and Arthur promised they would have a big meal at the end of the day. He told her they did not have time to stop for a meal, considering the cattle had been spread all over the wild Wyoming range.

As she continued to herd the cattle, ignoring the cramping of her stomach and the weakness growing in her arms, Marlene noticed a few cows that did not carry the same brand as the others. She rode up to Arthur to ask him what to do about it.

Arthur grinned as he watched Marlene gallop up to him. He halted his horse and turned in the saddle to wait for her. She looked like a natural on a horse now. Seven hours of continuous riding could do that to a person, he guessed. Yet he mused about the funny sight of her hair falling in strands out of the ponytail and her face darkened with the dry brown dirt stuck to her sweaty forehead and cheeks. Beneath the dust her face was flushed.

"Arthur, there are a few cows with a different brand," she told him, panting.

He narrowed his eyes. "Can you chase them off from the others?" he asked. "I don't want to be called a thief."

Marlene gasped for air before she replied. The strong scent of sage mixed with the salty smell of sweat ran to her nose. That was the smell of Arthur. Her deodorant still barely prevailed over her smelling so strongly. Arthur stared at her seriously.

"Sure I can." Her answer was frank. She wanted to try. Arthur gave her a look of approval and his blue eyes shone kindly. It was a loving look, Marlene felt. How handsome he looked to her. She felt the look rising up on her face would reveal her feelings for him, so she glanced down. A branch of tumbleweed was stuck in the lip of Arthur's boot.

Arthur reached out an arm and patted her on the shoulder. "You've been doin' great today, Marlene. You've been a real help. I was wrong about you," he complimented her.

Marlene could not help but look up to meet his gaze at these words. They stared at each other for the longest five seconds Marlene could ever recall. Then she turned her horse to ride back to the cows. She did not need to look back to see Arthur staring intently after her. She could feel his eyes on her.

Arthur stared after Marlene as she rode away. He admired her. He thought she could not handle riding on the range, skipping meals and galloping along even when every muscle in her body ached, but she had proved him wrong. She had won his respect, and, perhaps, a bit more.

As Arthur whipped his reigns to ride ahead, he wondered why Marlene had come back. She had resisted when he tried to kiss her. When she left that day, he thought he would never see her again. After all, she was upset by Curt's repeating of his own words, and she had been distant once they reached the barn. But that ride with her had been wonderful.

Marlene managed to chase off the cows and then rounded up another straying calf. As she rode she thought about Arthur's compliment. Perhaps he liked her after all. Or was it merely respect? The ride the day before had drawn out something in her, something she would reveal to Arthur when the time was right. In her had been born a love to ride, and a curiousness as to what life as the wife of a cowboy would be. Thinking of Arthur and his compliment, a longing to be held closely in his arms rose up in her. Just before she was frightened by the idea, yet now she welcomed it. She knew she could trust him, knew that he was not some strange man. Though she did not know him well, she planned to get to know him much better.

Arthur invited Marlene, Curt, and Nancy over for supper that night. They had just piled the hot potatoes and roast beef onto their plates when Marlene asked if they could say prayers. It had been years since Arthur had said prayers before a meal, and it was a new idea entirely for Curt and Nancy. Yet Marlene's friends agreed, and she voiced her thanks to God for the food and her friends. Nancy asked Marlene question after question as they ate, wondering what she had been up to. Marlene was hungry, yet she did not want to appear rude, so she answered the questions and forestalled eating. After a while Arthur noticed this, and he engaged Nancy in conversation so that Marlene could eat. Marlene could not recall ever eating so much in her life.

When she had cleaned her plate for the second time, Marlene shoved it a few inches forward and slumped against the back of her chair. Arthur scooted his chair back and rose up. "Pie anyone?" he asked.

"How'd you have time to make pie?" Marlene queried.

"Yeah, and since when could you bake a pie?" Curt asked.

All eyes were on Arthur. He shrugged and pointed to Nancy. "Nancy brought it over."

"That explains why ya brought thet box in. I didn't know it had our desert," Curt commented, smiling at Nancy.

Arthur was in the kitchen by now and called from there, "So, any takers?"

Marlene groaned as she thought of the several helpings of roast and two whole baked potatoes she had consumed. "I wish I could, but I'm full," she replied.

"I'll have a slice, and maybe more," Curt called.

"Me too," Nancy added. "I'll leave the pie here, Marlene, so you can have a slice tomorrow."

Arthur walked back from the kitchen with two plates, listening attentively for Marlene's reply. Marlene watched him as he set the plates down and waited to go back into the kitchen. "Actually, I'm heading back to Laramie tomorrow. But thanks," she told Nancy, though she was looking at Arthur.

Arthur met her eyes. "Your headin' back tomorrow?" he questioned her, as if he had not already heard the answer.

"Yeah. I need to get back," Marlene answered simply, though Arthur could hear the waver in her voice.

"Dang, Marlene! I was hopin' you'd help us another day! Arthur and me are startin' the buildin' of my cross buck fence tomorrow!" Curt complained.

"Curt! Watch your language!" Nancy reprimanded.

"All I said was dang," Curt replied with a shrug. He glanced at Arthur. "See what I have ta put up with? Arthur, ya should keep from gettin' hitched as long as ya can."

"Well!" Nancy cried, kicking Curt under the table. He let out a shout, but did not complain anymore.

Marlene and Arthur could not help but laugh at the two. Arthur continued to laugh even when he reached the kitchen to grab one more slice of pie. When he returned, Marlene looked serious again. "Arthur, I really am going tomorrow," she told him. Arthur nodded silently as he sat down. He cut into the pie and began eating.

"Say, Curt, yer one lucky cowboy! This apple pie is delicious!" Arthur voiced after savoring the first bite.

"Why thank you," Nancy replied before taking a bite.

"Well, thet's good. I never did ask Nancy for cooking credentials before I proposed," Curt commented. "Ya hear about thet cowboy who starved, Arthur? It was 'cause his wife couldn't cook."

"Really? Ya don't say?" Arthur mused.

Nancy kicked Curt under the table again. "You knew I could cook! I cooked you several meals when ya had me over," she cried indignantly. Curt grinned at her, and she could not help but smile back at him.

Later that night, Nancy and Curt had gone home, and only Marlene remained at Arthur's. They still sat at the table, and Arthur was telling Marlene cowboy jokes. He had avoided talking about more serious things, yet. Marlene waited and waited for him to ask about them, and finally she could wait no more.

"Arthur?"

Arthur stopped in the middle of telling his joke. With a smile he replied, "Yes?"

"I like your jokes just fine, but I was wondering if we could talk about something else, since I'm leaving tomorrow."

"Will you stop by before you go?"

"I might, but you might be at Curt's, working on his fence by then."

"What did you want to talk about then, Marlene?" Arthur's face turned serious.

"Us, Arthur. That is, if there is an 'us'. I need to know."

Arthur stood up and slowly walked towards the fireplace, which was not lit. Marlene stood up and followed him. He beckoned her to sit down on the rocking chair, and he remained standing, staring out the window. "I was wondering about that too, Marlene."

"Well, are we going to see each other again?"

Arthur turned to face her, gathering all the courage he could muster. "It's not likely, Marlene. We live two different kinds of lives."

"So?" Marlene snapped. "I came here to see what your life was like. It doesn't bother me that it's different. Is it me, then, and the way that I live that bothers you?"

"No, no!" Arthur cried, raising up his hands in self defense. "It's just that I don't know if it would work. And I don't just want to date for fun. That usually leads to someone gettin' their heart broken."

Marlene stood up and stared at Arthur, her nose inches away from his. "I didn't mean dating for fun, Arthur. I want to date you, and, and..." She drifted off. He was staring at her with that intent look in his eyes.

"We're separated by a couple hundred miles. How are we gonna date?" Arthur asked her, placing his hands on her shoulders.

"I don't know. I just know if I never date you, I'll never be sure if you were the right one. And I think if we really want to date, we'll find a way. My mom says, if you want something to happen, you'll find a way." Marlene said this calmly, though her knees were shaking under her. She felt like leaning forward and meeting Arthur's lips.

Arthur felt the same temptation, but took a step back. "You have one smart mom, Marlene. And that's another thing. Would she approve?"

Marlene looked down at the floor. "I'm not sure," she mumbled to her feet. Then she looked up again. "But it doesn't matter."

Chapter Thirteen

"Throw me the Frisbee, Nate!" Marlene called to her brother. He threw the Frisbee hard and she caught it, laughing.

"Throw it here!" Ryan called. Marlene threw it towards him, but his wife, Judy, jumped in the way and grabbed it. "Hey, no fair!" Ryan complained.

"Your wife can catch better than you, anyway," Nate commented.

"Hey!" Ryan ran towards Nate, who was waiting for Judy to throw the Frisbee to him. Ryan tackled his brother and they tussled in the short grass.

"You two are gonna have a lot of grass stains," Marlene told them, laughing. Judy approached her as she watched her brothers scuffling.

"So, when's he going to get here?" Judy asked.

Ryan and Nate overheard her question and stopped fighting. Ryan stood up. "Yeah, where is this guy you said was coming?"

Marlene shrugged. "He'll be here."

"I think you just made him up, Sis," Ryan teased. Judy glared at him. "What?"

"You don't believe your sister?" Judy asked.

A horn honked as Ryan was about to answer. Nate jumped up. "I see a truck!" he shouted.

Marlene ran towards the parked truck as a tall young man stepped out, slapping a cowboy hat on his head. Her siblings watched as she raced into the young man's arms. "Arthur, I'm glad you got here. Ryan was beginning to question my sanity."

Arthur hugged her and they walked, hand in hand, towards the curious group of onlookers. "Hello, Arthur," Nate greeted, holding out his hand. Arthur took it and shook.

"Hey there, Nate. Good to see you."

"Arthur, this is Ryan and his wife Judy," Marlene introduced. "And Ryan, Judy, this is my boyfriend, Arthur."

"Glad to meet you," Ryan voiced as he shook Arthur's hand. "So, you own a ranch up in Meeteetse?"

"Near Meeteetse, yes."

An older couple sitting at a bench near a tree stood up and walked over. "Mom, Dad, this is Arthur," Marlene told them when they had joined the party.

"You can call me George, and my wife Pam," George offered.

"So, when are we going to eat?" Nate asked.

"Is that all you ever think about? Food?" Marlene teased.

"I'm just reading Arthur's mind is all, Sis. Sure he must be starved after that road trip," Nate returned.

"I am a bit hungry at thet," Arthur admitted.

"Well, we got sandwiches galore, and Pam insisted on making her potato salad as well. Let's go to the bench," George offered.

As they sat eating, Marlene leaned against Arthur's side. He talked with her parents as she reflected on the last couple of weeks. Arthur had come to visit her twice a week since that visit to Meeteetse, and their dates had been full of fun and meaning.

One of the dates had been after they went to mass together on a Sunday, and Arthur had driven Marlene up to the Snowy Range mountains, where they splashed each other at the shore of Lake Marie. Each time Arthur came down from his ranch to visit, they would spend the whole day together.

Then the fall semester started, and to Marlene's parents' dismay, Marlene had even skipped a couple days of school on the weekdays Arthur came. Every date had been memorable to Marlene, and it felt like a lot longer than a month that they had been dating steadily. It had not all been fun and games for every date, however, for arguments over little, stupid things had ended a few of them poorly. But Arthur would always call Marlene when he was back home, and they would talk things through until their anger at each other had subsided, and they would decide on the next time he would visit.

Arthur glanced at Marlene to see a dreamy look on her face. He reached down by the bench and Marlene heard the rustle of leaves, but she did not pay any attention. Suddenly his hand was at her back, and he was shoving something down her shirt. Marlene screamed and jumped up. Everyone but Marlene was laughing as she hopped about, pulling on her shirt, trying to shake out the leaves.

When she was successful at ridding her shirt of the dry, scratchy leaves, Marlene put her hands on her hips and frowned at Arthur. "Arthur Pressed! What's the idea?" Arthur was the only one snickering now.

"I'm sorry, Marlene, but I couldn't resist!" he admitted, covering his mouth, lest his laughter come out louder.

"Nice one!" Nate cheered, giving Arthur a high five.

Marlene bent down and grabbed a handful of leaves. Arthur stopped laughing, and his eyes grew wide. "What do you plan to do with that?" he asked cautiously.

"I'll show you!" Marlene stepped towards him, but he launched himself from the bench and took off running. She chased him with the leaves and they ran along the creek like two kids.

As they grew closer to the edge of the small gorge that the water ran through, Arthur tripped and rolled down towards the creek. Marlene chased after him, realizing too late that it would be hard to stop at the bottom. She ran right into the foot-deep water, splashing it on her and Arthur, who lay prone at the shore. Finally she came to a stop by running into the clay covered slope on the opposite side of the water. Her hands clasped the clay for a moment before her wet feet started sliding.

"Oh!" she screamed. Quick as a flash, Arthur was on his feet, and straddled the creek to catch Marlene as she fell backwards.

Marlene felt Arthur catch her, and she did not fight him. She leaned against him, not trying to regain her balance. "Do ya think ya could stand, so I don't fall into the water?" Arthur asked after a moment. Marlene glanced over her shoulder. One of Arthur's feet was on one side of the creek, and one was on the other. There was a span of about four feet between his feet. Quickly Marlene leaned forward, and Arthur stepped across to her side of the creek.

"Thanks," Arthur panted.

Marlene turned to face him and almost slipped again. "Thank you."

He stuck out his hand. "Should we return, My Lady?" he asked, nodding his head towards the opposite bank.

Marlene laughed, taking his hand. "You sound like a guy from Shakespeare," she told him as they crossed.

"Ever since you told me you were taking Shakespeare this semester, I thought I'd read up on it," he replied, looking forward.

"Really?"

"Yep."

They climbed up the bank side by side. Once they were on level ground again, Marlene asked "Do you miss not going to college, Arthur?"

Arthur shook his head. "It bothers some people, I suppose. But I'm happy with having a ranch. Even if I went to college, I'd still want to have the ranch afterwards, so I just skipped to it."

Marlene took a deep breath of air. Arthur sensed she was preparing to say something important. Indeed, she had been waiting for the right time to ask this question. "Does it bother you that I'll have a college degree after this spring?" she asked him.

Arthur turned to face her, and they stopped. Marlene stared down at her soggy white and pink shoes, where black mud was oozing through the holes at the top. Arthur reached out his hand and raised her chin. Now she was forced to see him staring attentively at her. "No, Marlene, it doesn't. I want you to have whatever education you want to get. Besides, it's good for your confidence. I've already got confidence, from what I do. I don't see any reason to be jealous of you. I just want the best for you."

"Really?" Marlene asked hoarsely, suddenly finding her mouth to be dry.

"Yep. Besides, maybe then you can teach me some things." Arthur grinned at Marlene. She grinned back and hugged him.

"Arthur, you make a wonderful—"

"Hey, you two! Come and finish eating!" Ryan's voice interrupted.

Marlene pressed her mud stained hand into Arthur's and they strutted back to the picnic bench. Pam and George could not help but laugh at the sight of them. Marlene's jeans were covered with dark red mud from the embankment, and her light blue shirt had splashes of water and black mud splotched on it. Her hair was disheveled, and her face was red. Yet her eyes danced as she gripped Arthur's hand and they swung their arms. Arthur's jeans were merely soaked, and water dripped from his shirt. He, too, looked happy despite the mess.

"I think those two are serious," Pam whispered to her husband.

"They sure have a lot of fun together," George whispered back.

The rest of the day Ryan, Nate, and Arthur tossed a football back and forth, while Marlene sat and talked to her sister in-law, between her mother's questions about Arthur. Pam wanted to find out everything she could about Arthur, so that she could decide if she approved. At first she was careful and tactful, hiding her reason for asking Marlene so many questions. Marlene, however, could see right through her. Finally Pam asked bluntly, "How do you feel about Arthur?"

Marlene glanced over her shoulder to see Nate tackling Arthur. She stared at her mother and answered sincerely, "I love him, Mom."

Pam smiled and patted her daughter's hand. "I thought so. I've never seen you so serious about a young man before."

George grinned mischievously and interposed, "What about that Andrew Wankton in high school?"

Marlene glared at her father and gasped dramatically. "Dad! You know that wasn't anything!"

"You did tell me you had a crush on him, Marlene," her mother added.

"Yeah, but—hey! You told Dad about that?"

"Sure. I tell him everything."

"How embarrassing. Every time I confided in you about a crush, you told Dad." Marlene paused and stared at the table. "But anyway, this isn't the same thing. It's not just a simple crush."

Pam looked to see if Arthur was near. He was about a hundred yards off, preparing to throw the football to Nate before Ryan tackled him. "Have you talked about serious matters, Marlene? Like where you would live, what you would do if you did get married?"

"No, not that yet. I do know how he feels about a lot of things, though, including family. He wants a lot of kids, like me. And I don't think he'd want to give up his ranch."

"You'd live on his ranch?" George questioned, his face drawn and serious as he stared at his daughter.

"I don't know, Dad. Gosh, we didn't even discuss it. Let me tell you later, okay," Marlene replied, standing up. "I think I'll join in that game of football."

Judy stood up as well, understanding that Marlene did not want to talk anymore. "I think I'll join you," she told Marlene.

Chapter Fourteen

Arthur was out on the range, riding his horse, when his cell phone rang. He took the reins in one hand and reached   in his jeans pocket with the other. Flipping open the slim phone, he answered. "Hello?"

"Hello? Arthur, where are you right now?" Marlene's voice wafted over the line, sounding desperate.

Arthur feared something was wrong. "I'm on my horse. What's up?"

"Can you come to Laramie, right now?" This time Arthur was sure he could hear the fear in her voice. He sensed trouble beyond what he could be prepared for.

"Sure. Why?"

"I'll tell you when you get here. Just meet me at the hospital."

"The hospital! My God, what happened? What's going on?"

"I've got to go, now. Just hurry!" Marlene cried. Arthur could hear her crying as she spoke these last words. Before he could reply, she hung up.

Arthur rode swiftly back to the barn, where he unsaddled his horse. He then ran inside the house to grab his car keys and a bottle of water. The truck started without trouble, and Arthur soon found himself driving full speed over the road, the vehicle rumbling over the bumps and washes and gullies. Marlene needed him. That's all he needed to know. Still, he wondered what the reason was, and a million thoughts and fears streaked through his mind as he headed for the highway. He coughed on the dust that flew in through his window. Gripping the wheel, he kept his eyes glued on the road ahead.

Meanwhile Marlene was hugging her crying mother, telling her everything was going to be alright. Susan and Albert were standing nearby, talking in low voices. Albert had flown down as soon as he had heard the news. Sue had been visiting when it happened, so she had jumped in the van with her mother and they raced to the Laramie hospital together. Sue told Albert all that had occurred, at least all that she knew, with tears flowing freely from her eyes as she talked. Her face was pale and drawn.

Two hours after Marlene made the call to Arthur, Father Matthew arrived. He carried a small, black suitcase with him filled with items for communion and a few things needed for last rites. He offered half a smile to Marlene when she ran, like a child, to his open arms.

"Oh, Father Matthew, it's just horrible! We don't know if they're going to make it!" Marlene sobbed as the priest let her lean against him. Her wet cheeks pressed against his left shoulder. For the first time in his life, Matthew felt more like a father than a priest. He had prayed for this family the whole trip down from Gillette, hoping that things were not as serious as they seemed. Still, he had prepared for the worst.

He looked down at Marlene's disheveled brown hair and told her, "Let's just pray, Marlene. That's all we can do right now. God will have to do the rest, maybe through those doctors in there."

"What if, what if I never get to talk to my father again? We had an argument this morning before he left. I think he was upset with me. Oh, it's all my fault," Marlene mumbled.

Father Matthew took a small step back from her and lifted her chin with a tender hand. As Marlene stared at him, he smiled a confident smile. "Marlene, it wasn't your fault. And just have faith. Things can still turn out all right. Whatever happens, your father loves you very much. And so do your brothers," he replied to her.

Marlene nodded in agreement, though she still was not sure things would be all right. Just before the accident, everything in her life seemed to be fine, better, in fact, than they ever had before. Then suddenly, like an avalanche the world came crashing down on her, and all at once she felt smothered. She tried to come up for air, but with the feeling of hopelessness, it felt like concrete blocks had formed on her legs, dragging her deeper into the ruins.

The priest then walked over to her mother, who was sitting in a chair for support. He knelt down to be face to face with her, and took her hands in his. His face serious and filled with concern, he stared at Pam and spoke in a low, gentle voice to her. Marlene watched from a distance for a moment. Her mother nodded at intervals, and the tears stopped coming, but Marlene could tell they were on the verge of flooding out of those red, sore eyes any minute.

Marlene turned to stare at her brother and sister, who were still talking. She wanted to talk with them, and yet she wanted to be away from all these conversations about what might happen. The hospital waiting room felt cold to her, with its cleanliness and stillness. The only sounds that broke the silence were sounds of sobbing and low voices talking. A father and mother paced back and forth near the back corner of the room. Marlene had heard them speak of their daughter they were awaiting word of. Apparently their daughter was having a baby in a room a few stories above, and had asked them not to be in her room at this time.

Funny, Marlene thought, at a time when a baby is about to come into the world, coming into the lives of its new family, I feel like I'm losing my family. The room around her started to spin, and Marlene felt herself falling. It was like a dream, and she felt helpless to do anything. That was how her whole day had been. It did not even seem real that she was here in the emergency room.

With a thud Marlene hit the floor. Her knee hit the hard tile, followed by her back in weird, twisted motion. Though her eyes were open, the view before her was black. A swish of material revealed to her that someone was bending down over her, though she could not see who. "Marlene? Are you alright?" a voice called through the darkness.

Marlene recognized the voice, and she wished that she could see Arthur just then. "Arthur, is that you?" she replied, weakly, as she felt him gently tilt her head up and pull her against him as they sat on the floor.

Arthur gazed down at Marlene, concerned. She was looking up at him with a blank stare. And she spoke as if she could not see him. "Yes, Marlene, it's me. Can you see anything?" he asked her gently.

Marlene shook her head. "I guess my eyes must be closed, though they feel open."

The tall cowboy, sitting with the girl he loved so dearly laying with her head in his lap, frowned and replied, "No, Marlene. Your eyes are open."

Marlene's face took on a bewildered, frightened look. Arthur noticed how pale and devoid of color her face was. Her cheeks were wet, and more water began to flow through her eyes.

"Maybe the tears are blocking your view," Arthur offered. He softly wiped the tears from her eyes with a callused finger. "Can you see anything now?"

"No," Marlene told him. She tried to sit up, but it was like fumbling in a dark room. "Help me Arthur," she cried. Arthur helped her to stand up.

"How long have you not been able to see?" Arthur asked, more deeply concerned than before.

"Since I fainted a moment ago. At least I think it was just a moment ago." Marlene paused and felt for Arthur's face. Arthur took her hands in his, and pressed his forehead against hers. "I wanted to see you, so badly. Tell me everything's going to be alright, Arthur."

"Everything is going to be alright, Marlene," Arthur Pressed told her, still leaning in towards her. He did not know what she was talking about, but he figured it was more important to comfort her at this time.

"Will you pray for them, Arthur?" she requested, squeezing her hands together as Arthur held them tightly.

"I haven't prayed in years," Arthur admitted.

"Please, Arthur?"

"Sure." He paused, wondering if it would be okay if he said something more. "What happened, Marlene?"

"I told you, I fainted."

"No, I mean, why did you call me?"

"Can we sit down? My legs feel weak," Marlene replied.

Arthur brought her hands, clasped together in a praying form, to his lips and kissed them as he answered, "Sure, Marlene." He led her to a set of chairs, away from her mother and Father Matthew, away from the couple standing in the corner, away from all the commotion. "Here's a chair," he described, lowering her hands as she sat down.

Scooting a chair to be in front of Marlene, Arthur sat down. He stared across at Marlene, desperately wanting to know what was going on. They sat in silence for a few minutes. Marlene closed her eyes and leaned back in her chair. Arthur wondered if she was resting when she spoke. "Arthur, my dad was driving over here to talk to me, when he crashed into Nate's car. Ryan and Nate were both in the car, and Dad was in his little Volvo. After Nate's blazer crushed Dad's car, it somehow swerved off and rolled down the hill next to the road. And they say that Dad's in serious condition, and Nate, and Ryan, are in ICU, whatever that means. They had to fly them here in a helicopter, and they don't know if, if—" Marlene broke down into sobbing, and she hunched over, covering her face with her hands.

Arthur stared blankly a minute. The words had registered in his mind, but he did not believe they could be true. His only thought was, "God wouldn't let this happen to Marlene!" He stared up at the ceiling, glaring angrily as if he could see God up in heaven through the painted sheet rock. "God, you couldn't do this to Marlene!" he shouted suddenly. Marlene shook and lifted her head, as if to look at Arthur, though she still could not see.

"Arthur, you mustn't say that! God wouldn't do such a thing! It just happened," she cried.

Arthur shook his head, looking back down at her. "It can't be, Marlene, it just can't be. This must be some sort of nightmare."

"That's what it feels like, Arthur. That's what it felt like starting the moment I opened the door to see the highway patrolman standing there at my apartment door. The whole thing is unreal. But the part that scares me is, deep inside, as much as I hope I'll wake up as if from a dream and find everything is just fine, is that I know this isn't just a dream. It's real, Arthur, and that's what's eating away at me," Marlene returned. "I want God to heal my father and Nate and Ryan—I want it so badly!"

Just then a doctor walked into the room. Arthur heard his noisy steps on the tile and stood up. He swerved around to watch the man. The doctor's face was red, as if from embarrassment, and his white coat had drops of blood on it. "Mrs. Picket?" he called.

Pam Picket stood up from her chair and shakily walked over to take the doctor's outstretched hand. He shook her hand and told her, "I'm Doctor Wilabee. Are you Pam?"

"Yes. Can you tell me how my husband and sons are?"

Marlene stood up and called, "Arthur. Arthur?"

Doctor Wilabee looked past Pam at Marlene, who was feeling around like a blind girl for Arthur. Arthur took one of her hands and led her over to the doctor. "Is she blind?" he asked.

"No, not really. You see she just fainted a little while ago, and since then, she hasn't been able to see anything," Arthur tried to explain.

"Did she hit her head?"

"I don't know. I came right afterwards," Arthur answered with a shrug.

"Yes," Marlene told the doctor. She blinked and turned her head as if looking around, her eyes carrying a blank stare in them.

"I think we better have a look at you," Doctor Wilabee returned, grabbing his cell phone from a case on his belt. "Keith," he spoke into the phone, "I need you to take a look at someone."

"Marlene, are you alright?" Marlene heard her mother ask her.

"Yeah, Mom, I'm fine," Marlene's voice was as shaky as she felt.

Another doctor walked in. "Now Marlene, Doctor Palt here is going to take a look at you."

Doctor Keith Palt led Marlene away to another room. "Did you want to go with her?" Doctor Wilabee asked, noticing that Arthur was staring after her.

"I would," Arthur answered, "But I think she would want me to bring news of her father and brothers."

"Well, I'm only allowed to talk to the family about this. Are you family?"

"No, but I'm Marlene's boyfriend."

"I'm sorry. But we have a privacy policy. Would you come with me, Mrs. Picket? And is this your other son and daughter?"

Pam, Sue, and Albert followed the doctor down the hall, presumably to his office. Arthur watched them. His mind was spinning. He wanted to stop and catch a single thought, or at least make a decision as to what to do next.

"Arthur, did you want to talk?" a familiar voice asked.

Arthur spun around on his heel to see Father Matthew. "Hello Father. I didn't realize you were here." He stopped and stared up at the ceiling. "Think He knows what He's doing?"

"What do you mean, Arthur?"

"You know, making her family end up in the hospital, and causing her blindness and stuff. I mean, she must have felt lonely enough at not getting to see her brothers and father, but causing her vision to go? Marlene's a faithful girl. What's He pulling from up there?"

"Arthur, God's not pulling anything. He didn't make that accident happen, at least not as far as I can tell."

"Then how can He let it happen?!" Arthur snapped angrily, his face growing flush.

"Because, long ago God gave man the ability to make his own choices. He could control everything, true, if he wanted to. He could ease all the suffering in the world, end all the wars, make everybody happy, even make everyone believe in Him. But that's not how God works. He finds it all the sweeter when people choose to believe in Him on their own, after he may touch him with the Holy Spirit. And it's all the better when His children work for him to try to end the wars and poverty that cause suffering in the world."

"But God doesn't cause the wars."

"That's right. Men make wars, and they cause suffering. So when faithful people come along in God's name, choosing to risk everything, even their very lives, to make other lives better, following what Jesus did, God's glory grows greater, and the strength of people's love for God grows. This pleases Him, Arthur. He wants His people to love Him, to do His will."

"But what if He lets Marlene's family die? That's not going to make Marlene love Him more. She might come to hate Him, as I might, if He lets that happen."

"You mustn't say that, Arthur. Marlene might grow angry with God at first, but then she'll cling to him, stronger than before. I've seen things happen to faithful people like the Pickets. Tragedies like this might tear some families apart. But the families I know, who called me in to speak in God's name to their perishing family members, only grew closer together, and their faith in God only grew stronger. I know He has something to do with that. He doesn't want His people to hate him. But He gives them a choice. If He made everything good all the time, we would forget how good good things are, how important love and goodness are. We might not cherish His love, and the miracles that happen in life, if nothing ever went wrong."

"How can He work that way? How can you be sure?"

"We don't know everything about God, or even why He forgives us time and again with His unfathomable mercy and love. We only know three things about Him other than that He is three in one and that he sent down His only son: that He is the only God, He loves us, and He wants us to love Him and each other."

"I still don't see how bad things can be good."

"I didn't say that. What I meant was, well, let me give you a comparison. If you were a runner, and you were the fastest runner around, and you never lost a race, would winning always mean a lot to you? Or would you forget how special it was to win, and how neat it was that your family always supported you, and how amazing it was that you had such a gift at running."

"I guess you might forget. I remember a fast kid at my high school who was a jerk. He always expected to win, and was cocky to everyone."

"There you go. Now, take that kid who always gets last place, and who has to listen to the other runners talk about how great they are and how terrible he is. Life seems pretty bad for the kid, and though he persists for awhile, he finally just wants to give up. Then, suddenly, one race, another runner shows up and runs up to him in the race, as if to pass him. The slow kid is just about to stop, to give it all up. But instead of passing him, the new runner paces with him, cheering him on. He tells him that he thinks it's neat that he runs these races, no matter what the outcome. The slow kid complains to him that he's never won a race, never come in any place but last place. The new runner tells him that the races he's been running have never been about what place you get, but that you try, and that you keep on running. He adds a promise at the end that, in the end, when the kid runs the last race in his career, he'll be waiting there for him, with a prize better than any prize ever given to that cocky, first place runner." The priest stopped and watched Arthur's face contort in confusion.

"Interesting. Is there any more to your story?"

"A little. After that talk with the new runner, who then drops back, the slow kid takes heart. He starts speeding up, with renewed energy, acting as if this is the first race he's ever run. Then suddenly it's the end of the race. For the first time ever, the kid listens to the crowd, and he realizes that they're cheering for him. An official walks up and hands him a ribbon. And the kid realizes that the hope the new runner gave him helped him win the race. He asks about the runner, and no one around seems to know what he's talking about. They claim he was seeing things. But the kid knows he saw the runner, and tells everyone about him."

"I gotcha. The new runner is like Jesus, coming into our lives. And we'll run into people who claim He doesn't exist, but we give them the message that He does. And, after every time we mess up, or we lose a race, we have God's word to remind us what's really important. But what does that have to do with right here and right now?" Arthur asked.

"Right now the Pickets might be facing a losing race. But, if they truly have faith, and even only partially see things the way God wants them to, they will make it through to race another day for God."

Marlene sat in a chair as Doctor Palt pointed a flashlight first at one eye, than the other. "Can you see this light?" he asked her as he stared at her dilating pupils.

"I see some fuzzy brightness."

"Good."

"What's wrong with me, doctor? Why can't I see?"

"You struck a nerve at the back of your head, I believe. This nerve somehow connects to your eyes. I'm no specialist, but I think that fall caused you to temporarily go blind."

"When will it come back?"

"I don't know. I think you should see a specialist as soon as possible about this."

"But my family! I can't go see some specialist now. I need to find out what happened to Dad and Ryan and Nate!"

"If you want your vision to come back, you'd better see an eye doctor who can tell you exactly what's happened to your eyes right away."

"But my family!"

"What's your last name, Marlene?"

"Picket. Did you work on my Dad?"

"No. I helped the crew rush your siblings in, and then your Dad. He said something about 'Marlene Picket' when we asked if he had any family nearby. So we sent the highway patrolman who found and reported the accident to go find you."

"Do you know how they're doing?"

Marlene did not see Keith shake his head, but she heard him softly reply, "No. I'm sorry, Marlene."

Arthur walked into the room when the doctor was writing notes on a pad of paper. "So, Doc, what's the matter with Marlene? Why can't she see?"

"Who are you?" Keith asked, peering at a young, tall man with a cowboy hat covering wet, blond hair, and spur covered boots that jangled as he walked.

Arthur approached the young doctor. "Arthur Pressed. I'm Marlene's boyfriend."

Keith opened his mouth to speak, but all that came out was, "Oh."

Marlene heard Arthur and turned her head to face his direction. "Arthur, what'd that other doctor say? Are they going to be alright?" she asked.

Arthur stared at her face silently for a moment. It was convulsing with emotion. He strode over to her and bent over her. Marlene could hear his placid breathing. "I don't know, Marlene. Doctor Wilabee wouldn't let me hear. I guess we'll just have to ask your mom."

"Poor Mom. She's still in shock over the whole thing. I hope they're okay," Marlene spoke. Her voice quivered like her lips. Arthur squatted down and reached forward to hug her.

"Everything's going to be okay, Marlene. You just have to believe that," Arthur whispered in her ear. Marlene rested her cheek against his. He could hear her unsteady breathing as she tried not to cry again.

"I hope you're right," she whispered back. Her whole body shook against his.

After a few minutes Arthur stood up. "So, Doc?"

Dr. Palt turned from a counter. "She needs to see an eye specialist. As soon as possible. But I can understand the need to hear about her family, too, so try to get her to one once you hear about them."

Arthur strode up to Keith. "Thank you, Doctor—"

"Keith Palt. It's nice to meet you two, only I wish it were under happier circumstances. In my line of work, unfortunately, it usually isn't."

They shook hands, then Arthur returned to Marlene and helped her up. He led her out the door, down the hallway to the waiting room. The Pickets had not come back yet, so Arthur sat down next to Marlene in the corner to wait.

A few silent minutes passed, then Marlene spoke. "Arthur, there's something I need to tell you."

Arthur turned to study her face. "What's that?"

"I—I need to tell you why Dad drove up here in the first place."

"Was it to get you, so you guys could have your family reunion?"

"Partly, but there's more to it than that. You see, we were talking about you on the phone and, and he said it'd never work between us. I told him how serious we were, and he cussed and told me to stop dating you. He said you were a nice boy, but that you'd always be jealous of me for having a college degree, and that you'd force me to stay on your ranch if we got married, and never use my own degree. I told him that you weren't jealous of my education, and that you were smart too. Then he claimed you'd never amount to anything, Arthur. We started shouting back and forth, until I was crying and my father was using more foul language, then I said goodbye and was about to hang up when he said that he was going to come pick me up. It's all my fault, don't you see!"

Marlene began sobbing again, and Arthur wrapped his arm around her shoulders and drew her against him. He was starting to feel emotional from hearing her father's opinion of him, and started to feel anger build up within him, but he hid it from his voice. "Marlene, that doesn't make it your fault. Your dad was coming to pick you up anyway, wasn't he? I mean, you don't even have a car."

Marlene stopped crying a moment and sat up. She stared straight ahead with the blank look that was starting to bother Arthur. "I forgot to tell you that part of the conversation. I told my dad how I planned on calling you, and getting you to give me a ride up, so that you could also be at our family reunion. That's actually how the whole thing started. He had mentioned that he was going to pick me up, and I told him my plan involving you. Then he went raring off—oh, I shouldn't talk that way about him. I might not even see him again. Oh, God, what have I done?!" Marlene hunched over and covered her head with her hands.

Arthur stared at her, worried, confused, and unsure how to comfort her. Marlene had stuck up for him, but at what price? And was it all really worth it? Was this unlikely romance between a cowboy and a college girl even worth the pain and feeling of guilt it was causing Marlene? Was Arthur being selfish, hoping that one day maybe he and Marlene would marry and settle down on his ranch? Maybe her father was right. Maybe they did not belong together.

Suddenly Arthur felt he needed to get outside this hospital to think. He stood up. As he started to walk, his spurs jangled against the tile. Marlene heard him walking away and called out, "Arthur, where are you going?"

Arthur called back over his shoulder, "Outside. I need to think, Marlene."

"Arthur, don't go! Don't leave me here, all alone!" she cried out.

Arthur did not turn back around, but kept on walking toward the exit. He did not see Marlene stand up and try to follow the sound of his footsteps, ending with a fall as she bumped into a wall. He had to get away.

"Arthur!" Marlene cried in desperation. She had a sick feeling in the pit of her stomach, as she lay there upon the cold floor, that Arthur would not return. Suddenly she felt all alone. She was losing half her family, and now she was losing the man she loved. Just when she thought she could depend on him, just when she needed him desperately, he walked away and left her. How could God let her be so alone?

"Marlene!" a voice shouted from somewhere down the hall. Marlene heard fast pace footfalls upon the tile as her mother ran to her. Pam helped her daughter up, looking around for Arthur. "Where's Arthur?" she asked.

"He went outside to think, Mom. But what if he doesn't come back?"

Pam smiled at her daughter, for the first time that day. "And why wouldn't he?"

"I told him about what Dad said about him."

Pam frowned. She had been in the kitchen that morning when she heard her husband shouting into the phone in the living room. George had sounded angry and upset. When he slammed the phone down, she asked him what the phone call was all about. He gave her a brief synopsis before grabbing the car keys off the counter and taking off for Laramie in his small, blue Volvo.

"Oh," was all that Pam could think to say. She knew George did not approve of Marlene dating the cowboy, despite the young man's ambitions to have a big ranch someday. George was deep in the business world, and he felt strongly that his youngest daughter needed to make something of herself. He had tried to persuade her into going into something like engineering, where she would be guaranteed to make a lot of money. When Marlene refused, stubbornly as he liked to say, he asked her to at least plan for the future with some kind of realistic degree. Marlene chose business, with a minor in creative writing.

Next George hoped Marlene would marry a college man who would work side by side with her, and not be jealous of her fine education. To top off the whole thing, she had been talking a lot lately about her cowboy boyfriend, who never went to college and did not plan to. This made George's rage complete. Knowing how insulting it must have been for Arthur to hear all this, Pam had no argument to make against Marlene's fears of losing him. She wanted her daughter to be happy, and thought that Marlene and Arthur could perhaps make it, but now that the blow had been made, Pam did not know how to help Marlene recover and save her relationship. Pam only hoped that Marlene was not as serious about Arthur as she had appeared to be.

Arthur paced back and forth outside. He was frustrated with Marlene's father, and yet wondered if the man could be right. He wondered if he had been selfish, if he would be asking Marlene to sacrifice the possibly wonderful future she could have with her degree. Maybe there was some guy out there, waiting for her, who would be a big-shot in the business world, who she could work together with and make her parents proud. And maybe there was some girl out there, waiting for him, who did not have a college degree either, who was raised on a ranch, and who wanted to continue to live on a ranch. Maybe Arthur was not worthy of Marlene's family, or of her. He thought he was, he thought they were right for each other, but maybe they did not have enough in common, and maybe she was too good for him. After all, his plans were not too big for life. He just wanted to marry, have a family, like his father, and maybe do a little more than his family by making his ranch very successful and big. But was that what God had in store for him? Was God disappointed with him for not going to college, like his parents wanted? And now was God punishing him by making him hear such insults about him, by tearing him away from the only girl he ever loved?

He finally found himself next to his truck, his keys resting in his palm. Arthur had a choice. He could stay and face whatever Marlene's family might throw at him, or he could run away now, and never face them. It would be easy to run away. But Marlene needed him. She needed someone to be with her, come what may. Would she feel betrayed if he left? Certainly. He knew he would if she left him. Yet he could not face her family. He could not face her father, if he was still alive, nor her brothers, who might even think the same thing of him. Arthur moved the keys to be between his thumb and index finger, and stuck one key into the lock. Everything seemed like slow motion as he turned the key, opened the door, and hopped onto the driver's seat. Slowly he turned the key in the ignition, listening to the disruptive grinding of the engine before it took off in a steady roar. Already he was beginning to regret his decision, but he was feeling as stubborn as Marlene.

Pam watched through the waiting room window as that familiar blue truck raced out of the parking lot. Sure enough, her daughter was right in her fears. She turned to face Marlene. Marlene had her hand on her mother's shoulder. "What is it Mom? Did he leave?" she asked, noting her mother's silence.

"Yes, Dear. But I do have some good news to tell you."

"About Ryan, Nate, and Dad?"

"Yes, well, about Nate and your father—"

"Where is he, Mom?" a voice called. Judy ran in from the hospital entrance. She had been in Chicago, visiting family, when the accident happened.

"Mom, how are Nate and Dad?" Marlene asked.

"Dad is going to be just fine, and Nate, well, he will be all right, I think."

"What do you mean 'I think'?" Marlene asked. Her sister-in-law stood near her.

"His kidneys were damaged in accident. They need a donor, but then he'll be alright."

"What about Ryan?" Judy asked frantically. Pam watched as the blood rose to her face.

"He's in a comma, Judy. His body's not responding well, and, and—" Pam's voice sounded dry and husky. She could not finish.

Marlene prompted her. "Mother, and what?"

"The doctors don't think he'll make it through the night. They're already asking about how long we want him on life support, if his organs don't fail by then."

"Oh God!" Judy cried out. She turned away, tears in her eyes, and bumped into a familiar figure.

Arthur grabbed Judy and held her in his arms. "It's going to be alright, Judy."

Marlene heard his voice. "Arthur!"

Her mom also cried, "Arthur!"

Arthur gazed at the two surprised women over Judy's shoulder. "You don't understand, Arthur," Judy sobbed. "I went to Chicago to tell my family that I'm going to have a baby. Ryan was going to tell his family today."

Wide-eyed, Pam stepped over to Judy and hugged her and Arthur. "I'm so happy for you two, Judy."

Marlene stood alone. Suddenly she saw light, and then started to see the blurry forms of her mother and Arthur. She blinked, wondering how it could be that she could see again. Arthur gazed at her, watching as she stared back at him, a recognizing look in her eyes. He broke away from her sister-in-law and mother and strutted over to her.

"Marlene, can you see?" he asked her, standing a foot away.

Marlene nodded. Her face was wrinkled up as tears flowed down her cheeks. "God can't let this happen!" she screamed.

Arthur took a step closer and she ran away from him. "Marlene!" he shouted.

Marlene ran to the admittance desk. "What room is Ryan Picket in?" she asked the nurse there.

The nurse clicked the mouse next to her computer and typed in Ryan's name. "Room 208. But you can't visit him right now. Visiting hours don't start until five o'clock, if doctors are done with him by then," she conferred.

Marlene leaned against the counter, breathing heavily. "I need to see him, please!"

Arthur laid his hands gently on her shoulders and pulled her away from the desk. "Come on, Marlene, let's go see your father and then Nate."

"I thought you'd left, Arthur," Marlene replied.

"I couldn't leave you, Marlene. Not like this, anyway," Arthur told her.

Marlene, Arthur, Pam, and Judy visited George in his room. Sue and Albert had already visited him, and they left to buy lunch for everyone.

"Hi, dad," Marlene whispered when she was standing by his bedside.

"Hi, Marlene. Guess not even a car wreck can kick me out of life," George joked.

"I'm glad to see you're alright, Dear," Pam spoke softly. She bent over to kiss George.

George tried to lift his arm to wrap it around his wife, but found it would not move. He glanced down at, and cried out, horrified. "My arm! What happened to my arm?!"

Pam tried to hold back her tears, and to hide the fear in her voice. "They had to amputate it, Dear. It was smashed in the accident."

"Oh, God!" Marlene cried. She stared down at her father's shoulder, wrapped in a bandage.

"Everything's going to be okay, Marlene. Let's pray," Arthur whispered.

So, right there near the bed, Marlene and Arthur knelt down and prayed for her brothers and father. Pam hugged her husband and whispered to him, trying to comfort him. She dared not tell him yet the conditions of their sons.

Chapter Fifteen

The next few days passed by slowly. George was angry and depressed, and ever since that first visit from Marlene, he would not speak to her. He would just sulk and lay in his bed, his left arm crossed over his chest, as if to cross it with his missing right arm. George felt his career was over, now that his dominant arm and hand were gone. His wife tried to comfort him, but he only spoke a few words to her, revealing how bitter he was. Marlene had a deep, sinking feeling that her father blamed her, though out loud he only spoke angry words to God. He glared at Arthur the second time the young cowboy had come in, so after that Arthur waited outside the room while Marlene visited her father, day after day.

Several days after the accident, Arthur had the doctors test his blood type and his kidneys, to see if he could possibly be a match for Nate. He did not want Marlene to know, because he did not want to get her hopes up.

One week later, Arthur was still in Laramie, staying at a hotel so he could be near Marlene. George was out of the hospital now, and Nate had managed to survive on his failing kidneys so far. Ryan was still alive, but in a coma. His body was not responding well to the medicines the doctors gave him. Pam finally told her husband of their sons' conditions. George reacted angrily, tossing his food tray she had brought him across the room. After that he stared silently at the blueberry pie stain on the wall, while Pam strode out of the room. In the kitchen she burst into tears. No one else was home to see how Pam was suffering.

Arthur and Marlene had been visiting Saint Laurence O' Tool church at least once at day since the accident, to pray for Nate's and Ryan's recovery. They knew the odds were against them, and that it would take a miracle for them to recover. Yet Arthur had hope. Marlene was downhearted, and would not tell Arthur how she was truly feeling. He never asked her, but picked her up each day to pray, and to take her out to Wendy's for lunch.

Arthur still struggled with wondering if he and Marlene belonged together. He loved her, but he knew her father still did not approve of them. In fact, George had called him just that day to ask him to meet him in a few hours to talk about Marlene. Arthur had a terrible feeling that George was going to tell him to leave Laramie now, and to stop dating his daughter.

Despite Arthur's fears, he bravely showed up at the Picket's house in Cheyenne. As he stepped out of his car, he paused a moment to take in the view of the place where Marlene had grown up. It was a grand, two story house. Blue with white trim, it looked like something right out of the 1940's era. Blue curtains were drawn across all the front windows except one large window with three separated panes near the right corner of the house. A small garage stood next to that corner, connected, yet with a lower roof. There was a white mailbox with a picture of the Snowy Range Mountains on it that the Picket kids had painted when they were little. Taking a deep breath in, he knocked on the door. Hearing a hoarse voice call, "Come in," Arthur opened the door. It creaked on its hinges, as if in protest, as he shut it behind him.

In a plush, padded chair before a small color T.V. sat Mr. Picket, his feet rested up on a small cedar stool. Arthur hesitated in the hallway leading to the living room. George picked up a controller and pressed a button to turn off the T.V. Then he turned to stare at Arthur. It was not a welcoming stare, but rather an accusing one. After seeming to examine Arthur from head to toe, with his roaming eyes, George motioned for Arthur to come closer.

"You said you wanted to speak with me, Mr. Picket?" Arthur asked as he approached the chair.

George nodded. "Pull up a chair, young man, and listen to what I have to say."

Arthur complied, then sat patiently, yet nervously, as George cleared his throat. "Before you begin, sir, I just want you to know that I care about your daughter very much," Arthur mentioned, staring directly at Mr. Picket.

George averted his gaze from Arthur to look at a painting of a ship hung on the wall. "Arthur, do you have any idea what it took me to get where I am today?"

"No sir, I don't."

"My father never went to college, as he could not afford it. He spent long hours working, trying to provide for his family. Yet, despite all his work, he died a poor man. I scraped and saved from the time of my first job, delivering papers at twelve years old. Some called me ambitious, and I like to use that word myself. I managed to get into college, and get a job at a fine business, to support my wife and kids."

"I'd say you've done a fine job, Mr. Picket, but—"

"I'm not finished! You see, I managed to get every one of them into college. They all have fine minds, and will no doubt be famous and rich one day. So, what I want to know, since you take such a keen interest in my youngest daughter, is what you plan to do with your life."

Arthur shifted his feet around. As George stared at him, awaiting his answer, he decided it was now his turn to avert his gaze. He stared at the T.V., as if a movie was playing on it. Finally, he felt composed and answered, "Well, sir, I intend to ranch, just as I have done the past couple of years. I will hopefully have a bigger ranch soon, with good investment and perhaps a little luck, and help from God."

"No plans to go to college?"

"No sir."

"How old are you, Arthur?"

"Twenty-three, sir. I'll be twenty-four in December."

"Do you intend to get married, settle down and have a family?"

"Yes sir."

"And who do you intend to marry?"

Arthur raised his eyebrows and shot a glance at Mr. Picket. "I would like to marry your daughter, sir."

George frowned and stroked his chin with his hand. "Arthur, do you know why I'm in this condition, why I now only have one arm?"

"You were in an accident, sir. I know that."

"Do you know why I was heading to Laramie?"

Arthur remembered Marlene's depiction of the guilt she felt for the accident, and how she told him her father would no longer speak to her.

"Now, don't go blaming your daughter, Mr. Picket."

"I don't blame her—anymore. I realize it all happened because of you. It's because of you my daughter has no ambition to use her college degree once she graduates, and because of you that I was driving to Laramie in the first place."

"Now see here!" Arthur shouted, a surge of guilt washing through him.

Marlene was walking up the steps to visit her father, hoping he would finally talk to her. She heard raised voices as she approached the door. Stopping, she listened, with her ear to the door.

"It's true, isn't it? Look, mister cowboy, I don't have anything against you not having a college degree. I realize some people just can't afford college. But the fact that you don't plan on making anything of yourself, and anchoring yourself to my daughter, who would probably eventually have to work for the both of you, to support you, infuriates me!" Marlene recognized her father's rough voice.

"I wouldn't make her work! I make enough from ranching!" Arthur's voice was strained and angry.

"So you'd make her stay inside the house all day? She wouldn't get to use her education how she wants?"

"I didn't say that! DANG IT! You crooked old man! You twist every blasted word I say! Just git to the point!"

"Shut up, you young know it all. You want to know what my point is, you idiot?!! I don't want you near my daughter, ever! You hear me?!!"

"Yes I hear you! And I'd have to say that's up to your daughter! Why don't you ask her, huh? Rather than not speak to her? She's hurting inside!"

"DANG YOU! Get out of my house! If you ever come here again, I'll call the police!"

Marlene was not sure whether to enter now, or not. As she stood debating, Arthur opened the door and knocked into her. They both tumbled down the two steps leading up to the porch. Taken aback, Arthur stared at Marlene as they both stood up.

"Marlene, what, what are you doing here?" he asked her.

"I was coming to visit my father."

"Did you hear all that?" Arthur asked.

"I heard enough," Marlene replied, trembling. Arthur wanted to hold her in his arms, but instead he took a step away from her.

"I've got to go," he spoke softly. His face was pale. Marlene stepped towards him, and she reached her hand up towards his face. As she touched his cheek, he gently laid his hand over hers.

"Arthur, I'm going to go talk to him. He's being a fool. He doesn't know you like I do."

"But he's right about one thing."

"What, Arthur, what could my father possibly right about right now?"

"I'll never amount to anything. I don't have the ambition that your family does, Marlene. Your father will never accept me. I know that for sure now."

"Then let's go. We could elope, or something, Arthur," Marlene returned, desperately.

Arthur shook his head, pulling her hand from his face and dropping it so that she swung it back to her side. "It'll never work, Marlene. He blames me for all this. I, I can't convince him to forgive me, even if I go to college, and get a regular job."

Tears wet Marlene's eyes. "Arthur, you've got to understand. Grandpa never made it to college. Dad's been all for college ever since he went. Dad doesn't think Grandpa was successful."

"But do you?"

"I don't know. Grandpa Picket died of a heart attack when I was ten. I don't remember him very well."

Arthur nodded, knowingly. "Both sets of my grandparents died when I was young. Neither couples died very prosperous, in the money sense of the word. But before my grandma died, when I was in junior high, she called me to her bedside. Grandpa had gone the year before, and she was so lonely she wanted to join him. Well, I had always felt sorry for her and my mom, her oldest daughter, because they never had much. 'Grandpa worked fifty hours a week, and would come home, exhausted,' she told me. 'But,' she said, 'He was very prosperous and was the most successful man in the world.'

"'How can that be?' I asked her. 'You couldn't even ever afford a radio, much less a dishwasher.'

"'Not that kind of wealth,' she tenderly replied, squeezing my cheek as she always did. 'Walter kept me very happy over the years. Sure, we didn't have much, materially. But he was a good man, and he loved me and the kids very much. Though we couldn't afford many presents for Christmas, he and I always carefully picked out the ones we did get for your mother and her sisters. When Christmas Day came, I swear I couldn't tell who the kids were and who the grown-ups were. Your Grandpa was right in there, imagining he was the cop in the matchbox car, chasing the kids in their little red and blue cars. And, he never failed to set up the train around the tree. He knew that was my favorite tradition at Christmas time, other than going to mass.'

"'But Grandpa wasn't Catholic, was he?' I asked, confused. You see, my grandpa was a Christian, though he never objected to my grandma raising my mother and her sisters as Catholics.

"'No, that's true,' my grandmother replied, 'but he loved to go to mass with us, especially at Christmas. He had the whole congregation convinced he was raised Catholic. And when especially hard times fell on us, like when his small gas station burned down, he never took out his frustration on me or the kids. He and I would talk calmly at night, planning the saving we would have to do, spending as little as we could, so that we could continue to pay for our little three room house.' My grandma paused then for dramatic effect, and also to let a little thirteen year old boy soak in the importance of all that she had said. 'He may have died poor in money, but the wealth that he gained from the love in his family made him a very happy man. He told me so when he was dying.'"

Marlene stood silently for a moment. "I never thought of that before," she finally said to Arthur. Arthur nodded, then turned from her and strode towards his car. "Arthur, where are you going?" Marlene called, worried.

"I need to leave, Marlene. I've outstayed my welcome. But I hope everything turns out alright, and I hope you find the right guy for you. The one your family will approve of."

"Please don't go, Arthur!" Marlene cried, chasing after him.

Arthur opened his car door, saying, "Marlene, I must. I'm fed up with your materialistic family, and sick of takin' the heat fer stuff I didn't do wrong. Goodbye."

Off he drove, with Marlene staring after him. Once he glanced in the rearview mirror, to see her forlorn face, her tear-filled eyes staring longingly after him.

Marlene waited, hoping he would come back as before. But a half an hour later, still no cars had come down the street. She walked down the block, trying to think things through. She kept on walking, despite the cold wind that was blowing, and eventually found herself at a park. It was the same park she had played at with her brothers when she was little. Ryan used to race her on the monkey bars, and Nate loved to be "it" when Sue, Albert, Ryan, and Marlene would play freeze tag.

She sighed and sat down under a tall oak tree next to the playground. She had only seen Nate once at the hospital, and he looked pale, his face drawn. He looked like he felt hopeless, and he talked very little to her. He was obviously depressed about the whole situation. Oxygen tubes covered the bottom of his face, but they could not hide his expressions from her. The doctors still had not allowed her to see Ryan, saying that he was in critical condition. They kept saying he might die any day now, so she did not understand why they would not let her visit him, to at least say goodbye.

Marlene suddenly felt lonelier than she had ever felt before. This past week, although she felt like she had lost her family, she at least had Arthur. And she had felt so sure he would never leave her. Yet as suddenly as a life can be plucked away, Arthur had told her things would not work between them, and he left. It was so unfair. She gazed up at the cloud-filled blue sky. Its deep blue color reminded her of the lake here in Cheyenne that she and Arthur had visited to feed the ducks. They had a picnic lunch before breaking up pieces of stale bread to toss onto the surface of the glimmering pool of water. After a few bites, the ducks even grew brave enough to approach her and Arthur on land, waddling slowly up to them. Marlene giggled while Arthur laughed with his deep, rumbling laugh.

The memories of the dates and time she had spent with Arthur flooded back to her as she sat beneath the tree, shivering from the chill of the breeze. She wondered how God could give her something so great, such a great, caring family, and such a close relationship with a man, and then let it all fall apart. Why did she feel so empty now? Somehow it did not feel right to blame God for all that had gone wrong, as she did, nor did it feel right that she was so empty. At one memorable mass in church, when Marlene was confirmed, the priest had made a speech about basing your life on God. "God is the base," the wise young priest had said, "that never crumbles. Though the world may crumble around you, though your life may turn to ruin, you shall survive if you base your life on Him."

Back then, the message had been clear to Marlene, and, when she got to college, she felt that she was basing her life on God. Yet when the first big crisis ever crashed down upon her, she had fallen, and had blamed God for her ruin. As Marlene sat there, brushing her hand across the dry, bristly grass shooting up from the ground, a realization came to her. Though she had been praying to God, thanking Him and asking Him for things, and trying to do good for Him every once in a while, she had never truly trusted Him enough to base her life on Him. It was astonishing to think that she had not trusted her own creator. She had been so absorbed in her books, in her education, in her friendships, and in her relationship with Arthur, she had not let her life follow in the footsteps of Christ. It was not quite an obsession with a few things in her life, but it was to the point that she made those few things more important to her happiness than God. A feeling of deep and troubled guilt washed over her like a tall wave crashing down upon the sea.

Marlene silently stayed there, at the park, thinking the rest of the day. She stood up to watch the sun set in the distance, shading her eyes from the brightness as the colors started to flood the sky. The clouds absorbed the purple light, and a bright orange glowed behind them.

Then she returned to her friend's car that she had borrowed to come to Cheyenne. Getting in, she drove like a madwoman back to Laramie. She headed straight to her friend's apartment, dropped off the keys after parking, and walked briskly back to her own apartment. Though she could not make Arthur come back, and though she might lose Ryan and Nate, she had to have a positive attitude they would live, and change the way she thought about life altogether. It took a frantic situation to make her realize how precious were both life and God.

Chapter Sixteen

Arthur was about an hour from his ranch when he got the call. His cell phone rang three times before he pulled to the side of the road to answer it. "Hello?" Arthur answered.

"Hello. Am I speaking to Arthur Pressed?" a voice on the other line questioned.

"Yes, you are. And who are you?"

"I'm Sam Wilabee. We met at the hospital, I believe."

"Doctor Wilabee?" Arthur replied.

"Yes."

"Why're you callin' me, Doc?" Arthur asked, puzzled.

Sam heard the confusion in his voice. "Well, you took a test, didn't you?" Sam returned, confidently.

"Huh?" Arthur still was not making sense of this conversation. After a moment of silence between the lines, it all registered. "Oh, the test of my kidneys."

"Yes. Your kidneys are very healthy and—"

Arthur grew ecstatic. "They matched?"

"Yes. They were a perfect match for Marlene's brother, Nate. As a matter a fact, they are the only match we've had out of all the tests done so far. Several people from the university tried, and all the healthy members of Marlene's family. It seems odd to me that none of them matched, but you did."

"How is Nate?"

"I didn't want to have to tell you this, to make you feel pressured about this decision, but he's pretty bad off. The medicines have not helped, and infections are liable to set in as his body is now starting to shut down. He needs a, a new kidney immediately," replied Sam. He stuttered as he spoke, and, for the first time in the last ten years of his career, he felt nervous.

The line decreased to a foreboding silence. Arthur breathed hard into the phone as he tried to gather his thoughts. He would never see Marlene again. A tempting thought rang through his head. Why should he help Marlene's family when they were so ungrateful? Still, Nate had been nice to him. And even if he had not, what did it matter? Life was life, and Arthur had wanted to save it, ever since he watched his grandmother die of cancer. Every calf Arthur had brought into the world, every wounded horse he had tended to, he had thought of how important it was to save that life.

As the doctor waited on the other end, patiently giving him time to think it over, a memory flashed through Arthur's mind. He was a sixteen year old boy, and his father had just woken him up. A wolf had attacked a cow during the night, and William Pressed, Arthur's father, wanted his son's help to try to save the cow. It was a couple hours past midnight—the earliest Arthur had ever woken up.

"Son, shine that flashlight over here," William called.

Arthur turned the glare of the light onto the area his dad pointed to. There, in the field behind the house, they stared down at a bawling cow. The cow's side had been torn open. For Arthur, the sight had been most gruesome. He had seen his dad cut up dead deer before, but seeing a live animal in this shape shook him. Arthur glanced at the cow's face. Two large frightened eyes stared up at him, pleaded with him, from a head tilted up to look at its rescuers. Pain racked the poor animal's body, and it shook as William felt around and in the wound with his hands.

"Is she bad off, Pa?" Arthur asked his father, watching his father examine the cow.

"Yes, son, I reckon she is."

"Should we call the vet, Pa?"

"No. Doctor Benington couldn't possibly make it in time."

"In time? She isn't gonna make it?"

"No, son, I reckon not."

Arthur shone the flashlight on his father's face. "Dad, we've got to save her. We just hafta!"

"Son, the cow's bleedin' to death. There ain't nothin' we can do fer her," William told him frankly.

William Pressed stood up from his kneeling position and walked away, shaking his head. Arthur ran past him, into the house. Before his father could object, he called the vet's number. Doctor Benington told him he would head over as soon as he could. William watched as his son quickly heated up a poker in the fireplace and then ran outside. Arthur shone the flashlight on the cow, and he searched around until his saw the area where the cow was bleeding. "Please help me save this cow," Arthur prayed as he touched the poker to the bleeding flesh. The cow shook and tried to jump up.

Arthur was startled, and the cow might have kicked him had his father not been right behind him. William leaped into action. He jumped on the cow and held him down. "Do it again, Arthur. The bleedin's stoppin'."

Several more times Arthur repeated the process, and managed to sear the open veins. After that, he and his father stayed by the cow until Dr. Benington showed up. The veterinarian was amazed to see the cow still alive. He did some sewing up, and then shook Arthur's hand, proudly telling him, "You did a good thing here, Arthur. Not many people keep a cool head about this. You should be a vet, son."

When the doctor left, William hugged his son. "He's right, Arthur. You're a miracle worker. You should go to veterinary school when you graduate."

Arthur looked his father straight in the eyes and replied, "No, Dad. It wasn't me. I asked God for help, and He saved the cow."

William stared back silently, and he never did reply. He just turned around and headed back to the house to wash up. Arthur was not sure how the words had hit his father, nor what had caused him to speak them. Later William tried to convince his son to go to college to become a vet, but Arthur chose not to.

Reflecting over that late fall night, Arthur knew what he needed to do. And he hoped that God would once again help him.

"So, how soon do you need me to come to Laramie?" Arthur suddenly asked.

Doctor Wilabee was surprised. He had been thinking that Arthur was going to change his mind. After dwelling on doubt for the last few minutes, these words came as a startling shock. Rather than revealing his squelched doubts, the doctor moved forward. "You aren't still here?"

"No."

"I thought you and Marlene—well, never mind. It's none of my business. Can you come tomorrow? I know it's kind of late to come today."

"Sure. And when do you need to do the surgery?"

"Tomorrow. But first I have to tell you all the possible consequences of your decision, such as the high risk you'll be left with having only one kidney left."

"Alright, Doc. What time?"

"If you could come in the morning, say around nine or ten, I would appreciate it. The sooner the better."

"I'll see you then. Oh, and Doc?" Arthur returned.

"Yes?"

"Please, don't say a word about this to Marlene or her family. I want to be an anonymous donor."

Sam's respect of the rancher grew immensely at hearing him say these words. The young man did not want Marlene's family to base their feelings about him on this great deed. "You have my promise on that one, Mr. Pressed," he told Arthur.

"Thank you."

Chapter Seventeen

At the hospital, Arthur sat silently in Doctor Wilabee's office as the kind doctor explained the surgery to remove one of his kidneys, and the consequences. Arthur next signed a packet of papers, after reading through them. Then the doctor gave him a gown to change into, and he led Arthur to a room.

Marlene was stunned when Doctor Wilabee called the day after Arthur had left to tell her that a donor had turned up, and that Nate was going to get surgery today. Hearing the good news took her mind off of Arthur. Since it was a Sunday, Marlene went to mass with her parents and Judy. Marlene held Judy's hand tight during the Our Father prayer, and gave her a hug when mass was over. Judy looked pale and scared. She was actually Lutheran, but being so shook up about possibly losing Ryan, she wanted to stick close with Ryan's family. Judy was never very close to her parents, who lived in Chicago, and her older brother had been in Germany for the past five years. Ever since she and Ryan got married, the Picket's had become her family.

Sue and Albert had left that morning on two different planes, since they could take no more time off of work. In mass Marlene prayed hard that the transplant would work, and that she could see Nate back to his old self again. She did not know, however, that Nate would never be back to his old self.

Over the course of the week, with death drawing near, Nate looked back closely over his life, and reevaluated what was important. He had always been an eager young man, sure of himself, and never wanting a commitment. But now that he was possibly going to die, he had started to see things differently.

In surgery, just before the doctors gave him the medicine to knock him unconscious, Nate promised God that if he made it through, and lived, he would live his life to the fullest. No longer would he avoid girls and pursue just gaining knowledge and passing it on. He would see if God wanted him to marry, and he would do more than just teach history. Nate wanted to make a difference in the world, now, if he was given a second chance to do so.

Arthur woke up in a small room, separated from another room by a drawn curtain. It took him a few minutes to comprehend why he was there. The surgery to remove one of his kidneys must have been a success, unless this drab little place was heaven. Funny, he did not feel any different. He did not feel like he was missing anything. Before the doctors operated on him, he was extremely nervous about the whole thing. Then he whispered a prayer as they wheeled him into the operating room, and a calm peace filled him. After that he remembered nothing up to waking up just now.

A thin, wiry looking doctor walked in, with a nurse beside him. "Take his pulse, Kelly," the doctor ordered as he stared critically at Arthur.

"How's Nate?" Arthur asked.

"Nate's fine. He's still unconscious, but Doctor Wilabee and Doctor Jurt performed the surgery wonderfully. It all went as smooth as clockwork. As long as his body accepts the new kidney, he will be able to return to living a normal life."

"That's good to hear. By the way, who's Doctor Jurt? I've never met him."

"Her, Mr. Pressed. She's a specialist we called in. She actually works at the military hospital in Virginia, but she agreed to fly out here to help," the nurse, Kelly, told him.

"Well, it sounds like you had the best team you could have."

"Yeah, we were lucky. Thanks for donating. The Picket's will be thrilled to—" Kelly started off.

"Please, don't tell them my name, or anything about me. I want to be anonymous," Arthur interrupted.

"Well okay then," Kelly replied.

"You're doing good, Mr. Pressed. Your body seems to be functioning normally. Just to be safe, though, we're going to hold you overnight, and maybe tomorrow too," the thin doctor told Arthur.

"Whatever you say, Doc. You're the expert at this, and my health is in your hands," Arthur returned, shrugging.

Chapter Eighteen

Two days after Nate's transplant, Marlene visited him in the hospital. Color was starting to return to his face, and he already seemed to have more energy. As Marlene sat in a chair next to his bed, talking about college, since she had just started going back to class, Doctor Wilabee nearly ran into the room. His face was filled with excitement as Marlene and Nate stared at him.

"Your brother just woke up! He's even suddenly breathing on his own! It's a miracle!" Sam Wilabee shouted enthusiastically.

Marlene hurried after him to Ryan's room. The doctors had finally let her visit him the night before, since it looked like it would be his last night. They claimed that he was already dead, and that the machines were the only things keeping his organs working. But hearing Doctor Wilabee's news, Marlene knew they had been wrong.

There Ryan sat, propped up on pillows, sipping from a glass of water that a nurse held for him. Sam told Marlene that her parents would be there in about an hour to visit as well. When Marlene gazed upon her brother, awake for the first time in almost two weeks, her knees buckled and she fell to the floor. The doctor had to help her to her feet, and help support her as she unsteadily walked toward her brother.

Ryan turned his head to gaze at his younger sister. He had always felt protective of Marlene, and watched out for her even through high school. When a strange guy had flirted with her, the kind of guy he would never trust with his sister, he took his peer aside and threatened him never to date his sister. Unknowing of Ryan's reasons for threatening the guy who had asked her out, Marlene took her own sweet revenge on him that night when he was on a date with a friend of hers. At the time Ryan had been furious, but later, when he thought about it, it made sense.

Now, with foggy memories, Ryan stared at his sister as if for the first time. She was no longer the little girl he remembered, nor the naïve teenager that someone had to watch out for. He saw Marlene as a young woman. The nurse took away the glass from his lips, and he mouthed, "Marlene."

Marlene sat down on the edge of the bed. There were tears in her gentle, young face. Ryan could see the havoc wrought by accident in the wrinkles in her face. Slowly the worries melted away, and Marlene looked joyful. "Oh, Ryan! You're alive!" she cried, reaching forward and hugging him, despite the oxygen tube on his nose, the IV in his arm, and the nurse's warning.

Ryan smiled as his sister let go to sit upright on the bed again. "Ryan, Nate's okay too. And so is Dad," Marlene told him.

Ryan tried to respond, by moving his lips once again, but he could not get his voice to come. His sparkling eyes told Marlene how glad he was to hear the news. A brief flash of memory ran through his mind, and his eyes grew troubled as he recalled the accident.

Ryan and Nate were driving along on I-80 towards Cheyenne when a heavy rain started. Nate was driving calmly, so Ryan tipped his seat back and relaxed. The rain kept on pouring, and Nate had the windshield wipers stroking as fast as they could.

Suddenly Ryan felt the car turning in a jolting movement, and he heard Nate cuss. Ryan jumped up just in time to see that they had swerved onto a road connecting the west bound lanes to the east bound lanes. "Nate, what are you doing?!" Ryan cried. Then, horrified, he saw that a wash of mud had come off of the mountain cutout to their right, and was turning Nate's car just where he did not want it.

Finally the mud splashed past the car tires within a few minutes, and Nate braked. The blazer spun round onto a west bound lane. It slammed into something. Ryan only had a terrifying moment to see that they had crashed into a little blue Volvo, scrunching up its front. Then they were moving again, and Ryan watched the countryside outside spin as Nate's car tumbled down the hill. After that, everything was blank.

"Ryan, everything's going to be okay," Marlene spoke, trying to comfort Ryan, who sat sullenly. Ryan snapped back into the present. He saw Marlene stand up and leave, and tried to call out 'Goodbye,' but his voice still would not come. He then tried to raise his right arm to wave goodbye, but his arm would not move. Looking, he saw that the arm was still there, but it just felt numb. Wondering if there was anything else he could not move, Ryan tried to move his legs. His left leg moved just fine, but his right leg was numb like his arm. He had feeling in his left arm, though he dared not move it, since the giant needle of an IV was jabbed into it, up near the inside of his elbow.

Ryan glanced at the nurse by his side. She read his questioning gaze and sorrowfully looked down, knowing the doctor's diagnoses about his condition was true. Ryan stared at her nametag. It read 'Paula Wills'.

Outside of Ryan's room, Marlene bumped into Doctor Palt. "Oh, hi there Miss Picket," Keith said to her.

"Dr. Palt, what's wrong with my brother, Ryan? He won't speak. And he tried to move, but couldn't," Marlene asked.

Keith grunted and shifted his feet. He nervously spun his wedding ring around his finger like he always did when he had something hard to say. "Marlene, I don't know quite how to tell you this, but your brother had a sort of stroke from the accident."

"What do you mean?"

"He can't remember how to speak, just like a stroke victim, and we found he cannot move the limbs on the right side, signaling paralysis on that side, just like a stroke victim."

"Will he ever be able to talk again?"

"Sure, sure he will. We've had plenty of patients learn to talk again. Someone just has to teach them. As a matter a fact, the nurse carrying for him now, Paula, I believe, studied speech pathology. She could help."

"Thank you, Doctor Palt."

"You're welcome, Miss Picket."

Just then Judy came running down the hall. "Doctor, where's my husband? Where's Ryan?" she asked.

"I'll show you to his room," Keith offered. Marlene left. She knew Judy and Ryan would need some time alone. The nurse left soon after, to check on another patient, Nate Pressed.

Chapter Nineteen

It was early October, four weeks after the accident. Arthur was back on his ranch now, fixing broken down areas of cross buck fence on his land. He pounded hard with the hammer, driving a long nail hard into the thick log. His hands were raw and blistered from handling the rough, splintery wood. Arthur lost his leather gloves a few days ago, and had not bothered to get another pair yet. The pain in his bleeding hands, and the soreness in his arms and legs from his furious work at fixing up the ranch, took his mind off the pain in his heart.

As each day passed by, he longed to see Marlene's face again, to hold her gently in his arms, to hear her sweet voice again. He sometimes wondered if he should have stayed longer, rather than run away, and face George Picket's wrath. But he felt in his hurting heart that he had done the right thing. The only option for him and Marlene to stay together would be to elope, and he had a terrible feeling that that would drive a permanent wedge between her family and them. It was better in the long run that he never see her again, at least better for her. He did not want to cause estrangement between her and her stubborn father.

As Arthur stopped to take a break and sip from his canteen, he spied a cloud of dust moving down the road. The car grew closer and parked on the opposite side of the road from where he was. Out of the dark blue sports car stepped a tall, handsome young man. He squinted his eyes and then smiled, strutting across the quiet road. Arthur recognized him immediately. "Jim!"

"Is this Pressed Ranch?" Jim Pressed asked his brother as he hugged him.

The two stood facing each other. "It shore is. But what are ya doin' here?" Arthur queried.

"I got ta thinkin'. I haven't visited you in a long time, Arthur," Jim replied.

"Wall, it's shore a pleasure ta see ya now. An' thet car! Did ya steal it?" Arthur joked.

Jim laughed, glancing back over his shoulder at his small car. "No, Arthur. I bought it a couple months ago. My job's paying pretty well, and I saved up a lot. That's one thing you taught me how to do, Bro."

Arthur nodded knowingly, grinning. "Ever since you got that blue Matchbox car for Christmas, you told me you were going to get a real car, just like it. Though I've gotta say, this one doesn't look quite the same."

"Well, they don't make cars like that toy one anymore, and I wanted somethin' new."

"So, how long kin ya stay?"

"That depends. How long do you think you can put up with me?"

Arthur laughed deeply and gave his brother a noogie, messing up his nicely combed hair. "Hey, no fair!" Jim shouted, laughing as well.

Jim ducked his head and jumped behind Arthur. He tackled Arthur to the ground, while Arthur was trying to resist. When Jim stood back up, Arthur reached a hand up and grabbed one of Jim's legs, pulling him down.

Then Jim and Arthur spent the next moment trying to pin each other down. When Jim at last succeeded at pinning Arthur down, he yelled, "Say Uncle!"

Arthur grinned as Jim held him down. "Uncle!" Arthur shouted, and Jim let go of his hold. They both stood up and brushed the dirt off their jeans. It was just like the old days, when they were in junior high and high school. Jim had wanted to be a wrestler since he was twelve, so during the winter of ninth grade, he joined the high school wrestling team. When Arthur and Jim were in junior high, Arthur beat Jim almost every time the two of them wrestled. Jim kept challenging Arthur to wrestling matches for fun after school, although some of the matches were caused by a fight, and within a few minutes Arthur would have him pinned down. Jill would pick one of them to cheer for and yell their names as they wrestled. Sometimes Mr. Pressed would be home at the time, and yell for them to go wrestle outside, so he could sit and relax. After Jim joined the wrestling team, he grew stronger from weightlifting and exercises, and he learned special moves. From then on Jim won every match. It was around that time in Arthur's life when he grew more timid. Arthur used to be a noisy kid at school, but in high school, when his brother became popular, he toned down to a polite, quiet guy.

"Why don't we go ta my house?" Arthur asked his brother after a moment of reflecting upon the past.

"Sure. Just let me drive my car there. Hey, why don't you hop in?" Jim replied.

He drove down the dirt road leading to Arthur's house. They stepped out of the car and Jim whistled at the sight before him. "Woo-wee! This place is old-fashioned looking. It looks like it's falling apart."

Arthur turned red. "Well, I've been kinda busy with fencin'. I haven't had a chance ta fix it up."

Jim realized the cabin looked worse than it did when he, Arthur, and their father built it. He saw Arthur's face and decided it would be better to change the subject. "Say, where's your girlfriend? Shouldn't she be visiting or calling you constantly?" Jim teased.

"Who told you I had a girlfriend?" Arthur asked suspiciously as they walked long strides towards the house.

As they stepped inside, Jim returned, "You did. Over a month ago."

"Oh," Arthur replied, and then he was silent. He headed into the kitchen. "You kin sit down if ya want ta. Want anythin' ta drink?"

"Just water." Jim was puzzled by Arthur's avoidance of the question. "Everthin' alright, Arthur?"

Arthur poked his head around the corner at Jim. "Sure," he replied. "Why do ya ask?"

"I don't know. So, how is your girlfriend?"

"I wouldn't know."

Jim was too slow to recognize another perilous moment in conversation before plunging on. "Why wouldn't you know?"

Arthur walked into the living room with two glasses of water. His face was still red, and his mouth overturned in a frown. "Because we broke up."

"What? When?"

"Four weeks ago."

"Why, Arthur? You seemed so sure she was the right girl for you."

"Yeah, well, it has to be more than just me who thinks that."

"She didn't care about you?" Jim questioned, realizing now that he was inquiring about his brother's private matters.

"I don't know. I never asked. I stuck with her while she waited for her family to recover, and then her father told me to leave her alone—that it wouldn't work out."

"You listened to him? Why? Since when have you listened to the commands of anyone lately? You usually stick up for yourself, at least the past year you have been, against the banker and all that."

"Because, I got ta thinkin' that maybe he was right. An' even if he wasn't, eloping, like Marlene suggested, would only cause a rift in her family. And Marlene's close to her family." Arthur looked agitated.

Jim decided to change the subject. "So, did ya hear about Jill?" he asked Arthur. Arthur shook his head. "She's gonna have another kid."

Arthur looked down and mumbled, "I wonder if I'll ever git to have any kids."

It was clear to Jim that Arthur was stuck on the subject of Marlene. "Do you want to tell me about her, Arthur?"

So Arthur spent the rest of the afternoon and evening telling Jim about Marlene and her family. By the time they ate a late supper, Jim knew just how much Arthur cared about Marlene. He was excited to see his brother so in love, yet felt sorry for him that the relationship was broken.

When Arthur went to bed, Jim stayed up and sat in the rocking chair, looking out the window. The familiar view of his youth stared at him from the sky. Jim smiled as he realized that the view of the mountains here was unobstructed, and that there were not any lights of the city to damper the starlight. He had spent from high school on trying to get away from such isolated areas, to get a house in the city. While Arthur had always been satisfied with life in the country, Jim had always dreamed of living in the city. Now that he had it, with its big lights and noisy traffic, and people who often failed to greet each other as they walked by on the sidewalks, he could see what the country life had afforded. At night in the city, Jim would often gaze out his apartment window at the stars. But the stars were usually hard to see, what with lights still on in houses and businesses downtown. And then he would look for the looming form of mountains, as he used to see in his youth. But the mountains were hidden by layers of tall business and apartment buildings. Jim did not realize how much he had missed the simple pleasures of ranch life until he looked out that night at Arthur's barely habitable cabin.

The howling of a wolf out yonder startled Jim. He turned his gaze back towards the inside of his brother's home. "Arthur should really fix this place up," he thought. "It's not much of a home. If he wants Marlene to marry him and live here with him, he should have a house for her more like a modern rancher's. Mom and Dad had a nice, mostly modern house. Not only was there running water and electricity, but there was a good heating system, telephone lines, and walls, real nice looking, painted walls. Not the kind that made you feel like you were in the eighteenth century all the time, and that took a long nail and a powerful hammer to hang any paintings up on it."

Jim frowned. He had let himself forget that Marlene and Arthur were not together anymore. He felt bad for his brother. Arthur was a great guy, and he was not surprised when he heard he found a girl who appreciated him. Arthur deserved just as much happiness as Jill and him. Sure, Jim had yet to find a girl he really cared about, unlike the girl he thought he loved a year ago, but he was not jealous that Arthur had. Instead he just felt sorry for Arthur, and wanted him to be with Marlene. But how would that ever happen? Arthur had made some good points for leaving Marlene behind, yet there had to be some way, some peaceful way that would not cause a riot between him and her father, to get those two who seemed to be meant for each other back together. Jim sat thinking, rocking in his chair with the motion of the swaying of a ship.

Suddenly an idea hit Jim, like a big wave suddenly crashing down on him. He stopped his chair real fast, and almost fell out of it. He found himself shaking with excitement. Jim slowly stood up, and crept over to Arthur's room. Arthur was snoring loudly, and lay still in his bed, except for the rising and falling of his chest. Grinning, Jim crept back away and headed back for the living room. He grabbed his jacket and hopped outside.

Jim drove to Curt and Nancy Hawk's place, which was just a few miles from Arthur. Arthur had told him about his two good friends, and Jim had met Curt once a couple years ago. Jim knew Curt to be a trustworthy friend, who seemed to be willing to help in a time of need.

Curt was just closing his eyes when a blinding light poured in through his window. He jumped up, startled, thinking maybe it was some vision from God. Curt was hardly a religious fellow, but he feared God nonetheless. As Curt's senses sharpened and his mind became clearer, he noticed the sound of an engine purring like a kitten. Then the sound stopped, and there was the slamming of a door. Curt wondered who could be coming to his place at this hour. Unless something terrible had happened!

Curt raced to the door as he recalled the early morning that a priest showed up at his house, back when he was little. Ever since that priest showed up, and he answered the door to hear that his uncle, Derrick, had died from a seizure, Curt's nerves had been on edge with every door bell and every phone ring. Nervously Curt answered the door. There stood a man who resembled his best friend, Arthur, except he was a little shorter and narrower of shoulder. "Hi, Curt!" the man greeted.

Curt held the screen door open with his right foot while he rubbed his eyes. "Who are you?"

"I'm Jim Pressed, Arthur's brother. We met once," Jim told the sleepy eyed Curt.

"Who is it?" a voice called from the bedroom.

"Nancy, it's Jim, Arthur's brother!" Curt called back. "Come on in, Jim."

Curt led Jim to a table at the edge of the kitchen as he switched on the kitchen lights. They sat down at the table. "Want something to drink?"

Curt asked. Jim shook his head. Nancy soon joined them, wearing a purple robe over her pajamas.

"Jim, this is my wife, Nancy," Curt introduced. "Nancy, this is Jim Pressed."

"Nice to meet you Nancy," Jim spoke hurriedly. Nancy nodded.

"So, uh, why are you here, Jim?" Curt asked. "I don't mean to be rude, but it is pretty late."

"Yeah, sorry about that. I came because of Arthur."

Nancy jumped up. "He's okay, isn't he?"

"Yeah, yeah, don't worry, he's fine. It's just that, well, I want to, to— gee I just don't know how to say it."

"Go ahead," Curt encouraged.

"I think he and Marlene are meant to be together, and I've been thinking up a plan to get them back together."

"Great!" Curt shouted. "Does it involve us?"

"It sure does. Now, this entails the utmost secrecy. You can't tell Arthur or Marlene about it."

"Alrighty then. Let's get started. What's yer plan?" Curt asked, eagerly.

Jim smiled, knowing that he had come to the right place. "Well, first of all..."

Nate was deep in dreamland when the phone rang. He sat up and groped around in the dark for his telephone. Everything was dark and blurry. He managed to find his glasses, and then he could see the shadowy form of the lamp. Pulling the chain on the lamp and turning it on, he reached for the phone as it rang for the fifth time. "Hello?" he mumbled in a drowsy voice.

"Hello. Is this Nate Picket?" a voice asked.

"Yes. Who is this?" Nate blinked, as if trying to see the caller on the other line.

"This is Jim Pressed. You don't know me, but I believe you know my brother, Arthur."

"Yes, I do. What is this about? I haven't seen him for a month, since he dumped my sister." Nate held the phone close to his ear as he waited for a reply. The short cord was almost completely straight, and the base of the phone threatened to topple over the edge of his nightstand at any moment.

"How did you feel about Arthur dating your sister?" Jim continued, his voice sounding excited.

"I thought it was great, until he just drove off and left her crying. She's still upset about him. I can tell she misses him."

"Do you think they belonged together?"

"Well, yeah. They seemed so in love with each other, and they got along great. Say, what is this, an interview?" Nate returned.

"Sort of. How would you like to help get them back together?" Jim queried.

"Only if I was assured they were going to get married. I don't want to see my sister's heart broken twice," Nate replied. There was a pause. "Wait, what the heck is that supposed to mean?"

"I'll tell you, but only if I know you're on my side. Do you want them to get married?"

"Sure. Though I'm not sure how my father feels."

"Good. I'll tell you how your father feels, and why Arthur broke up with your sister," Jim told him sincerely.

"What, did you question him like me?" Nate laughed.

"Hey, I'm his brother. It's my job," Jim laughed back. "Okay, so here's what happened that day...."

Chapter Twenty

Arthur woke up to the roar of the wind. He looked out his window to see swirling snow. It was January 20th, and winter had settled in deep on the ranch. Jim had stayed for a week in October, but then he had to get back to work. After the first day of his visit, Jim had gotten Arthur to go to Cody with him every day, and he instructed Arthur to buy all sorts of household items that Arthur did not have. It was mysterious to Arthur, but he bought the items, and then enjoyed riding back to the ranch in the blue sports car with the roof open with Jim.

Arthur laid back down in bed, reflecting on the dream he had just woken from. It was the sort of dream he never wanted to end. It started with him and Marlene, talking as they walked around the lake at a Cheyenne park. Then he was proposing to Marlene, and she nodded and he kissed her, and held her tight in his arms. After that he was telling her what he had been up to since she was gone, with fixing up the ranch and the house. She listened eagerly, and Arthur held her tightly as they sat next to each other, under the shade of a tree.

Arthur told Marlene how much he loved her, and, to his great joy, she told him how much she loved him. Then the dream flashed forward to him putting on a tux, and Jim making jokes about how silly he looked, just like when Arthur was preparing for the senior prom—the only dance he ever went to. He was looking into the mirror as he straightened his tie, when a reflection of Marlene in a pure white wedding dress greeted his eyes.

Then a calf had bawled from the barn, and Arthur woke up. It took him a moment to realize that the whole thing was just a dream. In his heart he had wanted it to be true, the proposal to Marlene, the talk in the park, and then the wedding.

Checking his clock, Arthur saw that it was nine in the morning. Curt and Nancy would be over soon, if the snow was not too deep for Curt's Ford pickup truck. Though Curt had his own ranch to run, and the weather was too harsh and the snow too deep to do much outdoor work on the ranch, Curt had been coming over with his wife since Christmas to help Arthur fix up Arthur's cabin and barn.

With a groan Arthur slid out of the covers, to feel the freezing chill of winter air hit him. Swiftly he changed from his wool pajamas to his old pair of blue jeans and fading tan work shirt. As Arthur was pulling on his heavy woolen socks, he heard Curt pounding on the front door. Arthur hurried to answer it.

"Hey, Arthur," Curt greeted, stepping in, with Nancy close behind.

"Hey, Curt," Arthur replied. "What's all thet paint fer?"

Nancy raised up a can of light blue paint that her hands were wrapped around. "This is for your walls, Arthur," she told him.

"Walls! First you put insulation and sheet rock on them and the ceiling, covering my nice logs, and now you want to paint them!" Arthur exclaimed.

"Stop complaining, Arthur," Curt returned. "And you might as well know now, Luke Barbers, from Cody, is gonna come next week if the roads are clear, to install a furnace in here."

"Curt! That's expensive! This stuff is costin' me enough as it is, but a furnace! I got a nice fireplace here."

"But your house is still cold, even with that insulation we added. Oh, and your roof is sagging. Nancy noticed it outside as we were walkin' in. Much more snow and you'll be freezing with a roof as open as—well I don't know," Curt replied humorously.

"And besides, your ranch is payin' well now. Curt told me," Nancy added.

Arthur shrugged. Curt grinned at him as he carried two cans of paint over to the far wall, and set them beneath the window. As Curt stirred the paint with a stick, and Nancy set down newspapers, damp from the snow, Arthur began to eye his friends suspiciously.

"Why is it you two are so eager to make my house so 'hospitable looking,' as ya once said, in the first place? I like it the way it is."

"Just like you like to do your wash by hand, even in the winter," Nancy shot back.

"Washin' machines are expensive."

"Look, Arthur. Your house may seem fine to you, but if you want to have guests over, like yer brother, you've got to fix it up," Curt told him, pointing a brush at Arthur.

Arthur stood tall and stared hard at Curt. "You were talking to Jim? When?"

Curt looked surprised, like he had given away some secret. "After he visited you," he mumbled, awkwardly.

"Humph!" Arthur grunted. "Okay, give me a brush. I don't want my siblings ta be embarrassed of my house, or uncomfortable in it."

Curt showed Arthur how to stroke with the paintbrush, then he, Nancy, and Arthur each took a different wall of the room to paint. The white walls soon were disappearing into blue. After a while Arthur found his arm growing tired from the continuous up and down motion, so he switched the paintbrush to his other hand.

By sunset, almost every white space on the walls of the living room was gone. "Well, guess we should eat," Arthur said as he looked out at the setting sun.

"Not until we finish this room!" Nancy refuted, dipping her brush again. "And tomorrow we're going to paint the kitchen."

They finished the living room walls, and Arthur pulled a roast out of the oven, with baked potatoes sitting in the heavy metal roasting pan. After drawing the meat and potatoes out with a large fork and a long spoon, Arthur made gravy out of the dark meat juices by adding flour to the liquid. Then he carried the two main dishes to the table.

"I'm impressed at this table," Nancy commented as Curt pulled out a chair for her. "Where did it come from?"

"Well, you remember the week before last, when you two couldn't make it over because of the blizzard?" Arthur asked.

"Yeah," Nancy replied.

"I strode out into the snow and got some of that lumber from the pile in the back of the barn, and set right down next to the stalls to saw the boards. I decided I wanted a bigger table, for when you guys, or anyone else comes over. I even had the inspiration that maybe one day I could use it for my family, if I ever have one."

"But didn't you get cold?" Nancy queried.

"Shore. I got so cold that I was shiverin' uncontrollably, and my fingers got so numb I couldn't feel the saw anymore. So I dragged the sawed boards into the house, started a fire in the fireplace with some scrap wood, and continued to saw. Then I sanded it that Friday, used a can of stain and a can of some sort of clear coating I found in my closet to color it and protect it, and left it in my guest room until yesterday evening. When you two left, I decided to pull it out and start usin' it," Arthur explained.

"Nice, Arthur. I didn't know you were good in woodworkin'," Curt responded, feeling the smooth surface of the table by running the tips of his fingers across it. "And that explains the wood curls and sawdust I saw on your floor last week."

"It's very nice. You could sell something like this," Nancy told Arthur.

"I suppose so," Arthur rejoined, shrugging. "Well, let's eat."

As they sat eating, Nancy stared down at the floor. "Say, Arthur, you should think about getting some carpet," she suggested.

"No," Arthur refused, briefly. The rest of the meal was filled with a lonely silence.

That night, after Curt and Nancy left, Arthur sat by his fire, poking the dying embers with a stick. He got up to add more wood to fuel it, then eased back into his rocking chair as a flame rose up to lick the logs. Quietly Arthur stared at the flickering lights of the fire and then he turned to watch the shadows they cast upon the wall. It was nights like this, when the wind was howling outside, and a cold darkness blanketed the surroundings of the cabin that Arthur felt the most lonely. He had dreamed of sitting by the fire with Marlene, and having her just lay in his arms as they talked the whole night. Before he met Marlene, he never felt the lonely ach he felt now. He was satisfied with the company of one of his few books, such as the Bible. Many a winter night Arthur had turned page after page of the Bible that his parents had given him for his first communion.

Arthur reached towards the bookcase near him that he had built during the lonely night hours of Christmas Eve just that year, when he was without family or friend. He had built it while thinking of Marlene, and now it held the few books he owned. As Arthur slide the white-covered Bible off the shelf, he noticed another book was falling out. He caught the other book and took a moment to read the title on the cover. It was *Majesty's Rancho*, by Zane Grey. Arthur smiled as he blew the dust off the jacket. This was his favorite book, starting when he first read it the whole night after his father gave it to him for his sixteenth birthday. Seeing the cowboy rescuing the girl from a frenzied horse on the cover, Arthur frowned and slid the hard back book back onto the shelf. Seeing that picture reminded him of Marlene.

The Bible in his lap, Arthur flipped over to a random page, and started to read. The passage that greeted his eyes was one about how one should trust in the Lord. As Arthur read on, memories floated back to him, of when he was a junior in high school.

His parents had wanted him to go to confirmation class and to get confirmed, but Arthur refused. The year before Arthur had stopped going to "church school" as he called it. He no longer saw the point of going to classes to tell him about his Catholic faith. For no reason at all that Arthur knew, he just did not feel as strong in his faith that year as before. He even stopped going to church each weekend with his parents his junior year, staying home instead to ride the range on his horse. At school his best friend had teased him about being a Catholic, and Arthur rared back. Sometimes Arthur was mad at his supposed friend for the teasing that seemed to continue, but he just stopped talking back, and did not even fight, even though he grew angry at times and wanted to beat him to a pulp. No longer feeling able to speak out about his religion, Arthur all but gave it up.

He had prayed every once in a while, when something really bad was happening, but otherwise that, Arthur left God out of his life. Then, when Father Matthew invited Arthur to mass, and Arthur got in the accident, forcing him to stay in Cheyenne while his car got repaired, Arthur took it all as a sign. Going to mass for the first time in years had seemed strange, and he had felt nervous and out of place, yet when Marlene showed up, Arthur felt relief wash over him. He attended mass a few times in Cody after that, and started going to mass in Laramie with Marlene when they started dating.

When Marlene's family was tumbled in the crisis that fall, Arthur had been angry and bitter with God, for he found he cared a great deal about Marlene's siblings and parents. Then Father Matthew had given Arthur the sermon of a lifetime, and something quiet and new began in Arthur's heart.

Arthur found himself suddenly full of hope for Nate, Ryan, and George's recovery. He brought Marlene to the church to pray every day, and kept assuring her that things would turn out fine. When Marlene asked him how he knew, Arthur had no answer. He just felt it in him. And he felt a new hope for a more meaningful future with Marlene by his side. Arthur's faith began to grow, and soon it was noticeable to him that he was changing. Sure, he had been a polite, kind guy before, but now he was growing stronger in a way he had never imagined. For so many years Arthur had been meek and feeling too weak to put up a fight, except for when he was riding on the range. Then, when he had saved Marlene, he began to feel stronger, yet there was still something missing, something lacking in that strength.

Finally it hit Arthur. He put down the book. When he was with Marlene, he had started to trust and love God as never before. He had felt a new found strength springing up in him. George Picket had tested that faith, with arrogant, judging words. Arthur may have fought back a little too angrily, but he had been able to fight back. So why did he run away after that, like the meek high school kid he used to be? Why could he not stay any longer, to rebel against this unyielding father of the girl he loved? Maybe it was because George had shaken his confidence, but maybe it was something else. Could it be that that meekness that had caused him to leave was a gentleness, a true Christian gentleness, that would not allow him to go so far as to tear Marlene's family apart, just so that he could have her as his wife? Could it be that that gentleness, that he felt was not manly enough, and had tried to cover with his new, defending strength, had been a good, necessary quality in him? After all, he could not live his life without feeling. He had to be strong enough to stick up for his faith and all that he held dear, yet he had to feel that faith, and be able to love, and to feel pain.

Since the last time Arthur saw Marlene he had been trying to distract himself from that pain. He even prayed to God one night to ask that He take away the pain altogether. But suddenly Father's Matthew's words made more sense than ever. Without this pain, without the hardships and gritting challenges thrown before him, Arthur would not truly feel, not truly be able to understand why feelings more deep than the emotional kind, were important.

Chapter Twenty-One

Marlene flipped to the next page, her eyes scanning the text, but her mind drifting off. She glanced up at the clock in the library; it was three o' clock. Staring back at the page, and letting her chin touch her hand as she rested her head on her arm, she sighed. It was hard to concentrate with the deafening noise of construction vehicles digging up the ground. She looked at the page with her notes on it. A few minutes before she had written February 2nd on it. It was amazing that she was already two weeks into her last semester. Pretty soon she would have to tell her father the truth. She had lied to him her freshman year, telling him that she was majoring in business. Her father was so eager for her to get a degree in something "worthwhile." In reality Marlene would never major in business. She was so sick of her father talking about the raise he had gotten, the new clients his business had, and the great big retirement checks he would be getting in a couple years. Especially in the last four months Marlene had grown so exhausted at any talk of money that she would groan. It was because she knew money and success in her father's definition of the word were involved in the reasons why her father had rejected Arthur, and perhaps forced him to leave Laramie.

Marlene had planned to tell her parents the truth at the beginning of this spring semester, but had changed her mind when George had yelled at Arthur that fall. She knew her mother would actually be happier to know her real major, since she was a lot like Marlene. Since the breakup, Pam had called her daughter more often, and come up to visit on days when Marlene was feeling very low. Marlene knew her mother loved her very much, and was more concerned about her happiness than her income. However, she felt she could not tell her mother, as her mom tended to tell her father everything. Only Marlene's siblings knew her real major, out of all the members of her family, and she had also confided in Arthur. In a couple months, Marlene would invite her family to come to her graduation, and then her parents and aunts, uncles, and cousins would all finally know the truth: Marlene was going to be a journalist.

The thought of having to shake her father's hand upon receiving her degree both frightened and disgusted Marlene. She did not want his congratulations, yet she did. She feared he would yell at her, and disown her or something, when he found out she had majored in journalism. Yet she did not want to shake the hand of the man who had torn her away from Arthur.

Marlene only visited her parents for a few days at Christmastime that winter, and then spent the rest of the month-long vacation at her apartment. At home she hardly spoke with her father, except to ask him to pass the mashed potatoes and turkey at the dinner table, and to tell him Merry Christmas. She still had not forgiven him for making Arthur leave, and she doubted she ever would. Marlene acted cold around her father those few days, and ignored him most of the time.

At first George had acted just as cold back, but then he had started to melt. Marlene had not seen the change come over him, nor did she know how badly he was hurting, until her mother told her a week ago when she drove up to Laramie for a visit. Yet Marlene still could not bring herself to let go of her anger.

Her phone suddenly rang. Marlene drew it out of her pocket and spoke softly into it, not wanting to disturb the other students. "Hello?"

"Marlene, you've got to talk to your father. Now he's angry with you for not speaking to him," her mother spoke frantically.

"No, Mom. I've got to study," Marlene spoke briefly, and then hung up.

Looking back down at her book, she forced herself to read. One last semester, then she would be free from this agonizing studying. Yet this annoying, time-consuming studying had given her something to focus on other than thinking of Arthur. Though it still could be a pain—all the studying. She had a fifteen page paper due based on what she was reading right now, plus seven other sources.

Marlene would be glad when she was free of research papers and essays. She looked forward to getting off this campus, yet it held so many memories for her. She had met her good friends, Alice and Lilly here this last year, and she and Arthur had walked around the campus in the fall, looking at the changing leaves. They were a beautiful red and gold, and when they fell, they crunched beneath their feet. Marlene remembered how she and Arthur had raced down the hill, rolling like logs, back in August. Marlene had won, and she teased Arthur about it, but he preferred to say that he let her win.

She laughed sarcastically as she thought about Arthur's last words to her. He disliked the same materialistic ways of her family that she did. And yet those words had stung. Though she missed Arthur, she was also angry with him, and found herself blaming him at times for breaking up her relationship with her father. Still, the times with Arthur had been the best in her life so far. She would cherish those happy, and sometimes sad, memories with him forever.

"Hey, Marlene!" a voice called. Marlene snapped out of her reminiscing to shoot her head up. Lilly was walking toward her with Nate.

"Hi Lilly, Hi Nate!" Marlene called back as they walked over. "What are you doing here, Nate?"

"I was looking for you, and couldn't find you at your apartment. I bumped into Lilly and she told me you were here."

"And so I am. But why are you here?"

"You just can't stop questioning a guy, can you?" Nate joked.

"No, I reckon I can't," Marlene replied, imitating Arthur's drawl. She covered her mouth and looked shocked.

Lilly giggled, but Nate just stared at her, looking very serious. "You haven't gotten over him, have you Sis?" he asked quietly, sitting down at a chair across from her.

Marlene shook her head and turned her gaze back to her book. Lilly saw the rose in her cheeks and whispered to Nate, "Maybe you should leave her alone. Don't ask her now."

At hearing these words, Marlene looked back up. "Ask me what?"

"Nothing, Marlene. You're not in the mood for anything fun, anyhow," Nate replied.

"And what makes you think that? Just because I have a fifteen page research paper due this Friday, and an essay due Wednesday, you think that I have time for fun?" Marlene snapped, far from amused by her brother's taunting.

"Marlene, you know you can type like a jackrabbit. And it's only Saturday," her brother argued, flipping her book closed. Marlene stomped one foot and glared at him. She opened the book back up and started searching for a page.

Lilly bent down towards her and closed the book on her hands, then pulled the book out of the way. "Marlene, there's more to life than just studying, you know."

"I know that," Marlene quipped.

"You've been more focused on books than life lately, Marlene," her friend added. Marlene stared down at the table. She had no reply, for she knew Lilly was right. Marlene had tried to start off the New Year with a positive attitude, and with gumption that she could change things, but once school started again, she had started to wane.

"Well, enough lecturing. You're coming with Lilly and I to the dance in Fort Collins," Nate replied.

"I have a better idea," Lilly interposed. "Why don't you go with my friend, Paula."

Nate eyed her. "Say, what's this all about? You told me downstairs that you would go."

"That was before I thought of Paula Wills. Do you remember her?" Lilly asked.

Nate looked surprised. "Have you seen her lately? She told me she was moving to Indianapolis," he returned.

Marlene glanced back and forth between the two of them. "Who is Paula?" she finally asked Nate.

"The nurse who took care of me when I was recovering at the hospital. But I hadn't seen her since I checked out," Nate explained, looking wearily at his sister.

"She's in town for the weekend," Lilly told him.

"My gosh, does everyone know everyone around here?" Marlene joked.

"Do you have her phone number?" Nate queried. Lilly nodded and handed him her phone.

While he stepped away to call Paula, Lilly asked Marlene, "So, you going to the dance tonight?"

"With who?" Marlene asked.

"Your brother," Lilly replied shortly and confidently.

"But he already has a date—Paula," Marlene remarked.

"No, it turns out I haven't," Nate returned, closing his phone. "She's taking her grandmother out to dinner tonight, here in Laramie."

"Well, how about Lilly?" Marlene replied. "I can't believe I just said that," she added.

Lilly looked like she was about to say something, but then her phone rang. Picking it up, she answered it. "Hello?" she spoke into it. There was a pause. "Oh, I see. Yes, I'll be there. Okay, goodbye."

"Who was that?" Marlene asked.

Lilly looked disappointed as she answered. "That was someone from my church. There's an event going on tonight that I forgot about." She turned to Nate. "I'm sorry, Nate. Looks like I can't go either."

"That's alright. I'll just skip the dance," Nate spoke in a low voice.

Marlene eyed him suspiciously. "Why can't you just go alone?"

"Because I'd rather go with someone. And I'd planned it that way. I figured I'd find at least one person to go with me. And I was even going to buy her dinner."

Marlene grinned mischievously. "If you're buying dinner, I'll come along," she told her brother.

"Okay. It's a date," Nate declared. "I'll pick you up at four, then we'll head on up."

"What are you doing until then?"

"I've got some papers to grade, and this coming week's lessons to plan," Nate told her.

"Are you going all the way back up to Fort Collins?" Marlene questioned.

"No. I'll just swing over to Ryan's house and grade them there. I've got everything in my car." Nate turned to Marlene's friend. "Say, Lilly, what church do you go to anyway?"

"The Baptist church on the Fifteenth Street hill," Lilly answered.

"Between Harney Street and the high school?"

"Yeah."

"Cool. Have a good time," Nate responded.

"Thanks, I will. You too," Lilly returned. Marlene looked down just in time to miss Lilly winking at Nate.

Then both Nate and Lilly left, and Marlene was there alone. Marlene thought about how long Nate had been in Fort Collins. She figured it had been since he started teaching at one of the high schools down there in the fall, and coaching the sprinters on the track team. Nate loved his job, and he would often tell Marlene how much he enjoyed teaching history.

As Nate left the building, he opened his phone a dialed a now familiar number. "Hello?" He waited a moment, then spoke again. "Yeah, it's me. Yep, phase two completed." He paused. "Yeah, I'll call Ryan. I'd say better do it as soon as possible, so we know this thing's gonna work."

At that, Nate closed up his phone and grinned to himself. He hopped into his car and drove off. Marlene watched him drive off through the window. She could not hear what he was saying from two stories above, but she wondered what the phone call had been about.

Chapter Twenty-Two

"Wow! My house does look amazing!" Arthur exclaimed, staring from nearly a hundred yards away at the beautiful cabin that stood stolidly with the distant mountains in the background. The sun setting behind everything, adding its glowing gold touch to the roof, and a rosy hue to the mountain peaks, made the whole scene picturesque. If he had a camera, he would have taken a picture just then.

"Wait'll you see it from the inside," Curt replied after staring a moment himself. "But wait, I forgot, that's not done yet."

"It's done," Arthur returned. "I'm done working on it."

"You may be, but we're not," Nancy told him, winking at Curt.

"Well, we better get to church, Nancy," Curt told her, tapping the watch on his wrist.

"But what about the dance you were going to tell him about?" Nancy replied.

Arthur looked from Curt to Nancy. "Church? Dance?" he said, confused. He looked back at Curt. "Since when did you go to church, Curt?"

"A lot you know, old fellow. Since Nancy and I got married at her church."

"The Episcopalian one?"

"Yep."

"I thought you just believed in God, and that was about all."

"Aren't you happy?" Nancy asked Arthur.

"Shore, shore I'm happy."

"This is the thing, Arthur. I started going with Nancy just to support her. But then I started really gettin' interested in the masses, and askin' Nancy questions."

"Holy cow!" Arthur exclaimed. "And all it took was a girl to get you— why all those times when I was invitin' you to church this fall you turned me down."

"Well, during the past month especially, I've gotten to know Christ and God better, and—and—well now I want to be baptized into the Episcopalian church," Curt stuttered, watching Arthur's reactions. Arthur stared at Curt as if he had just pulled off a mask. Curt had never spoken so openly about his beliefs before.

"That's great!" Arthur exclaimed, heartily shaking Curt's hand.

"And now, the dance," Curt prompted.

"Arthur, there's going to be a dance in Cody on Tuesday night, and we thought you'd like to go with us," Nancy told Arthur.

Arthur eyed her suspiciously. "Say, I can't even dance. Are you two trying to set me up?"

Curt laughed. "No. I don't think it'd do any good. But we do think it'd be good fer ya to get out."

"Okay, you win," Arthur replied, shrugging. Curt looked astonished, but Nancy shot her husband a knowing look.

**The beautiful cabin stood stolidly with the distant mountains in the
background.**

When Nate arrived at Marlene's door, she answered it, wearing blue
jeans and a sweat shirt. Nate stepped in, upon Marlene's beckoning.

"I don't know what to wear," she confessed to her brother.

"Well, it's not a formal dance or anything, so just that would work.
Only I hope you have a short sleeve shirt under that sweat shirt. It tends to
get hot in there."

"I'll get one," Marlene replied, running to her room.

Nate waited by the door. He glanced about the room. It was a small
apartment, yet nice and clean. He noticed a paper on the table. Stepping
over, he read the words on it. It was a calendar from church, and had
different events on the dates. Every Praise and Worship event was circled
with a red pen on the blue paper. A few random drops of water caused
some of the printed black ink to smear and stain the page. Nate figured they
were tear drops. He could only guess that Marlene had just been staring at
the page, from November, and had started to cry.

Marlene had told Nate a couple days after he woke up from his coma
about how she planned to do stuff with the church more, and act more like a
Christian. On an impulse, Marlene had gone to a Praise and Worship, as it
was called, at St. Matthew's in town. She had made several friends, a
couple of them Lutheran, from going, and excitedly called her brother at ten
that night. Nate listened on the phone as Marlene told him about the

singing, and the friends she had made, and how she felt things were going to get better. It was the first time in three weeks that Marlene had acted that positive. That had been midway through October.

When November came, Marlene eagerly picked up a calendar of more church events, including Praise and Worship and Revive. Praise and Worship took place every other week, and switched between St. Matthews' and St. Paul's. It was an event where Christians of different denominations would get together to sing popular Christian songs, like the kind Nate had heard on the radio. Revive was less focused on singing, and more on fun and games. It was a sort of game and activity night for Christians at St. Paul's Newman Center. Marlene grew more and more upbeat the more times she went to Revive and Praise and Worship, and she started volunteering to help the church and then Habitat for Humanity.

Nate felt that his sister was getting over Arthur, and he was glad. His father had grumpily told him that Arthur had dumped Marlene. But then the tide of happiness receded, starting when Marlene came over to their parents' house for Christmas for a few days. It was as if seeing her father had opened a healing wound. Christmas night Nate woke up to the sounds of shouting. He peered out from the hallway, into the kitchen, to see and hear his father yelling at Marlene furiously, and Marlene yelling back. The day before Marlene had not spoken to her father at all, except to ask him to pass a roll at the dinner table. She had unwillingly received a present from their father on Christmas morning.

All day there had been an uneasy tension in the house, as if a storm was about to break out. And sure enough, just when the house was still that cold Christmas night, the thunder roared. Now Nate did not know whether Dad had confronted Marlene, or the other way around, but he did know that their dad looked fierce enough to break Marlene's arm. After a few more words, Marlene looked defeated. Yet she tried once more, and this time Nate was able to hear her. "Dad, this is why I didn't want to come. You had to ruin my positive attitude towards life, because you were jealous, and now you've ruined Christmas for me too. You're not a father, you're a monster!"

George boiled completely over at that moment and swept his only arm out to slap his daughter's face. Marlene screamed, and Nate ran into the kitchen, afraid of what George might do next. "Stop Dad!" he shouted, strategically placing himself between George and Marlene.

"You needn't defend her. I don't want to see you anymore, Marlene!" George snapped.

Nate glanced back at his tearful sister. She had one hand over her cheek, and the other rested by her side, clenched in a tight fist. "You don't have to worry!" she sobbed. "I'll never come back! And I'll never speak to you again."

Marlene stayed for one more day, and then left. Nate saw his father watching her drive away that day, and divined that he was hurting from the loss of his daughter's friendship. Marlene used to look up to her father, and shared her story ideas with him. Now George was realizing how much he had lost, especially Christmas night. Outside he was hostile, as if the guilt that must have been tearing him up inside was not there, but Nate had a feeling he was deeply aching. Nate avoided his father most of the time after that, and George avoided him. Their conversations on the phone were always brief, and the phone calls happened less and less often.

Nate noticed as Marlene spent more and more time studying when the new semester started, and less time doing anything else. She barely made it to church each weekend, and the fact that she made it at all happened with Nate's prompting. Each time she sat in the pew, however, Nate could tell she was glad to be there. She knelt down, sometimes even after the mass was over, just pouring her heart out in prayer. After a while dark circles grew under Marlene's eyes, obviously from lack of sleep. Whenever Nate saw her, and his observations were supported by Lilly's, Marlene looked as if she carried the weight of the world's sorrows upon her small shoulders. She walked about with her back somewhat stooped under her heavy backpack, and her face grew pale. As Nate saw this sad transformation, he started to wonder what had taken place between Arthur and George. Now he knew.

"How does this shirt look?" Marlene asked, snapping Nate back into the present. He turned his gaze from the paper to Marlene, who stood just behind him.

Nate stared at his little sister, stunned. She sure was not a little girl anymore. "Looks good!" he exclaimed. "Let's go!"

As Nate drove to Fort Collins he glanced at Marlene. She was smiling, and looked more excited than she had been in a long time. Her stooped shoulders were erect again, and color had come back in her face. Glancing at her again, he commented, "Say, you're going to make the other girls jealous. Every guy is going to want to dance with you."

Marlene gazed at him, startled. "But I'm not even wearing a dress, or anything fancy," she replied.

Nate grinned as Marlene stared at him, confused. "The way you were beaming, just then, any guy might fall for you."

Marlene blushed. "Nate, don't get too jealous," she joked.

Nate frowned as he stared up ahead. "I can't promise that. As a matter a fact, I'm afraid I'll have to fight them all off. After all, you're **my** date."

Marlene laughed, and Nate's frown disappeared. He laughed too. "You're the funniest one of the family, Nate," Marlene told him, punching him lightly on the shoulder as she used to do when they played the slug bug game as kids. Nate had always packed a harder punch, and Marlene always complained, until that game of slugging each other at seeing a Volkswagen Beetle was banished by their mother.

At the dance, Marlene walked in and shyly stood by the door. "Come on!" Nate shouted to her as the music of a live band started to play. He reached out and grabbed her hand to pull her onto the dance floor.

"But I can't dance!" Marlene cried, frantically.

"Then you're with the right guy," Nate laughed. "I'll teach you."

"How did you learn?" Marlene questioned. "You never went to any dances in high school."

"Sure I did, but not as a high schooler. I've been going to these weekly dances ever since I started teaching in Fort Collins," Nate explained.

"Now, step like this. Side-step, side-step, step back. Good, now you're getting the feel of it. Come on, let's try to get up with the music."

It turned out Marlene had a wonderful feel for the rhythm of swing music. As the clarinetists jazzed up the music, Marlene's feet tapped the floor lightly. After Nate taught her to dance, and some of the dancers saw her dance right to the beat, college guy after college guy kept walking up to her and asking her to dance. Pretty soon Marlene stopped looking down at her feet to make sure they moved right, and started improvising with the dancers. She hopped, she spun, and she slapped her feet against the floor in the fast pace beat of the swing songs. One young man even taught her the Charleston, and she soon got the feel of kicking her feet. The emptiness in Marlene that had been tearing a hole in her heart started to drift away, and she felt something new beginning in her. It was a sort of contentment in life just for being at the stage she was. She did not have to have everything going her way, or have all her dreams come true at the moment. She was still finding out who she was, and finally enjoying that adventure. Marlene was suddenly happy just to be there, out on the dance floor, enjoying this stage of her life.

Chapter Twenty-Three

George picket was opening the screen door to go out for a walk when he bumped into a young man. George staggered backward, and the young man fell to the ground. "Who are you?" George gruffly questioned the young man.

The stranger stood up and dusted off his pants, as if it was a habit. "The name's Jim." Jim squinted as he stared behind George. "Say, is Ryan here? I was supposed to meet him."

George glared at him suspiciously. "If you mean my son, Ryan, I don't know why'd he'd be here. He lives in—"

George was interrupted by the sight of Ryan hobbling up the sidewalk towards them, after stepping out of a dark blue sedan. "Hey, Dad! Hey, Jim!"

"You really do know my son," George spoke softly, relieved. He brushed past Jim, apparently wanting to start his walk.

Ryan stopped in the middle of the sidewalk to block his path. "Say, where you going, Dad?" he asked him.

"Out for a walk. What does it look like to you, son?" George snapped, growing aggravated at the friendliness he had encountered. Ever since that fall George had been hostile to everyone, and he enjoyed being left alone because of it. George tried to go around his son.

"Dad, we need to talk," Ryan commanded, reaching out his left arm to block his father.

George grunted and pushed past his son. "George Picket, we need to talk," Ryan called after his father.

George stopped in his tracks and swung around. "No son of mine calls me by my first name," he growled.

"Mr. Picket, you might as well know my last name while you're so heated up already," Jim called to him.

The older man eyed Jim. "Go on," he prompted.

"I'm Jim Pressed. Arthur Pressed, the great guy you rejected because of your sour standards, is my older brother," Jim told him, staring him straight in the eyes from across the yard. George's face grew red, and he looked like he was ready to tackle Jim.

Ryan stepped towards his father and grabbed him by his a plastic and metal prosthetic arm with his left hand. Jim approached and grabbed George's other arm. Despite George's protests, they dragged him back into his own home. It was a nice, quiet Monday afternoon.

A lot of yelling drifted out of that house at first. The yelling could be heard from a few houses down. Slowly, however, the yelling quieted down, until suddenly no yelling rose up at all, but instead the soft murmur of talk. The talk sounded gentle, like the quiet gurgling of a brook. By evening, anyone listening at the front door would have heard sobbing.

It was such sobbing that Pam heard when she returned to her home at seven that night. She had been out later than usual, though in the past couple of months she had purposely stayed out for most of each day. For the first few months that George was home she had endured his crabby, snappy attitude, that, had she not been in love with him, would have driven

Pam away long ago. But her solution was to avoid her dear husband as much as possible, to avoid going crazy or become panic-stricken or depressed like her husband. She was a forgiving woman, who put up with almost anything without a fight, but her fear of fighting had started to tear her up inside. Pam did not realize that there were some times when it was right to fight, and to speak the truth.

When Pam heard sobbing inside, at first she thought that George had hurt someone. He had been cold, and acted ruthless, though he had not physically damaged anyone yet. Still, a fear had hung in the back of Pam's mind that he might hurt someone someday soon, with the way he was heading. Then, as she was opening the screen door, she recognized the crying as George's as he tried to speak through tears.

As Pam stepped in, she heard a voice behind her. "Good evening, Mrs. Picket," the voice called. She swiveled around to see Father Matthew, who carried a look of surprise, yet gladness on the tides of emotion washing over his face.

"What's going on in there?" Pam asked him, searching his eyes with her own. She judged that Father Matthew had some connection with this unusual event. And so he did.

"Sounds like crying," Matthew told her.

"Yes, but it's George's. I can hardly believe it. He hasn't cried for half a year it seems," Pam replied.

"Guess that's why Ryan called me," Father Matthew returned, shrugging. He tried to hide his feelings, but Pam could see that relief and happiness shone on his face.

"Ryan's here? But why?" queried Pam, still not understanding.

Someone opened the wooden front door and beckoned for Pam and Father Matthew to come in. "Who are you?" Pam asked, following the young man in.

"The name's Jim Pressed, Ma'am," Jim drawled, extending his hand.

Pam took it and shook. "I'm Pam Picket."

"I figured," Jim returned.

"But how? And why are you—" Pam began. But then a shocking thought froze her tongue for a moment. "Are you Arthur's brother?" Arthur had told her of his brother and sister one day, and the name finally registered.

"Yes Ma'am," Jim replied, nodding, as he let go of Pam's hand. "Father Matthew, he's in the livin' room."

Father Matthew walked past them to the room spoken of. Pam heard him greet her husband. "Hello, George."

"Hello, Father Matthew." George's voice sounded shaky.

"Ryan called me. He said it was urgent," Father Matthew responded.

"It is—for my soul at least. Considering I don't know what may happen tomorrow, I've got to confess and repent today." Pam poked her head around the corner to glance at her husband before Jim pulled her away.

"Do you want to go to the church?" Matthew offered.

"Can we do it here?"

"Yes."

Ryan left the room, following Pam and Jim out to the front lawn. "We should give him some privacy," Ryan explained. Pam stared at her son. She knew instinctively that he had something to do with George's confession. And it had come just in time. Pam felt her knees wobble, and Ryan helped her sit down in a lawn chair beneath the only willow tree in the yard. Ryan had grown to be a wise young man after the accident. She could tell he looked at life from a different perspective through those soft, green eyes. Doctor Palt had told her, when Ryan woke up from his coma, that Ryan might be able to talk again, if someone patient enough would teach him. That someone ended up being his true love, Judy.

"You're going to make a wonderful father," Pam spoke to her son out of the clear blue.

Ryan smiled. Jim glanced at him, surprised. "Judy's going to have a baby? You didn't tell me that. Congratulations!"

"Jim, may I ask what this is all about?" Pam asked Jim, now looking very serious.

Jim hesitated, as if he had been caught in the midst of a heist. After a moment, he found his voice. "Mrs. Picket—"

"Please, just call me Pam."

"Okay, Pam. Can I count on you, for help I mean?"

"Help for what?" Pam asked, feeling rather impatient suddenly.

"For operation forgiveness."

"Huh? Wait, this is about George?"

"Partially, yes. And you, and your whole family, and—ahem, uh—" Jim hesitated, not quite sure what Pam thought of his brother.

"Who?" Pam asked.

"And Arthur Pressed," Ryan spoke for Jim.

"Hallelujah!" Pam cried out, standing up.

Ryan and Jim exchanged knowing glances. They were going to pull this off.

It was strange for Arthur to enter into that large room, and to see those people dancing wildly to the music. He had not been to a dance since high school. Yet he was intrigued at the thought that he might actually learn how to swing dance. Curt and Nancy practically leapt upon the creaking wooden dance floor, while Arthur observed the dancers. Then he saw one girl sitting alone in one of the chairs lining the wall. Though Arthur had only danced a little in his past, he decided to take a chance on going out to dance right away. Approaching the young woman, who was intently watching the dancers, Arthur asked, "May I have this dance?"

The girl looked at him, startled. Then an expression of recognition flooded her face. "Arthur Pressed?" she spoke softly.

Arthur stared down at her for a moment, before recognizing the stewardess. "Jane Fult!"

"I hoped to see you again, which is why I came to Wyoming for a visit, but I didn't think to find you so soon," Jane told him. It was at this speech that Arthur realized what an impression he had made on her.

"How's the airplane business?" Arthur asked casually, trying to hide the tremor in his voice as he stared at her beautiful face. Could it be this was the girl who was right for him?

"Good. How's ranching?" Jane responded.

"Good," Arthur replied. He shook his head lightly at himself, glancing down. He was in love with Marlene, and not even another girl's crush on him would ever change that.

"Did you say you wanted to dance?" she asked Arthur, watching him curiously.

Arthur looked back up at her and nodded. "Yeah, though I'm not very good."

She shrugged and giggled at this admittance. "Neither am I. Guess we'll both have to learn." And so they did.

Arthur and Jane watched the steps of the other dancers and tried to imitate. When they had tried for a while, Nancy and Curt spotted them. "Why don't we switch partners?" Curt suggested. "Nancy and I can teach the two of you how to really swing dance."

Curt then proceeded to dance with Jane, while Nancy taught Arthur. "Arthur, step like this," she told him. As they began to dance, Nancy asked Arthur, "Do you know that girl?"

"Yeah," Arthur replied, nodding. He glanced across the floor at Jane. "And I think she likes me. She came to Wyoming just to find me."

Nancy eyed him cautiously as she questioned, "What about Marlene?"

Arthur stared at Nancy. "I still love her. And that's the part that kills me. I'm afraid I can never go on," he admitted.

Nancy smiled at him. "Who says you have to?"

Before Arthur could reply, the song changed to a faster one. He found himself watching his feet on the floor. "You have terrible rhythm," Nancy laughed, trying to change the subject.

"I'll get it," Arthur replied stubbornly. He refused to admit he had no rhythm.

It took the whole dance for Arthur to finally get a sense of rhythm, and to learn how to dance. During the last dance, he strutted his stuff. His slick black shoes tapped the floor, and he swung his partner, a girl from Cody, around the floor with ease. He spun her quickly, and caught her hands to continue dancing smoothly. Curt and Nancy watched him from the corner of the room. "Think it'll work?" Curt asked. Nancy nodded, squeezing his hand as she smiled.

Chapter Twenty-Four

Thursday night found Marlene singing at her church, along with her friends. She felt renewed ever since she went to that dance with her brother the weekend before. It was amazing how one event could remind you that there was more than just school in life. She sang loudly and tried to harmonize with the other singers. Then they were all singing low and soft. The songs they were singing just now sounded as smooth as honey to Marlene. A smile came upon her lips, and she thought about the dance. How much fun it had been to whirl around the dance floor and forget her troubles.

Then one of the directors of Praise and Worship told everyone to spread out in the worship space and silently think and pray. Marlene hesitantly moved from the comfort of her friends to a pew in the back. It was lonely and dark there, for only one light was on in the entire room, and that light was pouring its light over the altar. She sat below a stained glass window, on a padded bench, and then she knelt down. Her legs quivered as her knees pressed against the kneeler. She bowed her head down, resting her hands over the pew ahead of her. Clenching her hands together tight in a weaving pattern, she let her thoughts run. Like a river they flowed. Her anger with her father, her fear of having to see him again, her longing to have her family whole and close again, her grudge against Arthur for leaving her and breaking her family apart, and yet her longing to see him again all flooded back upon her. Tears flowed in evidence of her troubled mind. All these things were wrong in her life, and she did not know how to fix them. Then the worry of what she would do after graduation staggered her, as if she did not already have too much on her mind. Where would she go and what would she do when she graduated? She had not an inkling of where she wanted to work as a journalist, or where she wanted to live. And yet she had a feeling that she wanted to run away—to be as far away from Wyoming and her troubles as possible. "Oh, God!" she sobbed out loud. "What shall I do?"

Suddenly she felt like two hands were resting on her shoulders. A calmness swept over her. She glanced back behind her, but no one was there. When she shot her glance around, she saw most of the college students bowed down in prayer, while a few looked startled at her outburst. Who had touched her, comforted her? A chill ran down her spine. The moment seemed so mysterious to her.

It was Saturday morning when Jim came to visit Arthur again. "Hi, Jim!" Arthur greeted his brother at the door.

"Say, did I wake you up?" Jim asked, glancing at Arthur's outfit resembling pajamas.

"I reckon you did," Arthur replied with a yawn. "Glad to see you, though I have no idea why you're here."

"Just to visit. I barely recognized your house from the outside," Jim admitted, shrugging.

Arthur grinned. "Wait'll you see the inside. Some comment you made to Curt got him and Nancy involved with the upkeep of my house. Now it

looks more like a house, I reckon, and less like an old abandoned cabin."
He turned to the side to open up the entranceway and swept his arm to
beckon his brother in. "Come on in."

Jim whistled in surprise as he looked about the room. "Say, you
actually have regular walls and everything!" he cried. "Why Arthur, you
better watch out, I'm likely to buy this place right out from under you!"

"It'd be a little hard, considering I own it all now," Arthur told him,
seriously.

"You paid off the mortgage?"

"Yep. Reckon so. An' now I have it all to myself. Those bankers
were a little upset at thet, especially when one came to visit on Tuesday to
finally end the mortgage."

"Wow. And all those cattle, too. You're liable to be a rich young man,
Arthur. Be careful. I know plenty of young ladies who would love to
marry a rich bachelor," Jim joked.

Arthur laughed. "Yeah, probably. Hey, thet reminds me. When are
you getting married?'

"After you, brother. You know I haven't even met the right girl yet.
Plus I told you I was waiting until you hitched."

"No, I reckon it was the other way around. You said you'd beat me!"
Arthur told him, still grinning. He punched his brother in the shoulder.

"Well, I changed my—"

"Is this the Pressed Ranch?" a woman's voice called.

Jim and Arthur turned their heads to stare at the open doorway, where
Jane Fult stood. "Jane!" Arthur exclaimed.

Jim looked startled. "Who's this?" he asked.

"Jim, I want ya ta meet my friend, Jane Fult. She's an airline
stewardess. Jane, this is my brother, Jim," Arthur introduced.

Jane fluttered her eyelashes and blushed as Jim stepped toward her. He
tipped an imaginary hat toward her. She giggled at his imitation. Arthur
glanced back and forth from Jane to Jim a few times before he cleared his
throat. The two hesitantly took their gazes off each other to look at Arthur.

"It's a nice day. Why don't I git my ridin' clothes on and we'll go fer a
ride?" he asked.

"Sounds nice. I haven't ridden a horse in a long time," Jane replied,
smiling.

After Arthur dressed, the three walked over to his barn. "The barn too?
Holy cow, Arthur!" Jim exclaimed at seeing the newly painted red barn
from a few feet away.

"Yep. I reckon once I let thet Curt git started on my place, I jest
couldn't stop him. He had ta modernize the whole dang thang," Arthur
replied with a grin.

Jane, who stood next to Jim, commented, "I like it. Your whole place
seems very nice, Arthur."

Arthur shrugged and led them inside. "Jim, you want ta ride Rusty?"
Arthur asked. "He's probably the wildest horse I got. And Jane, how about
you ride Peal? She's a purdy gentle harse. Got her this fall." Jane
consented, and Jim offered to help her saddle up. Arthur watched the two at

work for a moment, then turned to Gerome. He purposely did not offer
Jane Belle, though she was his favorite mare, because he could only picture
Marlene riding her.

Once the horses were saddled up and led outside the barn, Arthur
swung himself upon his mustang. Jim watched as Jane tried to hop up upon
the horse and failed. "Here, let me help," he offered. He held her hand and
helped her mount.

"Thank you, Jim," she spoke calmly. Her blue eyes glowed as her
cheeks flushed.

"No problem, Jane," Jim replied, smirking. "Hey, Arthur, you got
riding gloves? I sure would hate to see Jane's purdy hands get all blistered
up."

"Oh, I forgot about that. Yeah, they're in the barn," Arthur returned.
Jim ran back into the barn and out again with a nice pair of leather gloves.
Seeing those gloves that Arthur had forgotten to offer to Marlene reminded
him of her. He grimaced. Must everything remind him of Marlene?

The ride was wonderful, and the cool winter breeze was contrasted by
the warm sunshine. It seemed Jim could not keep his eyes off of Jane. The
two rode side by side as Arthur rode up ahead. At times Jane would speed
up her horse to gallop beside Arthur's. During such times she would try to
ask Arthur what he had been up to, and she kept trying to flirt with him.
After a while, however, she grew out of breath and let her horse slow to
pace with Jim's once again. Jim engaged her in conversation, starting with
a compliment on her hair.

"You've got purdy red hair. Looks soft as silk," Jim told her.

Jane wondered why she had not spent the last half hour flirting with
Jim. After all, he at least seemed interested in her. She blushed at Jim's
compliment, though it could hardly be told with the cover of an already red
face due to exertion. "Thank you," she panted.

"So, where are you from? And how did you learn to ride a horse like
that?" Jim questioned her.

Arthur heard bits and pieces of their long, drawn out conversation, from
what was tossed to him by the wind. Mostly, though, he did not pay much
attention to the two, and stared at the wonderful view of mountain range
ahead. The sun sat high in the sky, and its light glinted off the snow on the
mountain peaks. The range was a mixture between dark and light blues,
and the closer hills looked rugged with their covering of dark green pines.
The clean smell of sage and pine scented the air. It made Arthur think of
the sweet smell of Marlene's perfume that contrasted so strongly with it.
"God," he whispered as he rode, "please help me. I know I spent many
years turned away from you, but I really need you now. I need your help.
If I don't ever see Marlene again, I'm afeard I'll go crazy. She brought me
back to Ya God, along with thet priest who got me ta go ta church agin.
She helped me ta see the beauty of this range was Yer doin'. I remember
when we were reminiscing about the ride together, when we were eatin'
dinner together last fall. She said, 'It sure is marvelous that God created
such beauty. Take that mountain range you can see from your cabin,
Arthur. The hands of God created it so perfectly. I can only imagine how it
must look with the sun setting behind it.' And then I got ta thinkin', God,

about all the blessings you've put in my life. Please help me, God, though I don't deserve Your help. Amen." Arthur chanced letting go of the reigns long enough to cross himself and whisper, "Father, Son, Holy Spirit, Amen."

On the ride back to Arthur's ranch, Arthur challenged his brother to a race. Jim acted hesitant about racing him, so Arthur added, "Well, if yer afraid you'll lose, then—"

"No way!" Jim shouted earnestly. "Where'll we race to?"

"The barn," Arthur replied.

"Looks like I'll see you two later," Jane commented.

"Can you make it back okay?" Jim asked her.

"Sure."

As Jim turned back to face ahead, Arthur whipped his reigns, yelling, "Ya, Ya!"

Jim tore out after him, and the race began. Jim caught up quickly to his brother, and the two raced their horses, nose to nose. Arthur laughed at the sight of his competitive brother, who suddenly resembled a chariot racer in *Ben Hur*.

The hooves pounded against the ground, thrashing the sage that sat before them at intervals, tearing up loose earth. Dust filled Arthur's nostrils and he coughed. He pulled his bandanna over his nose. Jim saw him do this and cried, "No fair. I don't have one anymore!" He could not see the grin that rose on Arthur's face at his complaint.

Finally, worn and out of breath the two reached the barn. Arthur beat his brother barely. As Arthur caught his breath, Jim panted, "Alright, you won." He glanced back to see Jane a fair distance back, riding steadily toward them.

"Good race," Arthur told his brother, smiling as he pulled the cloth from his mouth. Then his smile faded as he saw the serious look on Jim's face.

"Arthur, can I talk to you for a minute?" Jim asked his brother, nervously.

"Shore."

"Do you like Jane Fult? I mean, are you in love with her?" Jim boldly continued.

Arthur looked shocked. Then he laughed. "Is that what you thought, when she showed up?" Jim nodded. "I barely know her. I'll admit she keeps trying to flirt with me, I think, but I never gave her a second thought. You know there's only one girl for me."

Jim gazed at his brother and his tense face morphed to one of relief. No fault in the plans after all. "Then it's alright if I ask her on a date when she gets here?" he queried.

"Shore. I'm not her boyfriend," Arthur returned. He frowned. "You like her?"

"Yeah."

"Then ya should take her to dinner, and then ta a movie or somethin'," he advised his younger brother.

Jim laughed lightly. "You never will stop playing the older brother, will you?" he joked, nudging his elbow at Arthur's side.

Arthur smirked. "Guess not. Nor the matchmaker."

Chapter Twenty-Five

Arthur walked into the ballroom as the band was tuning up. He could not help but tap his feet to the instrumentalists' short spurts of tunes in excitement, once he sat down. He grinned at the thought that this would only be his second swing dance in a long time, yet he would show those college students a thing or two about dancing. Ever since that dance last week he had been humming the tunes to himself and practicing steps between breaking the ice in the water troughs and shoveling manure out of the barn. He had to admit it was not pleasant when he was practicing the Charleston and slipped on a moist road apple and fell to the floor, on top of his gathered pile, but he still kept on practicing.

Just this afternoon Arthur had driven down to Laramie, after Jim told him on Saturday about the dance. It was Thursday, and a snowy Valentine's Day. Arthur closed his eyes a minute as the clarinetist tuned his horn. He pictured the flurries of snow that had swept across his path, and the thick, grey fog that had concealed the road from him. Once, after ice had formed on his windshield, he had to pull to the side of the road to scrape it off. Another time he had to swerve to avoid a semi coming down his lane as the driver tried to pass a slow-moving camper. The wind continuously tried to pull Arthur's truck this way and that, so that he felt as if he was on a boat, rocking side to side.

Finally Arthur saw the exit sign for Laramie, and gladly took it. He heard from someone in the parking lot that the roads had been closed soon after. Now he was here, on the campus that Marlene had walked to every day from her apartment. The ballroom was rather spacious, and the howling wind could not be heard from in here. It was a lot warmer in here as well, in contrast to the freezing, finger numbing cold outside. Arthur snapped back to the present sounds as a young man, dressed in a forties-style suit, called out that there would be lessons now.

Standing up, Arthur glanced around. Everyone who was in the ballroom and not carrying an instrument was walking towards the dance floor. He decided to join them. "Alright. I want all the guys on this side of the room, and all the girls on this side," the same young man declared. Then a girl in a skirt and blouse approached the suited man and they danced a moment to demonstrate. "This is the Jitterbug. So girls, follow her, and guys, follow me." Arthur smiled. This would just be a refresher course for him.

Arthur was a little off the beat at first, and it took some effort and concentration to get it right. Then the guys had to pick a girl to dance with and everyone began to practice the steps. "Hi, I'm Arthur," Arthur introduced, tipping his hat to a girl.

The girl, wearing a blue sweater and a brown skirt, replied, "I'm Amanda. Nice to meet you."

The dancers practiced for the next half hour, and then it was time for the dance to start. The trombone player started the band off, and soon a fun, fast pace melody was playing. Arthur asked Amanda to dance again and fumbled with his feet to keep up. He kept stepping on her feet, and, by the end of the song, he had stepped on her left foot twice, and her right foot three times. It was no wonder that she quickly found another partner for the next dance, lest Arthur ask her again. Arthur told himself that he really was a good dancer, and that the song was just too fast for him.

A slower song started to play and Arthur found a short redheaded girl in a blue-jeans skirt and white shirt to dance with. Her name was Diana, she told him, and he better not try to spin her. The first time Arthur stepped on her foot she was done dancing with him. She let go of his sweaty hands and they parted, with one last complaint from her about his hands. Arthur swiftly walked back to the side of the room, his face red with embarrassment. It was there, as he was about to sit down, that he bumped into Walter Jertenson. "Hey, Arthur! So, you decided ta come ta the dance, too, eh?" he asked Arthur. Arthur nodded.

Jenny appeared from behind Arthur. "Arthur, would you finish this dance with me?" the older woman asked him. It was apparent that she had seen him on the floor a moment ago.

"Sure," Arthur replied.

Walter looked real serious a moment and said to Arthur, "Be sure to bring my wife right back afterwards. I sure don't want her runnin' off with no cowboy!" As Arthur laughed at this, Walter's face broke out into a smile, and he laughed too.

Jenny was patient and calm with Arthur, reminding him of his mother, who had tried to teach him to dance one rainy afternoon over ten years ago. Arthur had been pouting and upset because he wanted to ride his horse. It had been a sunny Saturday morning when he first woke up, but by the time he had finished his breakfast, dark clouds rolled in and heavy thunder was rumbling the house. Rain began to pour and so did Arthur's complaints. He would have ridden in the rain had not his mother stopped him. Instead, she suggested she teach him how to dance. Arthur's father had an old jukebox that he had bought from a pawn shop as a teenager and fixed up. He had a large collection of forties and fifties records, and so Arthur's mother put one on and gently took Arthur's hands. She instructed him where to step and when. No matter how hard she tried to help him, Arthur would always step at the wrong time during that song. So they continued all afternoon, while Jim and Jill played cowboys and Indians on the worn carpet floor.

Eventually, after dancing from mid morning to the evening, Arthur got the hang of it. He found he had a love for music. After that Arthur's mom would catch him listening to the radio, late at night before the school day.

It was in high school that Arthur stopped listening to music, even in his car. He did not know why, but for some reason he did not like it as much. Maybe it was because, when he tried out for choir in ninth grade, the teacher said he could not sing, and his friends told him music was not cool.

Now, dancing with Jenny Jertenson, Arthur got feel of the music. His feet stopped colliding with her shins, and he started making time with the music. Then, all too soon, the slow song was over. After a minute of silence, the band started to play a fast swing song, so Arthur strutted off the dance floor. As he headed for the exit, to get a drink of water from the fountain in the hallway, he suddenly saw the most beautiful girl he had ever seen. She was just coming in, and had not seen him. He stopped and stared. There was a touch of makeup on her face, soft brown hair bounced on her shoulders in twisted curls, she wore a red, short sleeved, velvet shirt, a heart dotted skirt that fell just below her knees, and a pair of polished white shoes that came to points over her toes. His gaze went back up to her face. Her cheeks were rosy and her soft eyes shone beautifully in the dimly lit room.

Marlene was walking into the ballroom, staring at the band, and then at the dancers, when her gaze met the eyes of the most handsome man she had ever seen. His fine, chiseled chin, sharp nose, combed hair, slick with gel, and blue vest over a light blue and white striped shirt looked magnificent. His hands were stuck in his pockets, with his thumbs sticking out. Suddenly she looked back up at his face, where she saw his eyes glimmering with tears. As a feeling of shock shook her body, she saw a similar look on Arthur's face.

Arthur stood motionless, staring at Marlene, as the song ended. Another song, more Arthur's pace, began. Not knowing what else to say, Arthur asked Marlene, "May I have this dance?" He reached out his hand for hers. Marlene felt awkward, but she took his hand and let him lead her in, to the dance floor.

Arthur took Marlene's other hand, shakily. It was as if he was in a dream. So many times he had imagined seeing Marlene again, talking to her again, seeing her beautiful visage and hearing her sweet voice. Never had he pictured it would happen like this.

As Arthur gripped Marlene's cold hands, he took the first step. She followed and soon they were dancing. Then Arthur spun Marlene around once, then twice, and then a third time. Was it just the spinning that made Marlene dizzy and gave her such a confused, wonderful feeling, or was it something more? Arthur's warm, blistered hands gripped hers tightly, as if he feared losing her. She could hardly concentrate on her dancing, as Arthur's warm, minty breath glided against her cheek.

The song drawing to a close, Arthur decided to chance a dip. He wrapped an arm around Marlene's waist, and though she looked surprised, she let herself fall with his arm. The intent, longing look of his eyes poured over her, and made her spine tingle. She wondered if he would dare to kiss her. She half felt that she would welcome it. The music ended, Arthur bent over Marlene. He was going to risk it. As his lips brushed hers she felt herself reach out her hand and slap him. Arthur's eyes widened and he let go of her. Marlene fell backwards and down, and her back and butt hit the floor. Marlene scorned herself in whisper. Why had she slapped him? She quickly stood back up and chased after Arthur, who was making his way towards the door.

"Wait, Arthur!" she called as she ran. She could feel the eyes of the dancers upon her, but she did not care. One shoe slipped off and Marlene nearly tripped, but she kept on running. Then the other shoe fell off.

As Marlene chased Arthur outside, and the band began to play *Rock Around the Clock*, two pairs of eyes watched from a window. Nate and Paula exchanged discouraged looks as Marlene was slowing down and Arthur was still heading full speed for his truck. Then Marlene seemed to have a second wind and began sprinting, her bare feet crunching through the thin layer of snow in the parking lot. She ran around the fence surrounding the construction vehicles that sat in the middle of the large parking lot. The light from the spread out parking lot lights glinted off the snow and lighted Marlene's way. Paula's face took on a look of hope, while Nate still looked skeptical. Arthur turned the key into the lock on his car door. He grunted as he pried the frozen door open. He certainly was not going to stay to talk to Marlene, or to dance any longer. "I'm sick and tired of being slapped around," Arthur whispered to himself. "That girl just better leave me alone."

Marlene was only a few strides from Arthur when she slipped on the snow. She slid a foot, then fell to the ground. "Arthur!" she cried as she held her skinned elbow. Arthur was just about to step into his truck. He glanced back with a grimace on his face, and looked as if he was going to get in. Then he glanced at Marlene's dark figure on the ground again and slammed his door shut. He swaggered over to her and bent his knees to crouch next to her.

Marlene could hardly believe her eyes. Arthur had come back to her after all. Quickly she tried to think of something apologetic to say. "I'm sorry, Arthur. I didn't mean to slap you," she found herself sobbing. Arthur gently took her by the elbows and lifted her up as he stood. He then let go of her and stared soberly at her, a confused look in his eyes.

"Then why did you?" he questioned, harshly. Arthur longed to say that it was okay, and that he wanted to date her again, but he could not find the courage.

Arthur's words made Marlene's blood boil. Instead of saying something kind that would win him back as she truly wanted to, she found herself saying, "Because, you're not my boyfriend anymore. And you tore my family apart."

"What?" Arthur questioned.

"I haven't even talked to my father since Christmas, when we fought because of you," Marlene snapped.

"I broke up with you so that I wouldn't split your egotistical family apart. Your father is a maniac, anyway. Don't blame all this on me!" Arthur growled, wanting to reach out and shake some sense into Marlene.

"You've ruined my life, and you're just an ignorant cowboy with no manners and no feelings, just like my father said!" Marlene shouted, tears in her eyes.

Arthur's eyes were burning, and he felt heated with rage. "Look who's talking!" he cried, angrily, then turned and walked swiftly away.

As Marlene watched him drive off, she sank to her knees crying, "Oh God, what did I say!" The cold racked her body with shivers, but she felt numb inside. She had just muffed up the only chance she had at getting Arthur back. As the snow moistened her warm legs, warm tears moistened her eyes. She sat in that position for she knew not how long.

Despite the fact that Arthur should have stayed in Laramie, he took the highway out and headed northwest, for his ranch. The snow was falling hard now, and it grew thick on Arthur's windshield. After a couple hours, his wipers could barely move the piling snow. He turned on the heat and the snow started to melt, but the chilly winds turned the melting snow to ice, and the ice would not move. As he drove nervously through the blizzard, Arthur muttered angry things to himself. He was mad at Marlene and frustrated now with his whole life.

Then Arthur had to pass a slow moving snow plow on the highway. He shifted into the other lane to pass it, despite the fact that he could not see five feet beyond his front bumper. The ice started to melt, and Arthur could see a little farther now. Suddenly Arthur heard a loud honking, and a pair of bright lights blinded his eyes. He gripped the wheel tightly and drew in a sharp breath.

Marlene's eyes were getting heavy when she heard Nate's voice. "Marlene! Stop sitting there or you'll get pneumonia!"

She blinked until the snow on her eyelashes cleared away. Her brother was reaching his hands out, and she took them. She stood up and gazed at her brother. "Where's Arthur?" she asked.

Nate stared seriously at her. "Is that why you took off running out of the ballroom? You were chasing Arthur?" he asked.

"Yes," Marlene replied, quietly.

"Well, he's not around here, so he must have left. Sorry, Sis."

"It's okay. Nate?"

"Yeah?"

"Can I get a ride home?" Marlene requested.

"Sure. I don't feel like dancing anymore, either," Nate replied.

Chapter Twenty-Six

"Nate, you've got to get to Ivinson Hospital for me. I can't make it, since the roads are all closed. Arthur's in serious condition there," Jim panted into the phone.

"What? What happened?"

"He was driving back up to his ranch, I guess, and he hit a semi, head on."

"Oh my God! I'll head right over, as soon as I tell Marlene."

Nate found Marlene resting in her bed, coughing. "Nate, I think I have pneumonia," she admitted to him as he walked in.

The sun shone into her room, pouring rays of warmth onto her. She had skipped all her classes that morning to stay in bed. "Marlene, I've got some bad news," Nate told her.

Marlene nearly jumped. She stared at Nate, waiting quietly for him to continue. "Arthur hit into a semi on his way home last night and is in serious condition," Nate told her.

Marlene looked surprised, and then she burst into tears. Hearing that news was as if someone had torn her arm off. "Oh, God!" she cried out. "Where is he?"

"At Ivinson. I'm heading over now to visit him."

"I'll come," Marlene offered. She coughed, and grabbed a kleenex to spit mucus into it.

"No, you can't come. You're sick. You'll bring tons of germs into the hospital. I'll get a card for you to sign," Nate told her.

"Okay," Marlene replied, giving in.

Nate hurried past the automatic doors to the front desk. "I'm looking for Arthur Pressed," he told the nurse.

Paula ran down the hallway toward him. "Nate! Are you looking for Arthur?" she asked.

"Yeah," Nate replied.

"You can't see him right now. He needs a blood transfusion. He lost a lot of blood from the accident," she told him, reaching him now.

"I'll donate," Nate replied.

It turned out Nate had the same blood type. Doctor Wilabee showed up to take Nate's blood. "I'm glad you're helping out, Nate. With your help, we might be able to save Arthur's life," he thanked Nate as he pulled out a sterilized needle.

"I'm just glad I could help," Nate returned. "Ahh!" he groaned as Wilabee jabbed the needle into his skin. Nate started to feel light headed as he watched his dark red blood run through the tubes into a bag.

"Well, I gotta say, it's pretty neat, you helping him after he helped you," Doctor Wilabee commented.

"Yeah," Nate mumbled. Then, thinking of the doctor's words, he added, "What?"

Doctor Wilabee realized then that he had let some confidential information slip. "Oh, nothing," he muttered, trying to cover up.

"What did you mean, Doc? How did Arthur help me?"

"I can't say. He made me promise—"

"Tell me, Doc."

"Oh, alright. I guess I let it slip, anyway. Arthur was your kidney donor."

Nate's eyes grew wide and he held his breath a moment as he stared at the white coated doctor. "He did?"

"Uh, huh," Doctor Wilabee replied.

Then the world turned black before Nate's eyes, and he fainted.

Nate returned to Marlene's apartment after donating blood. He burst through the open door, excited. "Marlene, guess what?"

Marlene gazed at him anxiously. "What?"

"Arthur was the one who gave me my kidney. Doctor Wilabee just told me."

As the meaning of Nate's words sank in, all the anger that had built up inside of Marlene, like a solid wall around her heart, melted away. She suddenly forgave Arthur in her heart, and wanted to run to him. Jumping up, Marlene intended to do just that.

"Sit down, Marlene. Even if you were well you couldn't visit him. The doctors are working on him right now. Let's do our part and just pray that he gets well," Nate told her. His eyes were sparkling as he gazed at his little sister. He had a feeling she had finally forgiven Arthur for leaving her.

That night Marlene knelt in her bed and prayed. Tears glistened on her eyes and then dripped into her open mouth. "Please forgive me, God, for being so angry with Arthur. And God, please help him to forgive me and my family. And most of all, even if I never get to speak to him again, God, please heal him, and let him live. He's such an amazing guy, God, and I found that out too late. Please let him live."

She laid awake crying and coughing for half the night before she fell asleep. Her pillow was soaked with tears when she awoke the next day. She rubbed her sore eyes and stared out the window. The world outside was white. Sunshine glinted off the deep snow in the yard below, and off of rooftops around and above her. All was quiet except for the twittering of a few birds and the occasional car passing down the street. Even the street was hidden beneath a carpet of white, and an observer would have a hard time distinguishing it as a street, rather than a cleared ski and snowshoe path, except for the tread marks dented deep in four continuous parallel lines. A cross-country skier thrust herself forward with her poles, then glided down the gentle hill that the street ran down. As Marlene continued to stare, drinking in every sound and every sight, she pondered about the day before. It was a mystery to her how she could give up her anger against Arthur so easily, with just knowing that he saved her brother's life. It almost did not seem fair, that it would take her finding out something like that about him to finally cause her to forgive him.

Marlene looked out the window as she tried to understand her own feelings and her own actions. The laughter of two children caught her ears, and she glanced here and there until she finally spied them. A little boy was pulling a little girl in his sled, probably his younger sister, and they were laughing as he pulled as hard as he could to get the sled moving. Then, suddenly, he let go of the strings on the small purple sled, and his sister kept on going. She screamed as the sled continued to slide down their long driveway. When her brother reached her, she was crying. The little girl looked to be about two, and this seemed to be the first time she had ever been sledding. Her brother was about five, and eager to prove to her there was nothing scary about it. He bent down over her as she cried, concerned that she was hurt. Marlene watched as he talked to her, and she looked up at him angrily, her lower lip puckered out. Then he said one more thing, looking hurt, and her frowning lips turned upward into a grin. Her brother smiled back, and pulled her back up the driveway. He let go of her and she started to scream as before. Then, suddenly, her scream turned to squeals. Her brother had succeeded. Marlene smiled as she watched him run down after his sister and proceed to pull her up again. They were both enjoying the Saturday morning.

There was her answer, in the form of two children. The little girl did not take long to forgive her brother for suddenly letting go of her sled, and immediately went back to trusting him again. Turning her face away from the widow, Marlene kept on smiling. It was a wonderful feeling, to not be angry with Arthur anymore. Then she frowned, remembering that he was in the hospital, and that she might not ever get to see him again, nor let him know she forgave him. She sank to the floor, onto her knees, in desperation. Looking up to heaven, though her ceiling blocked the view, she prayed.

The doctors worked furiously to save Arthur's life. He had three broken ribs and internal bleeding. One rib was jutted all the way through his skin, and had torn it, when the ambulance found him after a good Samaritan call had brought them to the wreck sight. The truck driver had been unconscious when they found him, but he had no injury, save a few scratches, cuts, and bruises.

Blood kept trying to escape from a vein that had been cut on Arthur's wrist. After the windshield glass had cut his vein, Arthur had lost a lot of blood. Nate's donation was immediately used in the transfusion after the surgery. The whole time they worked on him, Arthur was in a state of unconsciousness. He had dreams, dark dreams of the past, and nightmares about his accident, and about his future. He dreamed that he would awaken to find both his legs amputated, and everyone in the world, including his own brother and sister and parents, hating him, and turning away from him as he cried out for help, telling him what a louse he was.

The next day, the day after the surgery that spanned between early morning and mid-afternoon of Friday, Arthur drifted in and out of consciousness. He would hear voices of nurses and doctors and open his eyes for a brief second to see them floating into his room, like ghosts, then gliding back out again. Then he would close his eyes, and drift back into a dreamy state. Nightmares once again haunted him, causing him to sweat. But that was not the only thing causing him to sweat. Doctor Palt checked Arthur's temperature late Saturday afternoon after a nurse commented to him that Arthur's composure was red and he felt hot. She would have checked his temperature herself, had not the doctor popped in at the same moment. Sure enough, it turned out Arthur had a fever. His temperature continued to rise through the day, as his limbs ached and his chest throbbed.

His heart beat heavily as his body tried to beat the fever. Arthur rolled from side to side in his small bed, and then he fell off. Doctor Palt found him on the floor and lifted him back into the bed. He watched as Arthur began to roll back and forth, moaning. Just as Keith Palt was about to call in for some medicines for Arthur as he watched over him, Arthur stopped and was quiet. He deep, husky breathing grew shallow, and he was breathing quick short breaths. Instead of calling for medicine, Keith monitored Arthur's heart, and watched on the monitor as the beat weakened.

Meanwhile, Marlene was throwing up mucus that she had swallowed. As she brushed her teeth afterward, an idea hit her. She spit out the minty substance from her mouth and ran several long strides to her phone. When she reached the phone, which sat upon her desk in her room, she was gasping for breath, and she coughed several times. She quickly dialed as she caught her breath. "Hello, Ryan?"

"Marlene? Are you okay? You sound hoarse," Ryan responded.

"Ryan, don't worry about me. I'll be fine. But I need you to pray for Arthur." Marlene's voice was strained.

"Arthur? Why, what's going on, Marlene?" Ryan's voice shook, as if she was talking about his own brother.

"He got in an accident. He was in serious condition yesterday. I don't know how he is now, but could you help me pray for him?" Marlene let out. This was the first time she had asked for such help before, but she was at her wit's end.

"Sure. Gosh, I'm sorry to hear that, Marlene. Yeah, sure I'll pray. Do you need to talk?"

"Not right now. I'll talk to you later, Ryan. Say hi to Judy for me."

"I will as soon as she can talk. She's kind of under a lot of stress right now."

"Huh? What do you mean?" Marlene asked. She heard groaning in the background.

"She's in labor right now. I took her to Ivinson Hospital this morning when she was complaining about her contractions. At least the baby had the courtesy to wait until I was off work," Ryan explained, humorously.

"That's great, Ryan! I'll talk to you again when you're a dad, Ryan," Marlene replied, excited. She was about to become an aunt again. As she hung up the phone, she frowned. Just as one life was coming, another might be going. It was the second time in her life that she had felt that way. She shook her head in disgust. She should not be so negative. Marlene decided she just needed to have more faith, and where she lacked that, she would get her family to help her out by praying.

Next Marlene called Susan, and then Albert. They both agreed to pray, and were even willing to come to Laramie to support her. Marlene thought she had never felt so much family support before. She told them to just stay where they were and pray.

As Marlene was calling her other siblings, Ryan was calling Father Matthew. A blizzard was still tearing across the road, so Father Matthew would not be able to make it up right now, but he told Ryan he would pray for Arthur, and ask his congregation to pray for him tonight. Ryan thanked him and hung up.

At the same moment, Marlene picked up the phone and slowly dialed the familiar number of her youth. This was it. She was going to talk to her dad without any fear of consequences. He and her mom were the only two family members she had not asked to pray, yet.

"Hello?"

"Mom?"

"Marlene! How are you doing? I haven't talked to you in a while," Pam responded.

"Mom, I've got a favor to ask of you, and then I really need to talk to Dad," Marlene told her mother. She could hear her mother catch her breath. This was the first time in half a year that Marlene had asked to speak to her father.

"Are you alright, Marlene? Is something wrong? Your voice sounds funny."

"That's just 'cause I'm a little sick. Otherwise I'm fine, Mom. But Arthur Pressed isn't."

"What?"

"He came to the dance, Mom, on Valentine's day, and we danced. Then I—well, then he left, and was heading back up to his ranch, when a semi hit into him, head on. He's in serious condition at the hospital."

"Oh my God!"

"Will you pray for him, Mom?"

"Of course I will Dear. Oh, that's horrible. I—"

"Could you hand the phone to Dad? I know he's probably waiting near you anyway," Marlene interrupted.

Sure enough, Mr. Picket was standing near his wife, wanting to hear the news of his daughter. "She wants to talk to you, Dear," Pam told her husband. He only gawked at her for a moment. "Really."

As George picked up the phone, his eyes grew misty. "Huh, huh, hello?" he stuttered.

Marlene was almost glad to hear her father's voice. "Dad? I need to ask you a favor."

"What, Marlene? What do you need? Are you—"

"Just listen, Dad. Don't ask me questions. Arthur Pressed is in the hospital. He was in serious condition yesterday, and I just got a call from Nate that he's in deteriorating condition. His heart is failing, Dad."

"Oh—"

"Dad, just let me finish. His only hope is a miracle. And, even though you don't like him, could you at least pray for him, for his life? Even if not for my sake, because I need him, Dad, at least for his. PLEASE DAD!"

George was too taken aback to speak. He had nothing against Arthur anymore, and had recently repented. Hearing his daughter ask for his help, like when she was little, made the tears spill over. She needed him. His little girl was speaking to him. And the man she loved, who he had tried to keep away from her, to his utmost regret, was dying. Finally, he found the words, and hoarsely spoke. "Yes, Marlene, I'll pray. And Marlene—" But Marlene had hung up at his words that he would pray. That was all she wanted to hear. She had barely found the strength to talk to him at all. It would take mountains of courage to continue to speak to him further. And her courage was minute compared to that which she needed.

Breathing heavily, Marlene slowly walked into her small kitchen. She opened up one of the cabinets where a bottle of cough syrup accompanied two bottles of aspirin and a bottle of allergy medicine. She took out the bottle of cough syrup, grabbed a spoon from the drawer which she commenced to fill, and then took a swallow of some bitter, 'cherry flavored' liquid.

George slowly walked over to the living room like a man in a dream. Instead of sitting on the couch, however, he knelt down and prayed. Pam watched him, and decided to do the same. At the same time, Ryan was kneeling in the hospital room, praying, as the cry of a baby girl filled the room. Nate knelt by Arthur's bed, while Keith Palt and Sam Wilabee talked in the corner about what they could do for the young man. Sam kept shaking his head at every suggestion Keith made, whispering things like, "It's too dangerous." Finally, after praying, Nate turned to the doctors and asked, "What's wrong with his heart?"

Sam turned from Keith to lay a strong hand on Nate's shoulder. "His heart is trying to cope with an infection. His heart itself could be infected."

"What are you going to do?" Nate asked.

Sam Wilabee stared at Arthur, who lay limply on the small, skinny hospital bed. The words came slowly from his mouth in reply. "I don't know."

Chapter Twenty-Seven

Arthur saw himself in a dark, desperate world, and he fought to escape from it. A tiny light shone in the distance, and he pulled himself toward it. But his body would not respond. He could barely see the form of chains, holding him to a giant concrete block, weighing him down, dragging him down farther and farther into this dark place. He felt like he was drifting down to the bottom of the sea. Just when he was about to give up the fight, he heard a voice.

"God, please help this young man. If, if you let him live, I promise not to criticize him anymore, and to let him have my daughter in marriage, if he wants to marry her. Please, God. He needs You. We all need You. We need Your help. This man doesn't deserve to die. He's got such a great future ahead of him, and he's got wisdom beyond him age. Please God!" the voice cried in desperation. It was a deep voice, a man's voice, and though it carried agitation, it also bore tenderness.

Those words cut into Arthur's unconsciousness, and he suddenly felt as if God was breaking those chains that weighed him down. Then he was running, towards the light. The next thing Arthur knew was that his eyes were open, and he had turned his head to stare at a man kneeling on the floor, with head bent down. At first Arthur did not recognize the man, but then he noticed the prosthetic in place of a missing arm. He only took his eyes off the man a moment to see a woman walking into the room. She was not a nurse. She was Marlene's mother.

As Arthur once again gazed down at the kneeling man, he drove his renewing strength into speaking. "George."

George lifted his head at hearing a weak voice calling out his name. At first he thought it was God, for his wife had left to get coffee, and Arthur was unconscious. But he stared into Arthur's face, and Arthur stared back with an amazed look. George was shocked. "Arthur!" he cried.

Arthur reached out an arm to George, despite the pain it caused to his chest, as if to quiet the older man. "It's ohh-kaaay," Arthur slowly drawled.

"He's awake!" George cried, incredulously. "Thank God!"

Then Arthur rolled back onto his back and his eyes closed. He did not have energy enough to keep them open. But, as Doctor Keith Palt ran into the room, Arthur's heartbeat picked up, and started beating with more enthusiasm. The young doctor's eyes shone. He did not say it, but he knew a miracle had occurred.

Marlene was laying in her bed, telling the headache that pounded in her head to go away, as she gazed out her window. She so desperately wanted to be well, so that she could go visit Arthur. The thought that she might never see him again, and that he might die at any moment was agonizing to her. Arthur had been there for her in the fall, when she needed someone to cling to, and now she could not be there for him. She felt so lonely and scared now, and wanted some hope, and someone to cling to.

Praying again, as she had been doing ever since she heard of Arthur being in the hospital, she turned her eyes to stare at the wall, where a small wooden cross hung. The figure of a man was carved upon it, with his hands and feet nailed to the cross. This man could have avoided death, had he wanted to. He could have avoided pain, and called down His father to wreak His wrath upon the men who were trying to kill Him. He could have condemned the sinners, made himself famous to the Romans, done anything He wanted. But that was not why He had come to the earth. He had let people crucify Him on the cross, after scourging him with whips, beating Him, and mocking Him. He came to the troubled world to comfort those in need of comforting, to turn sinners towards God, to forgive them, to save those oppressed in spirit from their oppression. He did not come to conquer an earthly empire so that the Jews and others could be free of physical oppression. Instead He did something much greater. He worked miracles, the greatest one being after He took on the pain, the suffering, and the sins of the world and died for them. The greatest miracle, His rising from the dead, had made it possible for men and women to go to heaven, to live on, even after their deaths on earth.

The thought of Arthur going to heaven, to see God, should, perhaps, have been comforting to Marlene. Instead it just made her more sad, to think that she might have to wait until the end of her life to see him again, if he died. What did comfort her was the thought of Jesus working miracles, the thought that God might work a miracle on Arthur. If Jesus, if God, was so willing to do so much for His people back then, almost two thousand years ago, then would He not be willing to help one of His flock now? Comfort from God drew itself around her like a blanket. Her faith was growing.

Suddenly Marlene heard a knock at her door, shattering her deep thoughts. She jumped up and ran, forgetting that she was still in pajamas. When she answered the door, she was befuddled and stunned to see her father standing there, alone. "Your mother's with Ryan and Judy right now, holding little Jean Marlene Picket," George offered, as his daughter continued to gawk at him.

"Come in," Marlene offered after a moment.

As her father sat down at her small table that only fit four chairs, Marlene spoke again. "So Judy and Ryan are parents now? And the baby is a girl?" George nodded. "What did you say her name was?" she asked, eager despite the thoughts of Arthur weighing heavily on her mind.

"Jean Marlene Picket. I thought it sounded kind of silly," George joked, laughing lightly.

Marlene stared at her father, confused. When was the last time he had joked like that? And why did he look so happy? Well, of course it was because of the girl. Then it hit her. Ryan and Judy had given the baby her name for the middle name. She began to realize just how much Ryan thought of her.

While his daughter stood, staring at the window across the room, George continued. "But I didn't just come to tell you that. I thought you might be interested to hear news about a certain cowboy fella."

Marlene swung her gaze back to her father's face. "What?!" she exclaimed. She observed, briefly, that there was a twinkle in his eye.

"Marlene, Arthur's still alive. He woke up today. He's going to be okay."

Marlene barely heard the words before she fainted. Her father caught her and set her in a chair. She awoke when he brushed a cloth of cold water across her forehead, minutes later. Her first question then was, "Can I see him?"

"No, Marlene. You're still sick. And they're not allowing any more visitors for a while while Arthur recovers," George gently told his daughter.

"Dad," Marlene spoke, swallowing hard as she did so.

"Yes?" her father replied.

"I love him. I still love him. And even if you don't approve, I want to be with him, the rest of my life."

She waited, fearfully, for her father to react. Instead of acting in anger as she feared he would, however, he nodded. "I know, Marlene. And I hope you'll forgive me for trying to keep you two apart."

Marlene's jaw dropped, and her heart nearly jumped to her throat. "Really?" she asked in disbelief. She felt almost as if she would faint again.

"Yes, Marlene."

"I forgive you, Dad." She hugged her father, tightly, as tears poured down her cheeks, onto his shoulder. Finally this strong, stubborn, angry man had broken down and let forth with feeling. She did not question how it happened, or why he had changed. She was just thankful that he had changed.

Chapter Twenty-Eight

Jim glanced down nervously at his wristwatch. It was a quarter to four. "Arthur, are ya almost ready? I gotta pick up Jane when we git there, an' it's already almost four!" he called.

Arthur did not respond. A moment later, however, he emerged from his room, wearing a dark blue suit coat over a light blue dress shirt and tan tie. He glanced down at his black dress pants to make sure they were not wrinkled then turned his eyes to his brother. "How do I look?" he asked.

"Great," Jim replied. "Now, let's go." He turned around. "Mom, Dad, Jill, we're ready to head out," Jim called. As Arthur and Jim walked to the kitchen, their parents and sister stood up from the table.

Jill opened the door as Robert Turn drove up. "Hey, Honey. Sorry I'm running late."

"I thought you were meeting us in Laramie," Jill replied, smiling.

"I wanted to see you as soon as possible. You've been here at Arthur's for almost two weeks now, you know," Robert told his wife. He walked up to her and kissed her.

"Oh, brother," Jim teased. "Can you two stop kissing in front of me? It's gross!" He grinned at his sister and brother-in-law.

"Pretty soon I'll get to tease you back, Jim. I hear we're going to mass in Laramie all because you're sweet on some girl there."

Jim's face flushed and he pushed past Robert, through the open door. "Let's go," he mumbled.

"Daddy!" two children shouted in unison as they ran toward their father.

"Hey, you little tikes!" Robert shouted back, embracing his kids.

"You look very handsome, Arthur," Arthur's mother, Helen, told him.

"You look good in that suit, son," his father, William Pressed, added, patting his son on the back. Arthur shrugged.

As William drove his wife and sons southward, to Laramie, Jim studied his brother's face. Arthur thought about Marlene, and wondered if she would be at the Easter mass. He and his family were all going to Easter vigil mass, and Jim told Arthur he planned to propose to Jane Fult.

In Cody, a week ago, Arthur had gone with Jim to help him pick the ring out. "This one?" Jim asked. Arthur just shrugged. "Okay, what ring would you give a girl you were proposing to?" Jim queried.

Arthur glanced about the jewelry store, at all the glass counters, his eyes aglow. He had thought of doing this many times after he and Marlene were getting serious. Finally his eyes rested on a golden band, with a red ruby in the crest. He pointed and said quietly, like a child, "That one."

So Jim asked the jeweler to remove the ring from the glass casing. He reached toward his pocket, to pull out his checkbook, then stopped. "Arthur, I forgot my wallet at home. Could you lend me the money?"

Arthur was about to reply, "That's a lot of money to lend," then stopped. Jim had been there for him many times in the past, so he was sure he could trust his own brother. Arthur paid for the ring.

On the way back to the ranch, Jim explained that he actually was running really low on money right now, so he was wondering if he could pay Arthur back in two months, when he would get his next full pay check. Hesitantly Arthur agreed that it was okay, especially since he had already purchased the ring.

Jim, William, and Helen had come down to Laramie the day the doctors finally allowed visitors. It was not much longer before they took Arthur back up to his ranch. When they arrived, so did Jill. She brought her son and daughter along, since it was their spring break. Robert drove them there, and then he had to return for work. For the next week Arthur's family stayed at his ranch with him, cooking for him, doing his laundry, and even keeping an eye on the livestock. He was fully recovered now, though his parents insisted on doing the driving to Laramie.

"Arthur, are you alright?" Jim asked.

Arthur returned to the present from his thoughts of the past. He looked at his brother. "Yeah, I'm fine. Why?"

"Just curious."

Marlene sat down in a pew, and her parents followed. A moment later, she saw Ryan and Judy, with little Jean cradled in her arms, walking down the aisle from the back towards them. Next Nate and Paula arrived. They were now officially engaged. Nate had proposed to Paula two days ago, and they had announced it last night, at the fish dinner Marlene's parents hosted for their family. George reached for his daughter's hand and squeezed it. Marlene glanced at her father. He smiled at her and whispered, "Happy Easter, Marlene."

Then the priest began to speak. The mumbling of the congregation hushed. Marlene glanced about the church walls, taking in the beauty of the stain glass windows with the sun pouring its last rays of light through them as it set. She focused on the priest again. He was explaining about the light of Christ. Then he used the Easter candle to light a smaller candle. Soon the candle each person held was lit. After all the candles were lit, someone stepped up to the podium. Marlene looked at the cross at the front a moment, then stared at the reader.

The reader was now reading about the making of the world. Suddenly Marlene heard the doors at the back of Saint Laurence O' Toole church open. With a muffled thump and two clicks they closed. Though this distracted her for a moment from the reading, Marlene did not turn around.

She heard footsteps up the aisle, and then whispering of unfamiliar voices, asking to sit in the crowded pew behind her. Then she focused again. The reading was finished, and the choir in the loft at the back of the church led everyone in a song. The reader stepped up again to give the second reading.

It was not until everyone stood for the reading of the Gospel quite a while later that Marlene heard the whispering. "Marlene. Marlene!" a voice called softly from behind her. Her eyes opened wide. Who could that be, calling her?

As the priest opened the book, Marlene turned around. She could hardly believe what she saw. "Arthur!" she gasped, for there was Arthur, standing right behind her, looking more handsome than ever in a suit coat and tie. Her heart beat wildly in her chest as she continued to stare at him.

Arthur smiled. "Happy Easter!" he whispered. Before Marlene could reply, Arthur pointed towards the priest. "I'll talk to you after mass," he spoke softly, "but first, let's listen to what he has to say."

Marlene took Arthur's advice, and paid attention to what the priest had to say. It was hard, but it paid off. That mass was the most incredible Easter Vigil Mass Marlene had ever attended. She felt her heart beating with joy, and understood more of the meaning of Christ's death and resurrection than ever before, as His story was told.

Then they prayed the "Our Father" and Arthur squeezed Marlene's hand tightly when she offered her hand to him with the words, "Peace be with you, Arthur."

Arthur was surprised at first when Jim had led him up to the pew behind Marlene, and he recognized Marlene immediately, even in the dim candlelight. He called to Marlene until she finally turned around, and then joyfulness filled him at seeing her face. He had not seen her since that dance, and his heart had ached at the thought of not being with her.

As mass was ending, and the congregation was singing, Jim slipped something into Arthur's hand. Arthur glanced down. In his palm lay the ring that he had picked out for Jim to use. He looked back up at Jim, confused. Jim grinned and whispered, "You're going to need it first. Besides, it's been yours from the start."

Arthur gawked at his brother a moment before he could speak. "Thanks Jim," he finally replied.

After everyone else had filed out, Marlene and Arthur remained. She was kneeling, praying, and Arthur was waiting for her. When she dipped her head back up, Arthur was staring down at her from the pew ahead. Tears of joy coated her face, but there was also a look of fear. "Arthur," she began to speak, her voice shaking, "will you forgive me for all I've done to you, for all I've put you through?"

Arthur gently reached out to help her stand, then beckoned her out of the pew space, into the aisle. He smiled tenderly at her as he held her hands. "Yes, Marlene, I forgive you. Will you forgive me?" Marlene could not speak, for fear that her voice would only come out in sobs after hearing him, so she nodded.

Then Arthur swiftly dropped down on one knee. He gazed up into Marlene's tear stained face as she wiped away the tears with her sleeve and sniffled. "Marlene, will you marry me?" he asked her, suddenly showing her a ring, gripped in his thumb and index finger.

Marlene's eyes shone at his words. How long had she dreamed of this moment, and how long had she wondered if it would ever come? As she rejoiced in her mind and heart, she found her voice to say, "Yes!"

Arthur stood up and kissed her, passionately. "I love you so much," he told her, slipping the ring on her finger.

"I love you, Arthur," Marlene whispered.

Then they walked out, arm and arm, to meet back up with their waiting families. Jim grinned at his brother, knowing that Marlene had said yes. It was an Easter Marlene and Arthur would never forget.

They all headed over to Ryan's house to have a late dessert. Marlene did not feel like eating the coconut cake, and instead she and Arthur talked.

Pam watched the two, and prayed a silent prayer of thanksgiving to God. Not only had her husband and sons healed from the accident, but her daughter was going to get married now. It was a wondrous thing to her, that such good things could be happening.

Pam knew Nate and Paula would have a great future together, just as Arthur and Marlene would. And Ryan was a father, Judy a mother. She had her doubts about Ryan recovering, at first. But Judy was the most patient person Pam had ever seen, and the most faithful. Judy helped Ryan, encouraged him, so that he finally could walk and talk normal again. Doctor Wilabee told her it was a miracle, and that he had never seen anyone recover completely from the partial paralysis, usually caused by a stroke, before. But Ryan showed no symptoms of his injuries anymore, and there was no longer a limp to his walk as at first. Another doctor claimed that, because he was so young, Ryan's body was able to heal better than those, usually older, who had strokes. Yet Sam Wilabee, a man who was known to have little faith before, insisted it was a miracle. And so did Ryan's family. Pam also was thankful that George had let go of his anger, and become a better man. He was more loving and caring now, and strove to stop worrying about money and business so much. Then she thought about the miracle of Arthur Pressed's recovery.

"Did you want some of your own cake, Pam?" Helen Pressed asked. Pam jumped out of her reminiscing.

"Sure," Pam replied.

Helen cut her a slice and handed it to her on a plate, with a fork. "It's so good to have finally met you, Mrs. Picket," Helen added.

"It's good to meet you, too. I think we'll be seeing a lot of each other in the years to come."

"I hope so. Your daughter is a wonderful person."

"So is your son. Oh, have you met my husband, George?"

"No, I don't think so. You met William, didn't you?"

Pam nodded. "George, come over here and meet Arthur's family," she called to her husband.

George, who had been quiet and acted shy all evening, came forth from the shadows of the corner to meet Arthur's parents, sister and brother in-law. He had already met the cunning and clever, yet kind, Jim.

Jim and Jane talked with Nate and Paula as they ate cake at the table. Arthur and Marlene were finally interrupted by Judy, so that Arthur could meet his soon to be niece, little Jean Marlene Picket. He glanced at Ryan, who stood talking to William, at hearing the baby's name. He knew Ryan had to do with the picking of Jean's middle name, and thought well of him for it.

Eventually, around two in the morning, everyone but Arthur and Marlene was tired out. Jill and Robert had already left for a hotel, since their kids had fallen asleep. The rest of Arthur's family retired to a hotel, and Marlene's siblings and parents went to bed. Paula and Jane headed out for Jane's house. Jane had moved to Laramie a month ago, when she got a job at the local airport as a stewardess. She had a feeling she would not be working there much longer, however.

Arthur and Marlene stayed up in Ryan's living room, talking. They talked all night about their plans and dreams for the future. They decided they would get married that summer, and then move to Arthur's ranch. Marlene told Arthur her dreams of writing, and he agreed that she should write both as a journalist for a newspaper, and on her own, since that was what she wanted.

Chapter Twenty-Nine

At the beginning of the summer, in May, Marlene walked up to the front of the stage to receive her degree. She had finally told her father that day, after dressing in her graduation gown, what her real major was. He was taken aback for only a moment before he hugged her and told her he was glad she was striving for her dreams. Her mother was not quite as surprised, but happy as well, for she knew how much Marlene loved to write.

The announcer called, "Marlene Rose Picket." Marlene could barely keep herself from running up to the dean of the college. He handed her the degree and whispered, "Congratulations," as she shook his hand. She paused for a moment shaking the man's hand as a flash of light blinded her for a second. Her father took a picture of her. Then she slowly walked back to her chair, stunned. After the rest of the names of those graduating were read, including Marlene's close friend, Lilly, it came time for the dean to announce that they had all officially graduated. Marlene felt a thrill as she turned the tassel to the other side of her mortar board and threw the hat into the air.

Arthur was the first to congratulate Marlene after she had tossed her hat up in the air. He ran to her and lifted her up, holding her by the waist. Marlene screamed in surprise at his actions, but was quick to embrace him when he lowered her back down. Jim, the sneaky fellow, snapped a shot with his digital camera of Marlene and Arthur kissing afterwards.

Both Marlene's whole family and Arthur's had come to watch her graduate. They had a big party for her afterwards. At one point during the party, George took his daughter aside. "Would you mind going on a short walk with me?" he asked her.

Marlene shrugged. "Sure."

They walked away from the green lawn of the park where the families were. At first George was silent, and Marlene wondered if he lacked the guts to say what he wanted to. But then he spoke. "Marlene, I'm proud of you."

"Thanks, Dad. That means a lot, coming from you," Marlene replied.

"Do you know why I'm proud of you?" Marlene shook her head, sure he wanted to tell her. "Because, despite my stubbornness, and insisting that you follow a dream that wasn't yours, but mine, you followed your dream anyway. Four months ago I would have been proud, had you gotten a business major. But now that I have been coming to realize what is really important, I'm glad you were as stubborn as I am, and stuck to doing what you want to do. I know how much you love to write, now, so I'm sure you'll make a fine journalist," George finished.

Marlene could not find the words to speak, and tears were filling her eyes. So instead of trying to say words that just would not come, she leaned forward and hugged her father. He patted her on the back. "I hope you always keep your faith in God," George whispered in her ear before he let her go. Marlene nodded, still feeling mute.

Then they returned to the party, where Arthur was showing Nate and young Josh, Jill's son, his rope for roping cows. As soon as he laid eyes on

Marlene, and saw the tears in her eyes, he excused himself from his friend and nephew, and he made his way toward her. When he approached, he asked her, "Is everything alright?"

Marlene nodded. "My father just keeps on surprising me. He was congratulating me," she explained.

Now it was Pam's turn to take her daughter aside. "Marlene," she told her, "I'm so proud of you. Over this last year you have become quite a woman. And, more importantly, you reached for stars. You're finding your dreams. I know God is working in you, as I have seen your faith in Him growing."

"Mom, can I ask you something?"

"Sure, dear. What is it?"

"How did you make it through? With the accident, and Dad's hunger for money and material things, and all that?"

"I had faith in God, Dear. Though I must admit, at times I was heartbroken and my faith was weak. Your father really is a very caring man. He was when I married him. That's why I fell in love with him. Money was never as important to him as seeing you kids and me happy. During the past couple of years, when things started going wrong in his business, then you were kidnapped, he just slowly let go of his faith, especially after the accident, and turned to material things to fill him up. Then suddenly, when I was at the point where I just could not stand it anymore, God answered my prayers. Now, as you know, your father is transformed. He's finally returning to the man he used to be. And yet he's not. This time his faith is stronger, I think, just as mine is." Pam paused as she looked tenderly at her daughter.

"So, I hope that, no matter what trials you may face, you will always look to God to help you through them. Never stop relying on God. He is your refuge. And when things go right, don't forget to thank Him and bless His name. I know you are strong in your faith, and I hope your faith only grows as you continue in life. This graduation may mean the end of some things. Like feeling the freedom of a kid. You're going to have to start working a real job now, and you won't have three month-long summer vacations. But that doesn't mean you have to completely let go. This is just the beginning of a new stage in life. You'll bring along all that you've learned, felt, and been through in the past with you to this future. I hope you never forget what it feels like to be a child, for, if you have children, you'll want to play with them, and understand them. And you'll want to pass on your faith in God."

Marlene was choking on tears by this time. Her mother had never said so many things to her at once before. She always knew the woman was amazing. But to hear her heart speaking, giving her advice and praying for her, was incredible. "Thanks, Mom," Marlene sputtered through tears of joy, and yet sadness, knowing her mother was right about her taking on an adult role now.

The party continued, and Marlene enjoyed playing with her niece, Jean, and with Arthur's niece and nephew, Sarah and Josh. Nate, Ryan, Susan, and Albert gave her a special toast for her graduation, telling her how proud they were to have their little sister graduate. At the end of the toast, Nate added, "And when you publish your first book as an author, Sis, I want an autographed copy!" Everyone laughed at this, and Nate's eyes sparkled.

"The same goes for me," Albert told Marlene a minute later. "I want an autographed copy, too."

All day the celebration continued, and soon the graduation cake and punch were gone, along with the giant sub sandwiches that George had ordered for lunch, and only snacks and cans of pop remained to be eaten and drank. The kids were still hyper when the sun was setting. Josh and Sarah ran about, while little Jean just giggled and made baby sounds. When the sun finally sank into the sky, everyone knew it was time to go.

Pam tearfully hugged her daughter when she and George were leaving for home. Her daughter was no longer a little girl. She and Marlene had already started planning for Marlene's wedding, which was coming in a month. No longer would she see her daughter so often, and no longer would she see her as just a kid. Right now, she could still fool herself into thinking Marlene was still somewhat of a kid. In a month, though, Marlene would no longer be kid to Pam.

Chapter Twenty Nine

As the music started, Marlene took her first step toward the door. Her dress glided behind her, and Sarah and Josh tried hard not to step on the train as they followed. Sarah carried a basket of flowers and prepared to start tossing the petals out as soon as they were inside the church. Josh carried the ring, watching it carefully on the pillow, afraid it would slide off. Marlene glanced down a moment to see the boy looking up at her with big blue eyes. He already called her "Aunt Marlene." His curly, unruly hair had been combed carefully and pressed down with hair gel by his father that morning. Then she took a look at Sarah. Her red, wavy hair flowed down past her shoulders, and the little girl carried such a big smile upon her lips. The five year old was so proud to get to be a flower girl in her uncle's wedding.

George cleared his throat, and Marlene looked up to stare at him. Her father opened the door for her and took her arm in his. He smiled at her tearfully before they walked together down the aisle. The sun shone through the colored glass, pouring down bright yellows and blues, reds, and purples onto the people who sat in the pews, the people who were important in Marlene's life and Arthur's life. Marlene's mother and Arthur's parents sat across the aisle from each other, and cousins, aunts, and uncles sat behind them. Jim, Nate, Ryan, and Curt stood at Arthur's side at the front. Susan, Jill, Lilly, and Paula stood to the other side, awaiting Marlene. Behind Marlene, Sarah tossed the petals while Josh counted and carefully took each step.

It seemed all too short a time for George before he had to hand his daughter over to this other man, who he had come to know so well over the past month. "I'll always love you, Marlene," George whispered to his daughter as he slid his arm out. Marlene turned to him and hugged him. Then George stared at Arthur a moment; the young cowboy looked very handsome in his blue suit. "Take good care of her, son," he whispered to the young man. Arthur nodded. As George retreated back to his seat, next to Pam, Arthur took Marlene's arm.

"I love you, Marlene," Arthur spoke softly in her ear, before the priest began to speak.

Then Father Matthew started the mass, and Arthur and Marlene looked at him. Here was a man who had helped bring them together, when they had thought they lost each other. He had helped Arthur to find faith at one of the most desperate, despairing times. And now he was about to join Arthur and Marlene together as man and wife. The priest looked at the two proudly, sure they would stay together the rest of their lives, sure even before they gave their vows. Arthur and Marlene had purposely asked him to come down from Gillette to Laramie, to marry them at Saint Laurence O' Tool, where Arthur had proposed to Marlene.

Marlene and Arthur exchanged vows, promising to be true to each other, to be there for each other, to always stay together. Arthur's mother watched her son as he gently and carefully slipped the ring on Marlene's finger. Her eyes misted over. She was so glad Arthur had finally found the right girl, but she was sad at the thought that he was no longer the little boy,

who wrestled with his brother and teased his sister. Sure, he would
probably still do those sorts of things, but now he was married. A warm
smile crept up her face. William squeezed his wife's hand, knowing just
how she felt.

Before Marlene knew it, she was staring at Arthur, now her husband.
Arthur stared back, just as amazed and pleased. He could hardly believe
Marlene was his wife. Wrapping his arms around her, feeling the soft
material of her white dress beneath his fingers, he pulled Marlene to him.
As Arthur kissed her, a thrill shot through Marlene's spine.

Then Arthur and Marlene Pressed walked back down the aisle together,
to start a new life. Marlene smirked as she thought: and to think that their
romance started with a kidnapping. There were whoops and cheers all
around, and as they exited the church, birdseed was launched at the young
couple. Arthur placed a brand new, brown Stetson on his head in defense of
the outpouring.

They drove together to Ryan and Judy's house, where they would have
the wedding reception. When they arrived, Marlene was amazed to see the
cake her grandmother had carefully baked and decorated for this day. As
Marlene's and Arthur's parents, siblings, and other relatives arrived,
Marlene looked around for her grandmother, Rose Picket.

Rose arrived with George and Pam, and immediately took a seat in the
corner. Marlene hurried over to her. "Grandma, thank you so much for the
cake," Marlene thanked her, gently hugging the older woman. Rose Picket
was eighty-two years old. She used to be the finest baker in Denver,
working at her father's bakery until one day she met a handsome young
man who would not long after take her to Wyoming as his wife. Still she
had continued to bake, as her husband worked hard to support them. She
sold some cakes, but never made a wedding cake until her oldest son,
George, was going to get married and requested it. The cake she made for
Marlene was the second wedding cake she had ever made, and that was
astounding for more than one reason. For the past eight years, Rose and
had gotten such bad arthritis in her hands that she hardly baked anymore.
Marlene sensed what pain Rose must have endured to decorate the cake
with such fine rose colored ribbons of frosting, and intricate, carefully made
flowers.

Rose Picket gazed upward at her granddaughter. Out of all her
grandchildren, this one had always been the quietest, yet always the most
appreciative as well. "You're welcome, Dear," Rose replied after gazing at
the very image of herself on her wedding day.

As Rose smiled, Marlene smiled back, and then she took a seat beside
her grandmother. Arthur approached and asked, "Marlene, did you want to
greet everyone?"

Marlene turned her head towards Arthur to look at him and replied,
"Yeah, Arthur. But first I want to ask my grandmother something." She
did not need to say anymore. Arthur understood. He took and squeezed her
hand a moment before leaving her alone with her grandmother. Arthur
knew just what it was Marlene wanted to ask, though she had not told him
beforehand.

"What is it you wanted to ask me, Marlene?" Rose asked, staring at her beautiful granddaughter and patting her hand.

"Grandma, do you believe Grandpa was successful?" Marlene asked.

Wrinkles formed around Rose's dark brown eyes. Tears glistened off those eyes as Rose's mind drifted to the past, to a day, long, long ago, that she would never forget. It was one day, after Christmas mass, when Charles Picket hunched down, so that he was at the same level as his son, George, and daughter, Marie. "Son, do you know what the Christmas story is about?"

George looked confused at his father and replied, "A little boy, a king, being born in the manger."

"Yes, but it's about more than that," Charles replied. "It's about how much God loves us, so that He sent down His Son to be born. And that boy had come to teach us all that there's more, so much more, to life than making money, and becoming rich. He taught us that true success is made by following God, and not always doing what we desire, or buying what we desire, but doing what he calls us to do. His love for us makes life have meaning." Little George still did not understand, but Marie partly did.

"Then, Dad, you're successful!" little Marie told her father.

Rose flashed back to the present, her vision blocked with tears. She blinked them away. Today was not a day for tears. Looking around, she spotted Marie, who stood talking to her older brother. Marlene still waited. Finally Rose spoke. "Your grandfather was very successful. He concentrated not on money, but on raising our children with love, sheltering them and feeding them to keep them content, and on loving me as a faithful husband." Rose paused, picking up a glass of water from the table at her elbow and taking a sip from it.

"Your grandfather had such faith in God, and love for all His people. Sure, he never went to college. But it would not have made a difference except maybe to distract him from his focus. He worked at a grocery store for fifteen years, before he got a slightly better job working at a bicycle shop. And though he'd come home every day at five-thirty, just exhausted after starting work at seven-thirty, he hardly ever complained. I would give him a glass of ice water, after a hot summer day, or a mug of hot chocolate, in the winter, and we'd sit together on the swing and just talk. Sometimes we wouldn't even talk. But when we did, he'd always mention how much he loved me and the kids, and how he wouldn't trade his life and his family for anything.

"The money he earned did not matter to him, except that it meant a roof over our heads and food to fill us up. After resting a while with me on the swing, he'd run around the yard or house, playing tag and other games with the kids. And every night he and I would tuck the kids in, and then he and I would take turns telling them stories." Rose paused to take another sip of water.

By now all the guests had filed into Ryan's and Judy's house, but Arthur kept talking to them and telling them that Marlene would join him in just a moment. Marlene turned back to her grandmother. She looked much younger now as she reflected back. Rose looked straight at Marlene, but

Marlene could tell she was looking somewhere else, far off. Then Rose continued.

"Even when he was fired from the grocery store, after he made the new manager look bad by working harder and working honestly, he never lost faith in God. He came home tired and worn, looking ten years older than he was, that day, and I knew something was wrong. But he did not yell, or complain loudly about the injustice of it all. He did not take out his frustrations on me or the kids. He didn't even mention his job at all until the children were tucked into bed.

"Then he took me out to the kitchen and told me. I began to cry. I was so scared. We didn't have much saved up. How could we, with having four kids to feed along with ourselves, and a car and house to pay for? Though he looked scared too, he gently wiped my tears and said, 'It's going to be alright. We just have to trust God. Surely I'll get another job. But the main thing is, no one is hurt, and all our children are alive and well. And you and I are fine, too. That's what counts. I know we don't have much in the bank, and I'm scared to. I don't want you and the kids having to live out on the streets, starving. But there's nothing we can do right now but pray to God that it will all turn out all right.' And it did.

"A week later, an old high school friend of Charles, who had joined the army with him right after high school to fight in the war, called up Charles. He had just started a bicycle shop, and already he was prospering. He had heard Charles had lost his job, and knew Charles to be a hard and innovative worker, so he asked him if he'd like a job. When Charles came to the laundry room to tell me about the call that day, he was crazy with excitement. He looked as if the weight of the world had been cast off his shoulders. We prayed right there, amongst the pile of dirty laundry, to thank God for taking care of us.

"Later, several of his friends landed on hard times after we had, and he lent them money so that their families would manage until times got better for them. And on Mondays and Wednesdays, after he retired, he helped cook and serve food at the local soup kitchen for those in need.

"So, Marlene, I'd say that your Grandfather was one of the most successful men. He raised eight healthy children with me, and loved us all, and loved and trusted God above all. He was never above helping anyone in need, either. I can see that you have been turning towards God more and more lately, and I can tell Arthur has too. I hope Arthur makes you as happy as your Grandfather made me, and I hope you two are successful in doing God's will."

With tears now brimming over Marlene's eyes, she gently hugged her grandmother and thanked her. Then it was time to eat the supper laid out for everyone. After the meal, Marlene and Arthur cut the cake. Then Jim stood to toast his brother.

"Arthur, this is a toast to you and Marlene. As your brother, Arthur, I have seen you grow up from a little kid to grown man. I looked up to you, all those times when you did what was right, no matter how hard it was, and I look up to you still. Your faith in God is strong, and you find strength in caring about people. And now there's something I think you and Marlene might like to know, since it has to do with that dance you two saw each other at, among other things," Jim announced. The room, which was humming with whispers at the start of his speech, quieted down to complete silence. Arthur and Marlene's eyes were glued on Jim, waiting for him to continue.

Jim swallowed, then continued, "As you know, Arthur, Curt and Nancy Hawk encouraged you to dance, and you ended up going to a Valentine's Day dance, where you saw Marlene. This was not quite by chance. Marlene, your brothers helped me get you to go to that dance, and I got Arthur's friends to make him fix up his house, so that it would be suitable for a family.

"We can't, however, take credit for how well things turned out. It turns out, though I tried to play the matchmaker, God was the real matchmaker. He brought you two together from the very start, and kept bringing you two together time and again. And I know that you two have a wonderful life ahead together, because you have involved God in all your plans, hopes and dreams, and in your marriage. So I just want to finish by saying, congratulations, Arthur and Marlene!"

The room roared with claps and cheers for the new couple. Several more toasts were made. Then the band Arthur and Marlene had hired started playing a slow song. Marlene danced with her father, and Arthur danced with his mother. Then, during the next song, Marlene and Arthur danced together. The third song was a fast swing song, and everyone there who could dance danced to their hearts' delight. Arthur only stepped on Marlene's toes a couple times, and she was so filled with joy that she did not even complain about it.

Before Arthur and Marlene were ready for it, the party was over. After hugging parents and relatives, they left Ryan's house. They stepped into Arthur's truck and drove away, with cans hung on strings clanking behind the bed of the pickup. From Ryan's house they headed straight to the airport.

They flew to Hawaii and spent their week-long honeymoon enjoying lazy days under a hot sun. All too soon those days were over, and they took a plane back to Denver. When they returned to Wyoming, and drove to Arthur's ranch, Arthur surprised Marlene with his fixed up cabin. She was thrilled and could not stop talking for the rest of the day about how much it felt like a real home.

That night they sat on a porch swing Arthur had hewn from logs. They sat together, Arthur's arm wrapped around Marlene to rest at her waist, Marlene leaning toward him with her head resting on his shoulder. They watched the stars slowly come out, and listened to the hooting of an owl. "Arthur, think we'll have a great time, here on your ranch?" Marlene asked Arthur, breathing up at his chin as she spoke.

"Well, it won't be easy, to keep up with all the work. But Marlene, I think as long as we always love each other, and God above all, we'll be alright," Arthur told her. Marlene sat up to gaze lovingly at her husband. They both smiled.

4144277

Made in the USA
Charleston, SC
05 December 2009